'THAT'S THE KIND OF GROUP I REPRESENT, LYNCH. A GROUP OF PATRIOTIC AMERICANS WHO BELIEVE THE CIVILIZED WORLD IS FACING A THREAT AS EVIL AND AS INSIDIOUS AS NAZISM.'

'Terrorists are the enemies of civilization,' Halloran continued, 'and our group has resolved to seek out and destroy them wherever they hide. Sure, it's vigilanteism on a global scale. Sure, it's against all principles of international law and, sure, our governments will express their outrage. It's getting down to the same level as the terrorist and fighting him on his own terms. And it's about time! Our governments can't—or won't—do what's needed despite the clear and express wishes of the people, so we will! Using good, old-fashioned private enterprise. That's why we want you, Lynch.'

The industrialist paused briefly, measuring the Briton with his gaze. Then he went on. 'We want you to take part in an operation against the greatest single source of terrorism in the world today. It is an operation involving the assassination of another country's leader.'

'Let us make my meaning indelibly plain, Lynch. We want you to go after that rug-biter Gaddafi . . . and blow his goddamn head right off!'

PINNACLE BRINGS YOU THE FINEST IN FICTION

THE HAND OF LAZARUS   (100-2, $4.50)
by Warren Murphy & Molly Cochran
The IRA's most bloodthirsty and elusive murderer has chosen the
small Irish village of Ardath as the site for a supreme act of terror
destined to rock the world: the brutal assassination of the Pope!
From the bestselling authors of GRANDMASTER!

LAST JUDGMENT   (114-2, $4.50)
by Richard Hugo
Only former S.A.S. agent James Ross can prevent a centuries-old
vision of the Apocalypse from becoming reality . . . as the malevo-
lent instrument of Adolf Hitler's ultimate revenge falls into the
hands of the most fiendish assassin on Earth!
           "RIVETING...A VERY FINE BOOK"
                    — NEW YORK TIMES

TRUK LAGOON   (121-5, $3.95)
Mitchell Sam Rossi
Two bizarre destinies inseparably linked over forty years unleash a
savage storm of violence on a tropic island paradise — as the most
incredible covert operation in military history is about to be uncovered at the bottom of TRUK LAGOON!

THE LINZ TESTAMENT   (117-6, $4.50)
Lewis Perdue
An ex-cop's search for his missing wife traps him a terrifying secret
war, as the deadliest organizations on Earth battle for possession
of an ancient relic that could shatter the foundations of Western
religion: the Shroud of Veronica, irrefutable evidence of a second
Messiah!

*Available wherever paperbacks are sold, or order direct from the
Publisher. Send cover price plus 50¢ per copy for mailing and handling to Zebra Books, Dept. 160, 475 Park Avenue South, New
York, N.Y. 10016. Residents of New York, New Jersey and Pennsylvania must include sales tax. DO NOT SEND CASH.*

PRIME OBJECTIVE

PAUL MANN

PINNACLE BOOKS
WINDSOR PUBLISHING CORP.

PINNACLE BOOKS

are published by

Windsor Publishing Corp.
475 Park Avenue South
New York, NY 10016

First Pinnacle Books printing: January, 1989

Printed in the United States of America

CONTENTS

1 The Outrage   9

2 The Decision   39

3 The Meeting   55

4 The Deception   75

5 The Departure   87

6 The Team   113

7 The Plan   137

8 The Tools   169

9 The Countdown   199

10 The Hit   225

'We have the right to take a legitimate and sacred action, an entire people liquidating its opponents inside and abroad in broad daylight.'

Colonel Muammar al-Gaddafi, Revolutionary Leader of the Socialist Republic of Libya.

Tripoli 1985.

1

THE OUTRAGE

London, Christmas 1988
Crowds had been gathering since dusk in Regent Street, to watch the Princess of Wales switch on the most celebrated Christmas lights in Europe. As he pushed through the heaving ranks of shoppers and royalty groupies the man in the shabby khaki raincoat couldn't help but speculate how efficiently a few kilos of IRA plastique would clear a space amidst such a mass of people. He also knew this would be the most heavily guarded street in London tonight. For days previously it would have been swept by men from the Royal Engineers using dogs and electronic sensors to detect explosives. Every ritzy shop in the street would have been visited by Scotland Yard, its premises searched, employees interviewed and their identities checked by Special Branch and MI5. Police snipers would have been on the rooftops since dawn and armed plainclothes men would be mingling with the crowd. Scores of uniformed police lined the kerb, facing the crowd, guarding the building where the princess would appear soon in a second-storey window—a window reinforced with bulletproof glass especially for the occasion.

The nondescript man in the raincoat knew, as he stepped on

a manhole cover in the footpath, that someone would be down there too and every sewer and service tunnel leading into the area would be guarded. He was so sure he toyed with the idea of rapping out a quick greeting in Morse with the heel of his shoe but let it pass. He had other things to do and no time for mischievous diversions.

When he reached the Aquascutum store he trotted up the steps, pausing only to glance back at the thousands of people spilling untidily off the footpath between agitated, complaining policemen and slowing even further the crawling lanes of traffic. Despite the police presence and the sinister threat of terrorist violence which now accompanied each Christmas season in the British capital it was a cheerful spectacle, an ocean of excited faces reddened by the cold and lit by the colourful blaze of light from shop windows. He pushed open the heavy glass doors and threaded his way into the big, busy store, losing himself among the regimented rows of neat, new raincoats.

'Can I help you, sir?'

He almost collided with a blue-suited, pinked-cheeked salesman who materialised in front of him.

'Ah ... I'm looking for a new raincoat,' he answered. He glanced self-consciously down at the shabby coat he was wearing, implying that further explanation shouldn't be necessary. It wasn't. Aquascutum salesmen are discrete.

'Yes sir,' the salesman smiled. 'Any particular style or colour in mind?'

'Khaki. I like khaki.'

'Classic colour, sir,' the salesman beamed his approval. 'May I show you our range in khaki and you can tell me if there's a particular style you favour?'

The man nodded and as he followed the salesman upstairs to another sales floor he carefully checked his watch. Two minutes to six. She would be appearing at the window any moment. He had to be in a position to see her clearly. The salesman

10

gestured towards a rack of coats and he automatically pointed to a Bogart-style trenchcoat.

'Absolutely classic, sir,' the salesman tattled. 'It will look good on you, too. Would you care to try it on?'

The man glanced at his watch again. 'Just give me a minute, would you?' he murmured politely. 'There's something I've got to see.' He walked over to one of the tall windows overlooking Regent Street and, as he had anticipated, found himself diagonally opposite the window which would protect the Princess of Wales. The salesman looked confused until realisation flooded his amiable face.

'Of course,' he said. 'I've been here so many years I'd forgotten. She's doing it this year isn't she? Yes, let's watch the show.'

Princess Diana appeared at the window some 50 metres further down the street and a cheer erupted from the crowd below. The man in the raincoat tensed. She seemed to fill the window with a luminous glow. Yellow, he realised, hardly believing it. She was wearing a full-length yellow coat and matching hat which told him exactly where her pretty, royal face would be. He could not have asked for better references for a head shot. She should have worn dark blue, he thought, to blend with the suits of the men standing around her. Just behind her, he suspected he saw another familiar figure.

The man slowly unbuttoned his raincoat, his back to the salesman, then let his hands fall gently by his sides, apparently quite relaxed. He heard the muffled tones of her voice float up from the speakers outside. Another few seconds and she would press the button, the huge Christmas decorations would explode with light, blinding everyone and rendering him temporarily invisible. His ears strained to hear her voice and anticipate her finger on the button. He heard the words '. . . wish you all a very happy and prosperous Christmas and I take pleasure in switching on these lights for Christmas 1988 . . .' The submachinegun in the custom-made holster inside his coat was loaded with 32 rounds. The first 16 had armour-piercing heads to rip through any bulletproof glass, the last 16 had mercuryfilled hollow tips to cause massive trauma and death with just a graze.

The gun's safety catch was already off and it was set to prolonged-burst mode. He reminded himself to compensate for the weight difference on the second squeeze of the trigger. Another second and it would be too late. He moved. In an effortless, well-rehearsed motion he pulled the gun from its holster, swung it up to the window and fired just as the entire street lit up with Christmas lights. He saw the window close in front of him dissolve in a splash of exploding glass, sending millions of slivers cascading onto the packed crowd underneath. A spider's web of lacy cracks had already appeared in the window over the street and a moment later its second bulletproof skin disappeared like a flimsy curtain pulled by an unseen hand. He fired the second burst and watched impassively as the slender figure in yellow staggered and fell. All around her he could see other dark shapes shivering under the barrage and then they were all gone. It had taken less than three seconds. His ears roared with noise and as he looked up Regent Street he thought it resembled a ghastly stage set. The awful unreality of what had happened was split by screams from below. He felt the cold night air rushing through the jagged hole he had blown in the store window, beyond which the great Christmas lights shone merrily. He spun round and looked into the shocked eyes of the salesman then dropped him with a smart blow to the temple from the butt of his gun. He stepped over the body, dropped the gun onto the carpeted floor and walked quickly and calmly back down the stairs and into the chaos below where he was carried away on a tide of panic . . .

Colin James Lynch saw it all. He felt it, even smelled it. In his mind. This was the most terrible scenario he could imagine and he knew too well how all these shocking images could become reality. Then the sudden flare of the Christmas lights switching on brought him back with a start. Lynch plunged his hands deep into his raincoat pockets and blinked away the dazzle.

She was still there. An elegant yellow slash in the window. The crowd cheered, the children gasped and merchants the length of Regent Street wore smug smiles as the Princess of Wales successfully launched the annual Christmas shopping blitz. Lynch turned away, his eyes smarting with neon snowflakes.

'I say,' the salesman remarked as their eyes readjusted to the more subdued lighting inside the store. 'Wasn't that Charles with her tonight?'

Lynch nodded. It was Prince Charles. He could have got them both in one hit if that had been his line of work. There would have to be a snotty report to Control about lapses in security, he decided, even though protection of the royal family wasn't really his department. Lynch switched his mind off work and back to the business of buying a new winter coat. The salesman held up a beautifully-tailored khaki trenchcoat for him to slip on but he hesitated.

'I don't think so,' he decided eventually. 'Too fussy. Not really me, if you know what I mean. Let's look at something a little less melodramatic, shall we?'

Three weeks later Lynch had drawn night duty, on Christmas Eve at Heathrow Airport. Twelve hours straight from six pm Christmas Eve till six am Christmas Day. He didn't mind. He was content to let the married men spend Christmas with their families while he and the other single men of the counter terrorist unit permanently attached to Heathrow did the overnight shift. Ever since the Christmas 1985 attacks on Rome and Vienna airports by the Abu Nidal group and the subsequent British-

13

backed American air raids on Libya, British airports had been a prime target for attacks by Libyan-sponsored terrorists.

Lynch's squad was one of 27 assigned to the major civilian airports throughout the United Kingdom. Each squad comprised six men, drawn almost exclusively from highly-trained fighting units of the British armed forces such as the SAS, SBS and Royal Marines. These paramilitary counterterrorist squads were part of an autonomous new department formed early in 1986 and administered by Sir Malcolm Porter, a former SAS commanding officer, answerable only to the Home Secretary and the Prime Minister. The London-based squads included a few officers from Scotland Yard's Special Branch on limited assignment but most units throughout the rest of the UK consisted of military men who had completed regular service in the armed forces and who could not see an appropriate role for themselves on civvy street.

Lynch had been a naval lieutenant attached to the SBS, the Special Boat Squadron, that branch of the Royal Navy which specialises in coastal reconnaissance, infiltration, sabotage and, occasionally, assassination. He had left the SBS two years after the end of the war in the Falklands. For him, the highlight had been leading the unit which navigated the minefield on South Georgia island at night and captured the Argentine garrison— without losing a man. When he had completed his service in 1984 he had been reluctant to sign for another term but civilian life held few attractions for him. Unlike some of his colleagues, he could not see himself accepting mercenary work, or following the well-trodden path to a desk job with a government department like Her Majesty's Customs and Excise. One of his fellow officers had become a bodyguard at high pay to an industrialist who travelled the world but Lynch could not quite see himself in that role either. He had begun to fear that his years with the SBS had made him unemployable in the outside world and had stayed with the navy on special attachment to the diving school

14

at Portsmouth, while he considered his choices. Eventually he had heard a few whispers about a proposed network of counter-terrorist squads formed specially to defend British seaports and airports against attack.

Until 1986, the SAS had performed this role as occasion demanded but the Special Air Service had neither the manpower nor the desire to maintain the kind of force now needed to defend every major Port in the British Isles. When Counter Terrorism Command became a reality Lynch applied for a job, glided through the selection process, and signed up for 12 months. After that first year he had been promoted to squad leader and had stayed on for a further year. Now, with the end of 1988 fast approaching, Colin James Lynch still had no idea what to do with his life after years of active service.

Lynch had been born 37 years earlier in Dumfries on the Scottish west coast. The son of a railway guard, he had always faced life with a necessarily limited range of options. Although he had done well at school his parents could not afford to send him to university and three years of subsisting on a government grant had not appealed to him. He joined the Royal Navy and went to the officer training college at Dartmouth. On graduation he had been assigned as a midshipman to the minesweeper HMS *Aden*, where he had demonstrated an aptitude for disarming mines. Following a decade of service on the navy's new generation of missile destroyers and a tour of duty with the aircraft carrier HMS *Invincible*, Lynch, now a lieutenant, had been asked if he would like to forego the struggle for captain's rank—in a navy with more captains than ships—and instead undergo special duty with the SBS. He had leaped at the opportunity and spent several years becoming a skilled diver and underwater demolitions expert. With the SBS he had taken part in covert actions in the Persian Gulf, the Baltic Sea, the Black Sea and the Mediterranean. By the time of the Falklands War, Lynch was master of seaborne sabotage and assassination.

He had married and divorced along the way. His wife, like many navy wives, was unable to stand the endless separations. There were no children and he had neither seen nor heard from his wife in six years. He had returned to Dumfries to visit his parents between leaving the navy and joining Counter Terrorism Command, but had left with the impression that his mother and father had accepted his loss years earlier.

On the drive back to London he had stopped off to see his elder brother in Carlisle on the English side of the border and declined the sincere but naïve offer of a partnership in his brother's successful market-garden business.

Training with his new counter-terrorist unit had been harder than he anticipated. After the SBS, he was confident he would breeze through the three-month training programme. But the emphasis on ultra-quick decision-making and expert marksmanship under great duress had tested him. There had been exercises involving simulated sieges and storming of passenger aircraft, ships and buildings and full-scale exercises at military airports and shipyards, with other officers and instructors playing the roles of panicking, obstructive passengers. There had been nights when he had crawled into bed, only to be dragged out of a deep sleep 90 minutes later and thrown into simulated combat. When it was over, Lynch believed his reflexes and all his combat instincts were sharper than they had ever been. He could assess a dangerous situation, distinguish between hostile and passive targets and make the decision to shoot in less than a second. Then, despite his SBS training, with the infallible logic of military and paramilitary bureaucracies everywhere, instead of a post at a seaport, he had been sent to Heathrow Airport. Temporarily. With him he had taken the most ominous piece of advice he had received throughout his training. An instructor, an SAS man, warned him that the only emergency action he wasn't prepared for now was his first real one.

Lynch was the oldest man on the squad by several years. The

16

others on duty with him this Christmas Eve were all in their late twenties. They included a former SAS captain, three former Royal Marine commandos and an inspector from Scotland Yard's Special Branch on special experience duty.

When he stepped off the tube from Hammersmith, Lynch made a point of strolling slowly through the subway tunnels and up the escalator to Europa terminal where he made a long, watchful circuit. It was bedlam. International terrorism had been off the front pages for a few months and passenger flow had surged for the Christmas holiday period. He scrutinised young, middle-class couples checking their skis for trips to the snow-fields of Austria and France. He saw that all the seats in every waiting area were jammed. People were squatting on the floor talking, reading, playing card games. Flustered mothers pursued overexcited children, long queues meandered everywhere, the bars were packed and the turnstiles at the duty-free store spun like tops with the traffic. The sound of jolly Christmas songs echoed tinnily over the speaker system punctuated by airline announcements. The noise was terrific. Lynch wondered if a gunshot would even be heard over such a din.

He passed two patrolling policemen, Heckler and Koch MP5s cradled in their arms, and they each returned his nod of recognition. There would be two more downstairs at arrivals. Somewhere in the crowd, he knew, there would be a couple of plainclothes men. These armed men, both uniformed and out of uniform, were the first line of defence. It would be their job to deter or contain any terrorist action until Lynch's squad could get to the scene. Lynch glanced through one of the vast windows overlooking the wet tarmac and noticed a few snow-flakes flirting with the winter wind.

'For Christ's sake, don't let it snow,' Lynch heard a young man in a silver ski jacket complain to his girlfriend. 'Half an inch of snow on the runway and British Airways can't get off the bloody ground. We should have caught the 'overcraft and

17

skied to bloody Austria.' His girlfriend giggled and Lynch smiled. Some things, he thought, like the British gift for complaining, would never change.

Completing his tour of the terminal, Lynch took a door marked 'Strictly No Admittance' and before closing it took another look at the teeming, defenceless crowds. He wasn't in any sense religious, but the words formed involuntarily in his mind: 'Please God ... not tonight.'

He shut the door and jogged down a bleak, grey stairwell to a locked red metal door at ground level. There was a button on the wall and he gave it a shove. There was a pause and he grinned up at the camera watching him from its perch in a corner, then the door swung open and he was greeted by an airport security guard with a pistol on his hip.

'Evening, Mr Lynch,' welcomed the guard. 'Merry Christmas eh?'

'Merry Christmas, George,' he answered. 'How late do you work tonight?'

'Till twelve, Mr Lynch. Late enough to see Santa get his arse in gear then get home to the wife and kids, eh?'

'Lucky man,' said Lynch. And he meant it.

'Not really, Mr Lynch. You haven't met my wife and kids.'

Lynch smiled. He had known George since the squad had started duty at Heathrow and had grown fond of his breezy, self-deprecating sense of humour. The two men were in a small security room with one desk, a chair and a couple of TV monitors, one focused on the stairwell, the other linked to a series of cameras showing the crowds upstairs. There were two phones on the wall, one red, the other black. Neither had a dial. This ugly little room was where George spent most of his shift. The only other piece of furniture in the room was a black plastic moulded bench near the only other door, which led outside. Lynch sat on the bench and looked at a digital clock near the TV monitors. It was almost twenty minutes before six.

18

'You squad leader tonight?' George asked.

Lynch nodded. He sat quietly for a few minutes looking over the security guard's shoulder at the monitors, then decided: 'I won't wait for the others tonight, George. Can you call me a car now?'

George obediently picked up the black phone and waited for the automatic connection to security central. 'Europa security reception here,' he said. 'Can you send a car for one passenger?' As soon as he had his acknowledgement, he turned back to Lynch. 'New raincoat?' he asked amiably.

Lynch glanced down at the sober, single-breasted blue raincoat he had finally chosen. 'A Christmas present I bought for myself,' he said.

'Thought so,' said George. 'Doesn't look new but it smells new.'

'You'll make Scotland Yard yet, George,' Lynch smiled. A moment later they heard the sound of a car pulling up outside followed by the jarring rattle of a loud buzzer as the driver pushed the button outside.

'Like fingernails down a fucking blackboard,' George muttered as he released the lock on the outside door. Lynch said goodnight and stepped outside into the freezing night air. The ride in the white Ford van with 'Catering' painted on its side took less than half a minute across an empty expanse of windblasted tarmac and they were at security central. Heathrow security central for Counter Terrorism Command had its own corner of a service hangar and the only way in was through a large set of double doors marked 'Fire Control', or by a smaller door to the side. Squad members often referred to themselves drolly as firemen though, in almost two years of duty, they hadn't seen one genuine emergency action. There had been plenty of exercises and weekend courses but never the real thing. The Prime Minister and the Home Secretary boasted privately that the mere awareness by various terrorist groups of the existence of highly-trained counter-terrorist squads at all major British ports had acted as an effective deterrent.

Equally privately, many of the officers and men serving with the squads wondered how well the system would work if tested.

The ground crews and many other airline employees around Heathrow knew this hangar housed the airport's counter-terrorist squad but no unauthorised person could approach the building without being challenged and no-one got inside who could not be identified by the guard manning the inside guard post.

Once through this guard, Lynch found himself in the central control room, where a duty officer monitored a semi-circular wall of TV screens covering every floor of all five passenger terminals at Heathrow. By flicking switches on the console in front of him, the duty officer could switch to cameras at various locations inside and outside all terminals and activate close-ups and wide-screen scans. The installation of this surveillance system—with the co-operation of airport unions acting grudgingly in the national interest—had produced an unexpected bonus for travellers passing through Heathrow. The airport's notorious pilfering of luggage had dropped by almost 50 per cent. The duty officer also had access to a computer keyboard and VDU linked to Counter Terrorism Command's national headquarters at Whitehall, which enabled them to run instant ID checks on terrorist suspects. As far as the job went it was as much fun as working in the air traffic control tower on Christmas Eve. If air traffic control reported a man in a red suit with a white beard-aboard an unidentified flying object not cleared for landing, it would be CTC's job to take him prisoner.

Lynch hovered at the duty officer's shoulder. Everywhere the cameras faced there was a seething mass of people. On nights like this Lynch knew their task was next to impossible. Prevention of a hostile act was out of the question. Swift containment was the best they could hope for. And before that people would die.

'How many suspect arrivals tonight?' Lynch asked the duty officer.

'A few,' the latter answered, without lifting red-rimmed eyes from his monitors. 'We've got Olympic, one flight from Athens at 19.20 hours, a British Airways troop charter from Nicosia at 20.00 hours, an Egyptair flight from Cairo at 20.10 hours and an Air Yugoslavia flight from Zagreb at 21.40 hours.'

Lynch winced. 'We'll have to keep an eye on Olympic and the BA charter. Departures?'

The duty officer pursed his lips. 'The big one for tonight is El Al to Tel Aviv departing at 21.14 but airport security and their own people have been over it like a rash and luggage was cleared an hour ago. Even since that pregnant bird with the bomb in her handbag got caught, the El Al boys haven't trusted us to do anything right.'

'Who can blame them?' Lynch murmured.

'They've been thorough,' the duty officer added. 'Slows everybody down but they seem to accept it.'

Lynch nodded. 'And meanwhile the queues up there get longer and longer. Any more?'

'Alitalia to Rome at 22.00 hours, Lufthansa to Frankfurt at 22.10 and a TWA flight from New York stopping over en route to Vienna. We've got a couple more from the US and Canada terminating here and a Qantas flight from Sydney via Singapore and Bahrain due in at 22.40 hours but they're considered low risk for now.'

'Silent night,' Lynch remarked to himself. He glanced at the clock on the wall and it said 17.49. Time to gear up,' he added and just then the black phone on the wall near the side door buzzed loudly. It was picked up by the guard while the man who had driven Lynch sat on the opposite side of the guard's desk drinking coffee and reading that day's *Sun*. The guard listened for a moment then called over to Lynch: 'Three more of your blokes on the way, sir.' The driver reluctantly closed the paper on the page-three girl, collected his cap and left.

Lynch continued across the control room towards a heavy, metal-reinforced door, pushed it open and stepped into the squad room with its cramped changing facilities, rest area and armoury. The last was a single room built like a bank vault. Its door stood open 24 hours a day, unlike most armouries. The only time the door was closed was when all members of the squad were absent on an emergency action. One key was kept in the top drawer of the squad leader's desk and the only duplicates were held in a safe at Whitehall.

The moment Lynch appeared in the room there was a mock cheer from the six men his team would be relieving. Squad Leader Bill Fraser, a former commando with the Royal Marines, got up from the desk where he had just finished typing his duty report into the VDU and welcomed Lynch. The other men deserted the TV set on one wall and began climbing out of their uniforms. The squads all dressed in police-blue, snug-fitting jumpsuits, boots, utility belts packed with spare 30-round clips of 9 mm ammunition for the Heckler & Koch MP5s—the West German-made submachine-gun which was the standard combat weapon for all squads in the CTC. Bulletproof vests hung from a row of hooks beside the door leading back through security control. The MP5s rested on a rack just inside the armoury door, all loaded with conventional 9 mm rounds. Beyond this rack were cases of ammunition, including specially manufactured 9 mm low-velocity dum-dums—for the silenced MP5s used for close-in work on aircraft, when it was preferable to shoot terrorists without the bullets passing through their bodies and hitting passengers. There were cases of stun grenades, gas grenades, conventional grenades and an assortment of other weapons like the Winchester 12-gauge pump-action shotguns, the American 'alley cleaner' for scouring corners other weapons couldn't reach plus half a dozen AR18s fitted with sniper scopes. There were even a couple of modified Blowpipe one-man rocket launchers for particularly stubborn cases.

While Lynch changed into his uniform he listened as Fraser gave him a quick verbal summary of his report. At the same time three men from his squad arrived with the news that the other two were right behind. While the two squads changed shifts there was plenty of amiable banter and Lynch thought how innocent it all seemed. Like two teams of football players who had just enjoyed a good game instead of two squads of trained killers going about their daily duty. It made him realise how much a part of this world he was, how normal it all seemed to him ... and how much he needed it. He kept an eye on the clock. They always seemed to cut it fine, yet by six the change-over had been accomplished smoothly and Lynch's squad was fully geared while the outgoing men were still tying their shoe laces. They exchanged a final ironic flurry of Christmas wishes and then Lynch and his team had it all to themselves till morning. He sat down at the squad leader's desk, scanned Fraser's report on the VDU, punched in his own code, confirming he had seen and approved it, then keyed it through to the terminal next door.

Most of the men lounged around a long, green, metal folding table in the middle of the squad room where they gathered routinely at the start of every shift for a briefing. For the next 12 hours, unless there was an 'emergency action', not one man would leave the orbit of the squad room unless it was to go to the toilet or visit security control next door for a change of scenery and a chat with somebody different. The whole time they would stay in uniform, including ammo belts, leaving off only the heavy bulletproof vests which they would have to grab on the way out on an EA alert. Virtually everything in the room was some shade of green. The floor was painted dark green and the walls light green. Under the fluorescent lamps set in the ceiling the room took on a sickly, aquatic look, like a fish tank.

Furnishings were either military surplus or public service drab. A powerful heater rested on a high shelf, blowing warm air into the room. There were a few nude pin-ups on locker doors and the usual menagerie of cartoons on the bulletin board next to the toilet door.

Most of the cartoons lampooned the imbecility of politicians and bureaucrats, reflecting the professional soldier's traditional contempt for both. It was a room like a thousand, perhaps a million others all around the world where men in uniform spent long hours of tedious duty.

The only concession to seniority was the desk and chair with the VDU set in a small alcove for the squad leader. Apart from that 12 hours out of 24, nine days on, five days off every fortnight, the same men kept close company. A third squad was held in reserve to fill vacancies caused by sickness, accident, annual leave or absence for other reasons such as the occasional refresher course or promotion examination. Every three months the squads rotated and one of the duty squads went on reserve. This way the monotony of inactive service did not cause morale to suffer. The men drew reasonable overtime for the long shifts and because of the social constraints of the job most of them were able to hang onto a sizeable piece of their fortnightly pay cheques. Lynch did not know exactly how much money he had in his bank account but he knew it to be in excess of 15,000 pounds. His poky little flat in Hammersmith cost him very little, he didn't smoke or drink much and he wasn't a fussy dresser. His wife had not asked for maintenance and he had no need to spend a lot of money on women. With his athletic build, neat chestnut hair and the fair, freckled complexion of the Scot, Lynch was attractive to women but his relationships with them were invariably brief, transitory, superficial interludes in which he satisfied his sexual needs and little else.

There were many times when Lynch thought about the life he might have had, what a difference the birth of children could have made and he wondered what sort of man he had become ... but never for long. He knew the men in his squad far better than he had ever known his own family. If he was going to die, odds were that it would be in the company of these men. Most of them were ex-servicemen. The only exception was Timson, the young and ambitious inspector from Special Branch. Timson had been engaged for three years but he and his flancée kept putting off the wedding until his career settled down. The thought made Lynch smile. Hawkins, McCosker and Lacey were all ex-commandos in their late twenties and dedicated to the promiscuous joys of bachelorhood in the nation's capital. Roper was an ex-army captain who had served three years with the SAS and whose idea of a good time was to scale terrifying mountain peaks alone in Snowdonia.

Lynch ran quickly through the evening briefing, singling out the suspect flights and emphasising the boarding time of the El Al flight. He stressed the size and confusion of the crowds he had seen at Europa terminal and added that the other terminals were equally chaotic. When he had finished there were no questions. They all knew what they were there for. On the surface it looked rather routine but Lynch sensed undercurrents of tension, a mild electricity in the air because it was Christmas Eve and a high risk period.

When he had finished, Lacey, the triathlete with the face of a boy, suggested a few hours of Trivial Pursuit.

'Movie edition?' he asked, looking around for takers.

'Yeah, that's only because you spend so much time wanking at the pictures,' complained his flatmate, McCosker. 'We'll do general.' Lynch left them to their familiar pastimes and strolled into the armoury to run the nightly weapons check, noticing as he did that the only man who didn't join in with the others was Roper, as usual. Captain Aidan Roper, ex-paratrooper, ex-SAS, walked quietly over to a sagging, iron-frame bunk and lay down with a book. It would be something light, Lynch knew, like the history of the Punic Wars. When he was satisfied with his check, he went back out to security control to spend a few minutes examining the TV monitors and the electronic net they cast over Heathrow. 'Fire Control' wasn't centrally located but drills showed they could reach every terminal in less than 60 seconds, either on foot to the closest terminals or by open Land Rover to Atlantic and Oceania terminals.

Drills had also showed that they could be at any point on any runway or within the airport perimeter in less than two minutes. In the event of a genuine emergency action, squad leaders carried enormous responsibility. Lynch had the authority to decide between siege action or ordering immediate assault when innocent lives were under clear and imminent threat. In the event of a siege, other officers, negotiators and psychologists seconded to CTC would eventually assume responsibility for all the decisions taken, but in the event of an assault the responsibility belonged exclusively to squad leaders. It was the kind of 'shoot first, ask questions later' policy once considered unthinkable in Britain but approved by the British cabinet in the climate of the times. Lynch was well aware of the awesome burden of the responsibility he carried and often speculated what the consequences would be, both public and private, on the day he or any of his colleagues had to issue such an order. It was a scenario which meant deaths were unavoidable and would ultimately have to be justified, however sanguine Whitehall pretended to be before the fact.

Lynch stood behind the duty officer and asked him to run through all the cameras at every arrivals and departures level in every terminal. It was just as he feared—even more confused and chaotic than it had been earlier. With the modern weaponry terrorists had in their possession, it would take only seconds to inflict appalling casualties before the officers on the spot could respond and Lynch's squad launch a containment action. On the hour he phoned the security desk at each terminal. Under standing orders, the guards manning these desks were to be informed of anything or anyone suspicious by patrolling police officers, airline security guards, customs and immigrations men, flight crews and plainclothes officers. Every scrap of information, every tip, every anxiety, no matter how bizarre or trivial, was checked by security central.

At 7.15 pm and again at five to eight Lynch interrupted his men and told them to stand by while he watched the flights from Athens and Nicosia arrive, both without incident. The Egyptair flight was running 90 minutes late and Lynch turned his attention to the boarding of the El Al flight to Tel Aviv. It too went smoothly. When it was airborne both Lynch and the duty officer heaved a sigh of relief. A few minutes later air traffic control reported the flight safely out of British air space.

The duty officer, a cockney, like George, swivelled in his chair to look at Lynch. 'You know,' he said, 'I realise it's wrong and all that because there's all colours wandering around out there.' And he pointed a thumb at the crowds on the TV monitors. 'There's black, white, yellow and bloody beige, and growing up in London you get used to seeing all sorts, but every time I see one of those shiftylooking wog types with hair like steel wool, I get a bit nervous. Know what I mean?'

Lynch smiled. He knew exactly what the duty officer meant. He decided to order in some coffee and sandwiches and strolled back to the squad room to ask his men if they wanted to place any orders. His fingers had just closed on the steel door handle when he heard a breathless 'Jesus Christ' from the duty officer. Lynch turned on his heel. The guard and the driver at the door jumped up and swapped fearful looks. The duty officer was half-standing, leaning over the console, eyes riveted to one of the TV screens on the bottom row as though he were unable to believe what was happening.

'Shooting,' he said shakily. Then the words came out firmer, just like another drill, except this time it wasn't. 'Shooting confirmed ... Atlantic terminal ... arrivals level.' He looked over to Lynch, his eyes wide with horror. 'Shit,' he gasped. 'It's on ... they're shooting people.'

Lynch rapped his orders out smartly: 'Order all mobile security personnel to Atlantic terminal now.'

The duty officer's fingers rippled over the console as he radioed every security officer at Heathrow, reciting Lynch's instruction and adding: 'Gunfire confirmed ... this is not a drill.'

Lynch was already through the squad-room door and on his way into the armoury. 'EA confirmed,' he snapped at his men. 'Weapons and follow me.' Adrenalin jolted him like a surge of electricity but he moved calmly, deliberately. He grabbed the nearest MP5, turned back to the door and quickly snapped on his bulletproof vest. As he strode back across the control room he clicked the safety catch off his gun. The double doors had been slid back and an open Land Rover waited with the driver at the wheel. Lynch was almost through the door with the squad filing quickly after him when the red phone on the wall buzzed. The guard grabbed it, then looked at Lynch. 'It's George,' he said blankly. 'There's shooting upstairs at Europa terminal, he says.' Then duty officer tore his eyes from the screens serving Atlantic and yelled to Lynch: 'Shooting confirmed ... Europa terminal ... departures level.'

A stunned silence filled the room and everyone stared at Lynch. 'Two attacks,' the duty officer said numbly. 'What are you going to do?'

It was the worst possible decision for any squad leader—two attacks, one almost certainly a decoy. But which? People were dying at both.

'Timson, Hawkins, McCosker—take the Rover to Atlantic,' Lynch barked. 'Lacey and Roper follow me.' With that he was sprinting across the blustery, wet tarmac towards brightly-lit Europa terminal from where he could already hear the crackle of automatic fire. As he ran Lynch calculated that the attack on Atlantic was probably the decoy but that was where shooting had been underway the longest. He had kept the two best men in his squad to contain the attack at Europa. If he was right, weight of numbers should overwhelm the attackers at Atlantic, and it was up to Roper, Lacey and himself to handle Europa.

Europa departures was on the second floor. Half a dozen staircases and escalators connected it with the ground floor. If the terrorists were still all on the departures floor he should try and force them up to the roof and isolate them there. He shouted orders to the two men running with him and they peeled away. Lacey could take the far left of the terminal, Roper could go right through the middle and Lynch would take the right.

People were running towards him on the tarmac, screaming. Lynch dodged his way through them and into the terminal. He found himself in a corner stairwell with the stairs jammed by a torrent of terrified people. He began shoving his way against the flow, upstairs towards departures, where the gunfire was much louder. Roper was next in. There was no door in the middle of the terminal overlooking the jet apron, so he checked quickly to make sure no-one was on the floor behind the plate glass, then blew out one window and stepped through. It was mayhem inside. The stairways and escalators were clogged with panicking people, falling and trampling each other as they tried to claw their way to safety. He saw children separated from their parents standing in bewilderment, tears streaming down their faces. The only escalator even half clear was the one moving up to the departures level. Roper ran for it.

To the far left of the terminal Lacey had found the stairwell impassable with sobbing, hysterical people and shoved his way into the main ground floor arrivals area, looking for another way upstairs.

By the time he reached the second floor, Lynch was quite cool. The people panicking all around him seemed oddly remote. Lynch had always possessed the ability to switch himself

29

into some kind of auto-pilot whenever he went into action. It had become fashionable to admit one's fear in combat. Navy doctors and psychologists in the CTC insisted that the expression and purging of fear was a healthy thing. Lynch had almost been ashamed to admit he rarely felt fear in battle. Usually he felt an odd kind of serenity and operated with perfect clarity in the midst of appalling chaos. He actually enjoyed the simplicity of purpose which accompanied warfare. And usually he felt nothing at all. Emotions, especially fear, only got in the way.

The top half of the stairwell was empty and when Lynch reached the entrance to the departures hall and peered carefully inside everything was eerily quiet and still. Those who had run and made their escape were lucky. The others, the people who had thrown themselves to the floor, were now trapped in a nightmare. The floor was littered with bodies. It was impossible to tell how many were dead, wounded or just lying and awaiting their fate. It was a surrealistic battlefield with bodies everywhere and a large, brightly-decorated Christmas tree in one corner of the garishly-lit hall. Lights on the Christmas tree flicked on and off and 'Winter Wonderland' was playing over the speaker system. Among the bodies were piles of luggage. Some had burst open spilling their intimate contents pathetically across the floor—underwear, toys, gaily-wrapped Christmas presents—the paper torn and ripped.

He could see four men standing in the centre of the hall. Three looked agitated and were holding Kalashnikovs. A fourth man, wearing a grey suit and carrying an automatic pistol, seemed almost relaxed by comparison. While his colleagues looked around he was bending down and appeared to be listening sympathetically to the pleas of an elderly man lying on the floor. Then he gripped the old man's hair, pulled his head up, held the pistol to the back of his skull and fired. Lynch snapped up the MP5 and fired a wide burst. He missed the man with the pistol but clipped one of the terrorists standing near by and watched with satisfaction as the man dropped his rifle and fell to his knees, scrabbling at his back and screaming in pain. Then a storm of bullets lashed the doorway and Lynch ducked back down the stairs as bullets and chips of brick and wood spattered around him like shrapnel. He waited for several minutes but the firing didn't stop. Lynch knew the Kalashnikov AK47 held 30 rounds of 7.62 mm bullets and had a firing rate of 600 rounds a minute. His own MP5 was only marginally faster at 650 rounds per minute. He was up against the finest assault rifle in the world and they could keep him pinned down indefinitely if Lacey or Roper didn't arrive soon to take the heat off. Then he heard the soft mutter of another MP5 opening up from the far side of the hall.

Lacey had seen Roper taking the up escalator and was only seconds behind him. When Roper rolled out onto the departures floor he took it all in at a glance. Three men, two with automatic rifles, one with a pistol, a fourth man writhing on the ground, just hit. The two with AK47s were spraying a distant doorway, taking it in turns to change clips. The man with the pistol was crouched down among the bodies of passengers, working his way towards a centre staircase. Roper got to one knee, took careful aim and fired. A sudden mist of blood spurted from the head of one of the terrorists holding an AK47 and he collapsed like a string of rags. The other gunman whirled and fired a long burst in Roper's direction and the ex-SAS man threw himself under the cover of a near by check-in counter, landing heavily on a woman in British Airways uniform. She whimpered and looked up at him, tears staining her face with ugly streaks of mascara, unable to speak. Roper began worming his way behind the line of check-in counters towards the men in the middle of the hall.

Lacey came off the escalator moments later and ran into a hail of bullets. They punched fist-sized holes in the metal walls of the escalator and one of them took his right calf away. The shock ran through his entire body and he fell, looking down at a ragged hole the size of a grapefruit where his calf muscle should have been. A wave of pain and nausea swamped him and he fought the urge to lapse into unconsciousness. He could see his own blood gushing onto the floor and knew that if he didn't stop the bleeding he would die from loss of blood. He wriggled behind a row of bodies and fumbled at his belt to improvise a tourniquet. A middle-aged man lay only a couple of metres away, watching him, and Lacey saw the fear and contempt in the man's eyes because he knew he was giving Lacey cover. The ex-marine looked away and began binding his leg.

The arrival of Roper and Lacey had given Lynch all the opportunity he needed. He knew Roper had knocked out another terrorist, leaving only two who posed a threat and he knew exactly where they were. One had hit the floor, using the trembling bodies of his hostages as a living shield;, the man with the pistol was trying to crawl towards a centre staircase and escape. Deciding on the strategy of relentless pressure Lynch leaped from the stairwell and began running across the departures hall. He jumped over a body, noticing the familiar uniform. It was George, the Europa security guard, pistol in his outstretched hand. His face was unmarked but his upper body was a mess of ripped flesh and an enormous red puddle had spread around him on the floor. A policeman's cap lay near by but there was no sign of its owner. He saw a little girl, aged no more than ten, with a pretty green ribbon in her hair, a matching green dress and both legs blown away. A woman in her late thirties lay beside her, eyes and mouth open, the back of her head dissolving into a stew of blood, hair and brain tissue. An Air France check-in counter near by was warped and scorched and Lynch knew it had to have been a grenade blast. Then the dreadful images became a blur as he ran with all the speed and strength in his body. He kept his eyes on two distant places, a heap of bodies where the man with the AK47 lay and another knot of bodies and baggage behind the first, where the man with the pistol had taken cover.

Roper peered through a gap in the check-in counters and saw what Lynch was doing. He fired a long burst into the ceiling in the middle of the hall, blowing out lights and spraying glass and shattered ceiling tiles everywhere. The man with the AK47 whirled around. It gave Lynch the extra seconds he needed. The man heard the sudden thud of boots and knew someone was almost on him. He squirmed furiously to bring the AK47 to bear but when he looked up and saw Lynch he knew he was a dead man. As he swung his rifle up an ugly, animalistic snarl escaped his lips, half-fear, half-fury. Lynch fired a burst at point-blank range and watched the contorted face explode into a hundred bloody fragments.

Three down, Lynch told himself. One to go. He paused in a half crouch, eyes seeking the man with the pistol and just caught sight of a round, black ball spinning through the air towards him. Instinctively he wanted to hurl himself under cover but he forced himself to stay put and focus on the grenade and its clumsy, tumbling trajectory. It was going to land short. He would be okay but the carpet of shivering bodies wouldn't. He leaped towards the grenade as it landed on an open patch of floor where a man with flossy white hair clutched two sobbing children desperately to him. The grenade didn't even have time to roll as it connected with the side of Lynch's boot and he kicked it towards the check-in counters and heaps of abandoned suitcases. He threw himself down as the grenade skittered noisily across the open floor. There was a loud, flat-sounding crack and he felt the sharp jab of the concussion on both ears followed by an upsurge of cries and sobs. He looked up and saw the Lufthansa counter had been blown apart and several suitcases burst open, spilling their smouldering contents like entrails across the polished floor. Lynch scanned the big room and saw the last terrorist sprinting for the down escalator near the main, central staircase. He crouched and fired off a couple of short bursts but missed. The man in the grey suit reached the top of the escalator and, as he began to disappear from view, turned and fired a couple of wild shots in retaliation at Lynch. Again Lynch hit the floor and when he looked up the man had gone. He got up and took after him but before he had gone two steps felt a rush at his side and saw Roper pass him at a full sprint. He knew Roper was the fittest man in the squad and would reach the escalator first. He pounded after the stocky, bobbing figure, jumping over the huddled bodies, and was about to yell a warning not to follow the terrorist down the escalator when the words died on his lips. Roper wasn't aiming for the escalator. He was running towards the second floor railing at full tilt. Then Lynch saw something he hadn't seen in a lifetime of active service with the navy, the SBS and CTC.

Roper leaped over the railing and into the empty space beyond as confidently as a sprinter who clears a hurdle on the athletics track. But touchdown for the SAS man was a hard floor, five metres below. The man with the pistol was more than half way down the moving staircase and looking frantically for his escape route when his pursuer sailed over the balcony above him. As nimbly as a cat twisting in mid-air Roper turned his body and brought his MP5 to bear as he plunged towards the floor. For a moment he seemed almost to hang in mid-air as though suspended by wires and the entire scene froze in Lynch's eyes like a moment of suspended animation. It was an exquisitely executed manœuvre and a breathtaking demonstration of acrobatic ability.

As the terrorist on the escalator saw Roper appear, materialising as if by magic out of thin air at the side of the moving staircase, his face took on a stricken look. Roper fired a long, withering burst and the bullets stitched across both the gunman's legs at mid-thigh, shredding flesh and bone and almost severing both limbs. With a strangely soft groan he collapsed in a bloody pile, his pistol falling from his fingers and clattering down the staircase ahead of him followed by a wave of his own blood turning the gleaming steel steps darkest red. Reaching the bottom, the gunman spilled onto the floor like a heap of sodden refuse.

Roper had already landed in a perfect roll and was back on his feet. He strode across to the dying man slumped at the bottom of the escalator and surveyed the shattered stumps of both legs. Lynch was already on his way down the near by main staircase when he hesitated. Something about Roper's behaviour caused him to stop. Even though Roper must have known Lynch was watching him he gave no sign that he was aware of anyone else. The ground floor was now deserted and Lynch was his only witness. Roper jabbed the gunman with the nose of his submachine-gun and when he didn't respond jabbed him again, harder. The amount of blood swilling onto the floor around Roper's boots indicated the terrorist would be dead in minutes.

Roper hooked the tip of the MP5 under the gunman's chin and forced his head up. He gazed into the dying terrorist's eyes for what seemed a long time. Lynch had the uneasy feeling he was watching some obscene act of psychopathic intimacy and that Roper *wanted* him to see it. Roper spoke a few words but Lynch couldn't hear what they were and there was no way of knowing whether the man heard them or not. Then Roper squeezed the trigger, blowing away the man's throat, and watched impassively as the severed head fell to the floor.

Forty-seven dead, 115 wounded, 63 of those seriously. Half a dozen of the wounded were not expected to live and a dozen more would learn that they were maimed for life once they emerged from operating theatres in hospitals all over London. Eleven of the dead and 26 of the wounded were children, one of those a boy of eight months whose body had been sliced by grenade shrapnel. Lynch stared numbly at the figures on the computer print-out he'd just been handed at security central. More than 14 hours had passed since the two attacks on Heathrow and these looked like final figures. Christmas Day had dawned outside as miserable and cold as Lynch felt inside. His eyes were red with fatigue and his stomach bilious with the bad coffee which had sustained him through the night. He wore the same clothes but had changed his boots because the soles had been sticky with blood.

The figures gave a rough breakdown of age, sex and nationality of the victims of the massacre at Europa terminal. The majority were Britons, Germans, Greeks and Italians. Only eight people had been killed at Atlantic terminal, five of them Americans and three Britons returning home for Christmas.

Security's response to the attack at Atlantic had been overwhelming and the three terrorists involved had died within minutes of launching their assault. It seemed most likely they were decoys and, inadequately trained perhaps, had bungled the attack. An armed, uniformed policeman at Atlantic had noticed the trio acting suspiciously and had approached them when they began pulling grenades out of a small sports bag. He had shot one dead but had to dive for cover when one of the remaining two pulled out an Uzi and began spraying the arrivals hall. This had triggered the first alarm. Both remaining terrorists were shot dead by Hawkins who had been first into the terminal. However, they had created enough of a diversion to draw airport security, giving the main team free rein at Europa until Lynch, Koper and Lacey reached the scene.

The only survivor of the two terrorist groups was the man Lynch had shot in the back, and he was under guard in the military hospital at Aldershot army camp. Lacey, crippled for life, would be invalided out of CTC with a pension.

The images of the attack on Europa terminal wouldn't leave

Lynch alone. He had seen dead people before. He had killed before, at close quarters, but he was still shocked by the amount of blood he had seen. Perhaps it was those polished floors. There was nowhere for the blood to go. It couldn't soak into the desert sand or the floor of the jungle. The floor at Europa terminal had been awash in it. And there was the memory of the little dead girl in the green dress with the matching ribbon in her hair and her mother near by, her head blown apart. Surmounting it all was the recurring image of Roper's grotesque execution of the terrorist leader.

Sir Malcolm Porter had arrived from a Christmas cocktail party within an hour of the attacks and launched an immediate departmental enquiry which would be superseded by a full government commission of enquiry. Sir Malcolm had gone to pains to reassure Lynch that he had taken the only action available to him under the circumstances and that he would have his chief's full support.

From the first shots at Atlantic to the death of the last gunman at Europa both attacks had lasted less than five minutes, yet they constituted the worst single act of terrorism ever to take place on the British mainland in peacetime. Reports of the atrocity had already flashed around the world, regular TV programmes were interrupted by newsflashes, newspapers brought out special editions carrying the first ghastly photographs of the carnage. The Prime Minister was expected to visit survivors in hospital that afternoon, the Queen's Christmas holiday at Sandringham had been interrupted and she too was expected to make a special trip back to London to visit survivors. Washington expressed outrage and threatened military reprisals against the perpetrators while Moscow expressed qualified regret.

There would be days, weeks, months of piecing it all together. What had gone wrong? What had they to learn? How could they prevent it happening again? Who was to blame? Then the

37

memory would be overtaken by another terrorist outrage. Because no-one doubted that there would be a next time.

It was a catastrophe and every time Lynch went over it the same chilly realisation flooded his thoughts—he had called it wrong. He had unnecessarily split his forces. He should have guessed that the second attack had the potential to be far more devastating than the first. It was the consummate failure of an otherwise successful career. It was a failure which would haunt him for the rest of his life. For the moment, he knew he had to stick with it all the way through to the final post mortem. He would have to shoulder most of the blame whatever Sir Malcolm had promised. And he knew what he would do when it was all over. Whatever the outcome, he knew he would resign from the CTC. He couldn't even begin to consider what might come afterwards. All he was sure of was that the last 24 hours had brought him to the end of a long and bloody road. He was finished with counter terrorism.

2

THE DECISION

London, spring 1989

The phone was ringing. The red phone again. This time, instead of the guard, Lynch picked it up. There was a man's voice at the other end, sonorous and accusatory, reciting the same thing over and over. A litany of numbers. The numbers of the dead and those maimed for life. And as the voice droned on, the faces of the victims floated in front of him. One face always recurred more than the others. The face of a little girl, perhaps ten years old, pretty fair hair tied with a green ribbon matching her green dress. And then the green was soaked with a tide of red as blood poured from her shattered body. In the distance the phone still seemed to be ringing. Lynch struggled foggily, gratefully out of the nightmare. The phone in the living-room was still ringing. It must have been ringing for some time. Whoever wanted to speak to him wouldn't give up easily.

Lynch still didn't feel like talking to anyone, even though he was glad that something had dragged him out of bed. Sleep was still the worst time. When he was awake he could banish the haunting images from his mind's eye by an effort of will but when he was asleep his defences crumbled and they always came back. It was a Monday in the middle of April, just after eight in the morning. As he shambled from his darkened bedroom into the living-room, wearing only a pair of crumpled underpants, the sunlight hurt his eyes. He had not closed the curtains the previous night and he saw that it was a beautiful spring day outside. One of those first days of a real English spring, when office girls risked catching colds by going to work in summer dresses which exposed their pasty limbs to the sun.

He stepped around the coffee table littered with the debris of last night's drinking—half a dozen empty beer cans squashed flat and an almost-empty bottle of Lamb's Navy Rum. There were some dregs of rum in the bottom of a glass and when the smell drifted up his stomach heaved. He wasn't used to it. He hadn't been a heavy drinker since his early days in the navy and had given it away altogether on joining the SBS. His head ached, a puddle of acid had congealed in the pit of his stomach and his mouth tasted foul, reminding him of the long-forgotten joys of a rum hangover. The ringing phone waited him out and, reluctantly, he picked it up.

'It's Roper,' the voice on the other end announced abruptly. 'I want to talk to you.'

'You don't owe me anything,' Lynch said, his voice flat and emotionless. He had not included in his report the bizarre circumstances in which the last terrorist had met his death. He had skirted it successfully during days of examination and cross-examination at the commission of enquiry and had not raised it at all with Roper. Lynch was aware that the latter knew he had been seen, but had not mentioned it either.

'It's important,' Roper pressed. Lynch was surprised to hear from his former colleague so soon after the close of the enquiry. He had neither expected nor wanted to hear from anyone in his old squad yet. The hearing had wound up only a month earlier, after sitting for six weeks straight. Just last Friday the judge who chaired the enquiry had issued his findings, singling

40

no-one out in particular for blame but criticising the CTC in general for 'inadequate all-contingency response' and recommending that security at all airports and seaports be stepped up 'appropriately'.

It seemed no-one but Lynch had expected anything else. Which was why his resignation came as a shock to CTC. Sir Malcolm had sympathised and suggested he was suffering from unnecessary feelings of guilt and urged him to take an extended leave to rest and reconsider. He had refused. His last official act before leaving the command was to recommend Roper as squad leader. He speculated that Roper knew and that was why he was calling.

'If it's about my recommendation that you replace me . . .'

'No, it isn't,' Roper interrupted. 'I didn't know. Thanks but no thanks. I'm not interested. What I want to talk to you about is more important than that.'

Lynch sighed. He held a quiet admiration for Roper though that had been tempered by what he had seen at the airport. Not that he intended to let it worry him. The armed forces were full of psychopaths. He just hadn't expected it from Roper. He had decided to file it mentally. After a lifetime of serving with men through periods of intense, sustained pressure, Lynch had grown accustomed to the unexpected where human nature was concerned. Random acts of cruelty in the heat of battle were nothing new. Roper was too valuable a man to throw away because of a single act of sadism, he decided. Jobs like this needed men like Roper. Lynch had simply decided that as he wouldn't be seeing anything of the man any more it would no longer be his problem. He also knew that Roper wouldn't ring him without good reason. If he said it was important then it probably was, though Lynch couldn't begin to imagine what it might be. He looked down at the dwindling half bottle of rum on the coffee table and frowned. 'All right,' he decided. 'Come to my place tonight. Around seven.'

41

Lynch hung up and went back to bed but couldn't sleep. After an hour of trying he got up, shaved and showered, put on jeans, sneakers and a light sweater and went out for the morning papers. By the time he'd had a little walk, some fresh air, returned to his flat, eaten breakfast and read the papers, he began to feel marginally better. He pushed open the window overlooking the street to let in some of the spring sunshine along with the roar and fumes of the passing traffic. When he turned his favourite chair at just the right angle he could put his feet up on the window sill and see a sliver of the Thames between the drab, sooty buildings which hemmed in his first floor terrace flat. He had taken the phone off the hook and turned the radio to a soft rock station. With a fresh cup of tea in his fist he settled down for a quiet morning. He eyed the remaining rum on the coffee table and considered adding a splash to his tea but thought better of it. He hadn't had much time for reflection since the events of last Christmas. He had lived in a virtual state of limbo, his life on hold, throughout the enquiry.

As the facts emerged, it transpired that the two groups of terrorists had not arrived at Heathrow aboard any aircraft. The squad which did most of the damage at Europa had arrived, like Lynch, on the tube, its members travelling separately with weapons concealed in cheap suitcases bought days earlier in London. They had not formed into a single cell until they had all arrived at the departures lounge, when the man in the grey suit had fired his pistol into the air signalling their attack to commence at 9.21 pm, exactly one minute after the attack at Atlantic terminal had begun. They had thrown grenades and fired indiscriminately into the crowd. Because all the other security guards were already en route to Atlantic terminal, George was the only guard left at Europa and he had fired two harmless shots before he had been killed. Then the terrorists had ordered everyone to lie on the floor and their leader had begun to pick his way among them systematically, seeking out Britons, Americans, Israelis and Jews of any nationality. Anyone who gave an answer he didn't like was executed. The decoy cell had arrived intact at Atlantic terminal by taxi. The taxi driver thought it strange that they only had one bag between three of them and that their leader had emptied his pockets to pay him off, giving him an eighty-pound tip, but hadn't thought to tell anyone on airport security.

MI6 had discovered that all the terrorists had arrived in Britain separately, over a period of two months, either by cross-channel ferry or by airplane from a friendly country. None were carrying any ID at the time of the attack, though it appeared they had all travelled on non-Arabic passports, probably Pakistani. This information was provided by the surviving terrorist, Muharram Bandar. Bandar gave his age as 22, and had told his interrogators that he was a Palestinian who lived in northern Lebanon. He had been trained in Libya and Syria. He said he was a member of the group calling itself Red Jihad, which had claimed responsibility for the attacks. Bandar had recovered from his wounds except for a permanent limp in his left leg caused by one of Lynch's bullets which had chipped his pelvis and been deflected down into his thigh before exiting, leaving a large wound. He was now a maximum security guest of Her Majesty awaiting trial on charges of multiple murder.

Bandar claimed to have travelled by road to Damascus and then by air to Karachi. He had stopped over for two weeks to collect a genuine Pakistani passport, doctored to carry his photograph and describing him as a student of agriculture. From Karachi he had flown direct to London where he had passed easily through immigration, posing as a student enrolled at Reading agricultural college. Due to his swarthy complexion, his ethnicity had not been queried. Once in London he had gone to a safe house in Fulham, rented for the duration of the operation. The arms and grenades were already there, he said, having been smuggled in earlier aboard an Eastern-Bloc freighter.

He had expected to die, he said, for the holy cause of the Palestinian people, and had been surprised when he woke up in a military-prison hospital instead of paradise. Examining psychiatrists had pronounced him immature and below average intelligence. After his trial he would probably be put away for the rest of his life at the expense of the British taxpayer, unless MI6 could find another use for him.

Within 48 hours of the Heathrow attacks a video cassette had been delivered to the Swiss envoy in Beirut. It showed an unnamed man at a desk in front of a backdrop of the Palestinian flag, claiming to represent Red Jihad, accepting responsibility for the attacks and promising to carry the war against 'all imperialists and enemies of the Palestinian people'. A day later, Colonel Gaddafi had apparently appeared on Libyan television praising the heroic action of 'all martyrs to the great Arab cause'. At the same time Gaddafi was careful to dissociate Libya from any active role in the attacks. Despite the bluster, he had been a more prudent man since the American bombing raids of March 1986.

Those raids had cost the Americans diplomatically but they had also rocked Gaddafi more than anyone outside the intelligence services of the Western democracies could know. However, in the interim period of calm, he had regained his grip on the country and his open support for such terrorism now constituted his most provocative behaviour for almost two years. After praising the attacks he had embarked on a familiar tirade, deriding Britain as a toothless lion and a lackey of the Americans. His appearance on the evening television news had been greeted with the standard mix of jeers and mock cheers in pubs and lounges around Britain. The government had huffed and puffed, Tory backbenchers described the attacks as an act of war and demanded that the RAF bomb Tripoli, but the PM refused to condone any kind of military response and had, instead, urged the free world to impose trade sanctions and isolate those states which supported terrorists.

Even the Americans, despite their five dead, appeared unsure of how or where to direct their fury this time. Once again the President threatened direct military action against Libya and Iran but, despite the implied support of those states, it was clear that this latest attack had been launched from Red Jihad's base somewhere in the bloody stew of Lebanon. The terrorist hierarchy, ever mindful of the importance of world opinion as an ally against military retaliation by the Americans, had been prompt in identifiying themselves as a new and autonomous Palestinian splinter group based in Lebanon. But though the surviving terrorist confirmed he had received training in both terrorist states, this attack had been launched from somewhere else, a country which could not be held accountable because it was no longer a country.

Frustrated by their inability to pinpoint Red Jihad's Lebanon base since it probably did not exist except as a propaganda ploy, Britain and America once again appeared impotent. Restrained by observance of the principles of international law the Americans seemed unable to find an appropriate response. Invasion of terrorist states such as Libya was out of the question, Lynch knew, however vexatious Gaddafi became. So was any kind of overt commando-style raid. Yet, he knew that unless the Western powers resolved to go directly to the source of terrorism and cut off its head, groups would continue to receive lavish funding and strike wherever and whenever they liked. The advantage always lay with the fanatic willing to die for his cause and as long as leaders like Gaddafi provided arms and support, terrorists would slaughter innocent people in the West.

Warships of the American Fifth Fleet once again cruised to the coast of Libya and penetrated the supposedly inviolate waters of the Gulf of Sidra but Gaddafi merely uttered taunts and did nothing to provoke direct military confrontation. Meanwhile the West presumably would try to isolate Libya further in the international community, a process Lynch knew was impossible as long as Gaddafi had the tacit support of the Eastern-Bloc nations and could rely on the shifting alliances of other Arab countries.

Covert attempts to destabilise Gaddafi's rule from within were a long-term prospect and Lynch wondered how many more women and children would die in the meantime. He crossed his feet on the window sill and thought about the lessons the West had failed to learn from the example of bloody regimes such as those of Gaddafi in Libya, Assad in Syria, Khomeini in Iran, and of the former lunatic dictator of Uganda, Idi Amin. Amin had committed crimes which had rivalled only the Third Reich in scale and horror. Yet the West's tacit acknowledgement of the sovereignty of madmen had permitted Amin to go his merry, murderous way for almost a decade. Like Amin, Gaddafi was living on borrowed time, but, Lynch asked himself, how could any government give back the lives of the innocents who died in that time?

The more he thought about it the more irritated he became. He tried to push these thoughts out of his mind. He would have to start thinking about his future soon. Money wasn't an immediate problem. He wasn't rich beyond the dreams of avarice but he had enough cash to last him a while. He still had a modest income from his navy pension and despite his abrupt resignation from CTC would receive a substantial pay-out of accumulated holiday pay, overtime and unclaimed leave. He would have to consider finding another way of earning a living eventually, but he had enough to buy time to think. Lynch needed to rid himself of the appalling malaise which had afflicted him in the aftermath of the Heathrow attacks. He had never been easily depressed, nor was he the type to wallow in self-pity but something was wrong, he knew, and he needed time to recover. Not from the guilt he felt at all those innocent deaths at the airport. He was too much of a pragmatist to assume all the blame. It was something else that haunted him, something worse. An overwhelming sense of futility tainted everything he had ever done. He was drained by the enervating conviction that no matter how good he was at his job, he was destined to dissipate his skills within the framework of a hopelessly defensive and inadequate political structure. He may as well try to hold back the tide.

The State had apparently accepted that there was no defence against this new kind of war and that the civilian population would just have to carry the casualties until terrorist groups somehow exhausted themselves. Squads such as the CTC were basically clean-up crews—always on the defensive. Diversions, surprise, multiple attack, sheer bloody-minded fanaticism would win every time. The initiative had been surrendered to the terrorists. And there seemed to be no shortage of fanatics willing to die for a transient, sordid victory. Western society could not be shielded from that kind of insanity. To Lynch, a whole way of life, a philosophy, the set of freedoms which held together the great democracies, were under siege by a tiny clique of zealots. And as long as men were restrained in their response to this threat, innocents would continue to die, old men in wheelchairs, old women, children whose lives had not yet begun. They were all victims of the terrorist initiative and Western impotence.

Lynch had gone into counter terrorism because he could think of nothing better he could do with his life. The first time that decision had been put to the test it had proved a terrible miscalculation. How naive he considered himself to have been. He also knew that if the people of this battered, beleaguered island knew just how inadequate their defences against terrorism really were, they would throw out the government in a week. His country was losing a war and as long as men like him were forbidden to fight on all fronts they would never turn the tide of that war. Rather than lose the battle, Lynch had decided to lay down his arms and walk away. Now, for the first time in his life, he had nowhere to go.

He decided to go for a drink.

Lynch strolled the few blocks to the Dove, his local Hammersmith pub—it was a name he had always thought singularly appropriate considering the nature of his profession—and passed a leisurely couple of hours sipping beer and enjoying the sunshine on the terrace overlooking the Thames. He sat through the lunchtime trade, which was light because it was Monday, read the early edition of the *Evening Standard* and exchanged mildly flirtatious glances with two pretty office girls. He took his time with the beer. He didn't want to be hung over when Roper came around. He wondered what could possibly be so important to Roper that he had arranged the meeting, but his speculation only led him back down the same dead end and he tried to put it out of his mind. Around two, he decided to take a long walk by the river to sweat some of the beer out of his system. After several months of idleness, sitting around in stuffy commission hearings, he had missed his regular exercise programme and had begun to feel both restless and lethargic. He had opted in favour of the lethargy for the moment and resumed drinking to subdue the restlessness. He knew he would have to be careful not to become too habitual a drinker but for now it was the sedative he needed and it helped him get to sleep at night.

The spring sunshine had held into the afternoon and the sky was storybook blue with only a few white puffs of cloud. Even a tired old tart of a town like London seemed rejuvenated and refreshed by a day like this and put on its prettier face for the visitors. By contrast Lynch felt old and careworn. His mind wandered back 15 years to the weekend trips he made up from Britannia Naval College at Dartmouth as a young naval officer, when life was just one magnificent adventure and no problem seemed insoluble in the face of limitless youth, energy and optimism. He was brought back with a jerk when he passed a gaggle of London's ageing punks with rainbow Mohawks and scrawny bodies bandaged in leather and chains. One of the men wore a necklace of what appeared to be rat's tails.

Lynch smiled to himself. They looked as tired and passé as he felt. With his crewneck sweater, blue jeans and closecropped hair he suspected that to them he just looked like an ageing skinhead. They were all dowdy patriarchs from two declining tribes of speedily-declining Britain.

He walked all the way to Tower Bridge and, enjoying himself, decided to cross the bridge and walk back along the south bank. A little after four his appetite flared and he stopped to buy fish and chips from a shop run by a Punjabi. He took his late lunch out to a scarred public bench and watched the river traffic while he ate. He looked back down the road leading from Tower Bridge at a man sitting in a light-blue van parked at the kerb in a no-parking area. Lynch thought he recognised the man from the Dove. About the same age as himself, receding motheaten hair, bad skin, cheap brown suit off the peg at Marks and Sparks. He wouldn't put it past Control to keep an eye on him for a while. He decided to phone Porter in a few days. He didn't want to appear overly concerned but decided they should know that he knew. Lynch finished his al fresco seafood lunch, stood up, faced the blue van and gave a loud, bilious belch. Then he started walking towards the van. The man in the brown suit stared resolutely at the windshield. As he passed the driver's open window Lynch screwed up the greasy wrapped paper from his lunch with its pungent cargo of fish scraps and slung it onto the driver's lap. The man did nothing. As he walked on Lynch became more positive the man was from Control. Suddenly an-

49

gered, he changed his mind about the walk and hurried to catch a bus back across the river. He was tired when he got back to his flat and lay down on the couch and quickly fell asleep. This time there were no dreams.

Lynch woke up a few minutes before seven, as though an internal alarm had gone off. It was a knack he'd learned in his early days in the navy. He made some tea, switched on the TV and idly watched an early-evening chat show. The door bell rang promptly at seven. Lynch buzzed his guest up and Roper strolled in, face expressionless as usual.

Lynch offered him tea and Roper shook his head, adding only two words: 'The pub.' Then he turned back down the stairs. Lynch shrugged, grabbed a jacket and followed him but he didn't like the implication in Roper's behaviour that his flat might be bugged.

'I didn't think you drank,' Lynch said, as they walked into the half-empty pub.

'I don't,' Roper answered.

Lynch glanced around at the faces of the drinkers in the Dove. He knew the man in the brown suit would not be there but wondered who might have replaced him. He ordered a pint of lager for himself and a Coke for Roper. The spring day had cooled and all the pub's customers were drinking inside, leaving the terrace empty. Lynch led the way out and picked a table. 'Quiet enough for you?' he asked and Roper answered by sitting down. Lynch joined him and took a long, satisfying pull on his drink, then waited in silence. It was Roper's move and as far as Lynch was concerned they could sit there till closing time.

Finally Roper spoke and as usual it was to the point. 'How do you feel about doing some freelance work?' he asked.

Lynch resisted the temptation to smile. So that was what it was about, he thought. He shook his head slowly. 'Not my style, mate. I don't go in for that kind of thing.'

'This isn't the usual mercenary deal,' Roper said. 'It's different. I can't give you much detail now except to tell you that it is something I believe you would want to be involved in.'

Again Lynch shook his head. 'Not good enough. I need a bit more than that before I even decide if this conversation is worth pursuing. There are other things I could be doing.'

'Like getting pissed?' Roper had seen the almost empty bottle of rum on the table in Lynch's flat.

'Yes, as a matter of fact,' Lynch replied evenly. 'I find it very therapeutic after all these years.' If Roper was attempting to redefine their relationship outside the squad they weren't getting off to a very good start, he thought. He was a little wary of the other man since the incident at the airport, even though he had kept it to himself. He wasn't exactly sure what kind of psychological undercurrents ran through Roper's mind. He let the silence lengthen.

'There's a guy I'd like you meet,' Roper said eventually. 'An American. A bloke with a proposition I think will be of considerable interest to you. I'll set up the meeting. The deal is that you listen. If you decide then that you're not interested then you can walk. But before that I want your word that, whatever happens, whatever is said, you will never disclose the nature of the offer that will be put to you. If you do, it could be bad for a lot of people.'

Lynch recognised the hint of a threat in Roper's words but despite himself he was intrigued. This was all highly atypical behaviour for Roper. Lynch had never seen him so intense. He decided to draw the normally taciturn ex-SAS man out a bit more.

'Not interested,' Lynch said. 'Sounds like a lot of trouble to me ... mysterious Americans ... secret meetings. I really don't need anything to do with our line of work for quite some time. I'm a man who needs a holiday.'

'You didn't resign just to have a holiday,' said Roper.

'A long holiday,' Lynch smiled. 'A whole new change of direction perhaps.'

There was another pause, then Roper said, in a voice intended to carry a weight of meaning: 'I think we can guarantee you that.'

Lynch hesitated, then changed the subject. 'How do you know my flat is bugged?' he asked.

'I don't.' Roper shrugged. 'Not for sure. But I think there's a fairly good chance it is. Don't you?'

'Control had a man following me today,' Lynch added casually. 'I wonder what they're afraid I'll do.'

'Occupational hazard,' said Roper. 'They'll keep an eye on you till they're satisfied you're not going crackers. That you're not going to start yapping to the newspapers. That you're not going involve yourself in some kind of mercenary skullduggery that might embarrass them.'

Lynch nodded. 'They'll get bored with me very quickly, then,' he said, draining his glass. 'Another?' Roper hadn't touched his Coke. He waited till Lynch had returned from the bar with his second pint, then asked: 'Will you give me your word on this meeting?'

'Aren't you afraid of being seen with a rogue elephant like me?' Lynch countered. 'Failed CTC squad leader. Embittered ex-serviceman, emotionally crippled, broken by failure and taking to the piss in a big way?'

Roper sighed with uncharacteristic impatience. 'Look,' he said. 'I'm going to tell you something I haven't told anybody else. Either you'll understand or you won't. If you don't, then I'm talking to the wrong man.' He hesitated, then hunched forward, body tense, hands clasped tight in front of him. Despite his wariness Lynch found himself drawn in by Roper's earnestness and he detected a note of deep anger in his voice when he started to speak again.

'Five years ago, there was a demonstration by Libyan students against the regime of Colonel Gaddafi outside their embassy in St James Square. You remember?'

Lynch nodded.

'A policewoman was shot by someone inside the embassy. She died 24 hours later. Her killer was never brought to justice. Subsequently, all those Libyans inside the London embassy, including the killer, were allowed to leave the country in exchange for a bunch of Britons Gaddafi took hostage in Tripoli.'

Lynch found himself transfixed by the look in Roper's eyes, a look of cold, controlled malevolence.

'I'd just joined the regiment,' Roper continued, using the term preferred by serving members of the SAS. 'I was in the mess with some of the lads when the shooting was shown on TV. I've never been able to get the image out of my mind of that poor bloody policewoman on the ground. Shot while doing her job. Just another day, another demo. Till one of Gaddafi's lunatics starts firing from the cover of the embassy into a street filled with unarmed civilians and a few harassed bloody coppers struggling to keep a lid on it. I went on stand-by with my unit while the whole business dragged on. We were ready to go. We could have taken them out in minutes. In the end we had to sit back and do nothing while those bastards got a police escort out of London. You can imagine how everybody felt about that.' He paused and rubbed a hand roughly over his face. 'Diplomatic immunity,' he said, the words coming like obscenities.

Lynch waited in silence. He had not anticipated such an outpouring of anger and frustration. Not from Roper.

'You know what it's like,' Roper smiled thinly. 'All dressed-up and nowhere to go.' He hesitated, then said: 'What really turned my stomach was the way Gaddafi welcomed them back like conquering heroes. Some toad shoots a defenceless policewoman and that makes him a hero.' He seemed to struggle for the words that might somehow put form to his fury. 'These people aren't just cowards,' he ground out. 'This is something

53

worse than cowardice. These people are beyond all shame and they have put themselves beyond all mercy. If they go unpunished then the life of that poor bloody copper and the lives of a great many other innocent people cease to have any meaning.' He paused and looked hard into Lynch's eyes. 'Don't try to talk to me about international law,' he said, anticipating an argument that did not materialise. 'International law only works when all sides play by the rules. That's the problem with this country. Civilisation is a wonderful concept but it seems we're the only ones playing the game. To hell with that. We've been buried by the law. What we need now is a little justice. That's where you and I come into the picture, Lynch. Our whole lives have been a preparation for an opportunity such as this.

'We have it in our power to see that justice—real justice— is done. It's something I've wanted for years. And unless I've misjudged you badly this is something you will want very much to be part of. Now,' he paused, 'do I have your word on the meeting?'

Roper straightened up and looked away and the two men sat in silence in the cold night shadows of the terrace overlooking the Thames. They could hear the rumble and roar of what had once been the most civilised city on earth all around them, the slap of water on the ancient stone wall at the river's edge, people talking and laughing behind them in the familiar warmth of the pub. A freighter hooted mournfully on its way to the empty Pool of London. It was a scene of soothing, restful decay and both men knew that neither of them belonged in it.

'You have my word,' Lynch said.

3

THE MEETING

London, summer 1989

The first Monday in May, Lynch phoned the office of Sir Malcolm Porter, his former boss of CTC, in Whitehall. It had been more than two weeks since his meeting with Roper but he had not heard further about the proposed meeting with the unnamed American. He was still drinking but trying to cut back and, disgusted by his own idleness and the fear that he would lose fitness, began exercising again. In the mornings he got up before rush hour and jogged along the Embankment. In the afternoons he would cross the river to Richmond Park and run around the perimeter a couple of times. He knew that the onset of the peak tourist season would soon put an end to that and decided to look for a gym.

He secured an appointment with Porter for two in the afternoon of the following day. Lynch believed he was still under observation and though he had scoured his flat for bugs the fact that he hadn't found any meant nothing. Directional eavesdropping devices in any of a hundred vehicles parked the length of the street could easily pick up a conversation in his flat, and recording his phone calls was child's play. The CTC had its own intelligence department which worked in close liaison with MI5 on security matters on the British mainland. CTC needed its own operatives both to maintain security within its own network and to monitor the activities of terrorist suspects, groups and organisations all over the world. It would be easy for Sir Malcolm to put Lynch on the surveillance list for a while, at least until he was satisfied that he wasn't likely to do anything which could embarrass the department.

The following day Lynch, wearing a smart navy blazer, tie, grey slacks and highly polished black shoes, walked through the doors of the Home Office's 'C' wing in Whitehall, where CTC occupied one whole floor. It took a few minutes to clear security inside and then he took the lift to the third floor, showed his visitor's pass to the guard there, and walked for what seemed like half a mile down drab cream and brown-painted corridors until he turned the corner which took him to Sir Malcolm's office, identified only as room C331. He opened the door without knocking and recognised Sir Malcolm's secretary, the tiny but efficient Jean Hamilton, a Scot like himself but with the prissier accent of a superior Edinburgh private school. He had met her several times since joining CTC, the last time on the occasion of his promotion to squad leader.

'Please take a seat, Lieutenant Lynch,' she said pleasantly. 'I'll tell Sir Malcolm you're here.' As she disappeared through the door to her employer's office Lynch realised she was one of the few people who always addressed him by his naval rank. There was precious little of what crossed Sir Malcolm's desk that his long-time secretary did not see and Lynch suspected she forgot even less. Lynch expected to be kept waiting as a matter of form and was mildly surprised when Jean Hamilton reappeared and told him to go straight in.

The head of CTC came around from behind his desk to welcome Lynch and shake his hand. 'Would you like something to

56

drink?' he offered. 'Tea, coffee, cold drink, something a little stronger perhaps?'

Lynch declined but had no doubt that Sir Malcolm already knew he was drinking quite heavily. He made himself comfortable in one of the two high-backed leather chairs facing Sir Malcolm's desk. From here he could look past his former boss through the high, Georgian window and see the tops of the elm trees just outside. Sir Malcolm did not occupy a grand office. It was big enough for his desk, bookshelves, and a few odd pieces of furniture but that was all.

The ubiquitous computer terminal squatted like a sleek, one-eyed toad on a corner of Sir Malcolm's desk, blinking at its master. On the walls were only two pictures, both portraits. One of the Queen, the other of Colonel David Stirling, founder of the SAS, Sir Malcolm's former regiment. He had been a major-general in the army before becoming CO of the SAS and then resigning from the army altogether to take on the task of establishing the CTC at the personal request of the Prime Minister. Though he was in his mid-fifties, he was still demonstrably fit, with the weathered complexion of the career soldier and crinkly brown hair only lightly tinged with grey.

'Reconsidered?' he asked Lynch abruptly.

Lynch shook his head. 'Sorry, sir. I meant what I said last time we spoke.' Lynch had informed Sir Malcolm of his intention to resign from the CTC whatever the findings of the government's commission of enquiry and had reaffirmed his decision with a letter of resignation the week its findings were handed down.

'Then I'm sorry too,' said Sir Malcolm and he sounded as though he meant it. 'Why did you ask to see me?'

'I want you to stop having me followed.'

'Can't do that,' Porter snapped back. 'Next?'

Lynch smiled despite himself. 'You can't afford to have me followed indefinitely.'

'No,' Porter agreed. 'Only until we're satisfied you're not at risk.'

'From whom?'

Porter arched his eyebrows as if to say: you tell me.

'It's very annoying, you know,' Lynch continued. 'And quite unnecessary.'

'My dear Colin,' Porter countered amiably, 'you simply don't know. We don't know. You could be a target for compromise. We may be doing you a favour. You've been through a deep emotional trauma, you may be susceptible to pressures which would not normally affect you.

'We'll have to keep an eye on you for a little while longer, just to make sure our friends in certain Eastern Bloc countries or in the Middle East don't decide that you've got all sorts of information worth knowing. It's department policy, old boy. Actually I'd much rather you stayed with the department, even on extended leave if you wish. The offer's still there. I do wish you'd consider it.'

Lynch realised he was getting nowhere. 'You know, I don't subscribe to that popular Whitehall theory that if I'm not with you then I must be against you,' he said. 'I think my record and my loyalties are above reproach. Yes, it's been an ordeal. No, I'm not about to go bonkers and offer my services to the IRA, the CIA, the KGB or the RSPCA. And I don't think I'm in possession of too many secrets our friends in the world of international terrorism don't already know. Our weaknesses are common knowledge. You're quite correct in suggesting that I need some extended leave. I should probably have got out after the Falklands, but the navy was still home to me and when my service was up I was happy to bide my time till I could join CTC and feel I was doing something useful. But people like me do wear out. It just takes us a while to admit it to ourselves, and when we do I wish people like you would let us go gracefully . . . sir.'

Porter looked at Lynch with an odd smile. 'People like you don't wear out, Colin,' he said. 'And you never go out gracefully. You're just suffering a little bit of metal fatigue, that's all.'

Lynch hesitated, then added: 'A favour?'

'What?'

'Stop bugging my flat and my phone.'

Porter shook his head. 'Sorry.'

Lynch stood up to leave. 'Okay,' he said. 'But at least try and put a couple of half-decent watchers on me. The last few have been getting under my feet. You never know, I might trip and hurt one of them by mistake.'

'Don't be naughty, Colin,' said Sir Malcolm, walking around his desk to see Lynch to the door.

The two men exchanged cordial goodbyes but just before Lynch left the old man's office Porter gave him a strangely loaded look and said: 'I'm sure we'll be seeing each other again, Colin. Quite sure.'

As he retraced his steps along the endless Whitehall corridors Lynch was puzzled and angry. His suspicions that his flat and phone were bugged had been willingly confirmed. So willingly, that Lynch had to conclude Porter was telling the truth; it was department policy and would cease in due course. In the meantime, he decided, he would have to be particularly circumspect, especially with Roper and any dealings he might have with the mysterious American.

In his office Porter had returned to his desk and asked Jean Hamilton to get him an important phone number. When he had been put through he spoke briefly: 'Lynch is aware we've been watching him, so it's all gone rather well this far. You can tell your people to make themselves a little less obvious now. And if he sees Aidan Roper again I want to know immediately.'

Outside at her desk Jean Hamilton saw the red light on her internal switch go out when Sir Malcolm hung up. It used to be a number she had little cause to dial yet she had rung it for the old man at least a dozen times in the past two weeks. It was a direct line to Sir Malcolm's opposite number at MI6, Britain's department of foreign intelligence.

The surveillance appeared to stop though Lynch knew it hadn't. Despite his initial irritation he wasn't overly concerned. His life had become pleasantly dull since leaving the CTC. He was delighted to see how little it cost him to live so long as he didn't throw too much money across the bar at the Dove. The pay-out from CTC had taken his modest nest egg to around 30,000 pounds. Enough to feed and clothe him and pay for the rent on his flat. His navy pension would cover most of his other costs and his four-year-old Ford Escort, parked in the street, was paid for.

He realised he no longer had to remain in London if he chose otherwise. He had enough money to buy a cottage on a few wild acres in the western highlands of Scotland and wondered how CTC might maintain an unobtrusive surveillance on him up there. But he still needed to go through a period of adjustment before making up his mind and he had promised Roper he would consider his promised deal. Another two weeks had passed and still he hadn't heard back. In the meantime he contented himself with building a new daily routine. He still went for his morning run but he had enlisted in a sweaty local gym and spent two hours a day there, working out on the machines and punch bag, occasionally sparring a few rounds with the predominantly West Indian clientele. Most evenings he had a couple of pints at the Dove or ate locally and then went home to watch television. He was usually in bed before midnight. In an effort to cut his alcohol consumption he had stopped bringing booze home but he still felt fidgety with the time it left on his hands. Convalescence for whatever sickness it was that afflicted his spirit was going to take time. He received few phone calls and made none. Hawkins, McCosker and the newly-recovered Lacey had invited him out for a night's drinking but he had refused, leaving them hurt and puzzled. There was nothing, Lynch was convinced, that could possibly stir the interest of the people who listened in on his life. Sometimes, out of boredom, when he went to the toilet he left the door open because, he decided, if they wanted to listen to him they may as well listen to everything.

It was almost the end of May when Roper called and arranged to meet Lynch for a drink. This time they stayed in the crowded bar of the Dove so their conversation would be drowned in the noisy babble around them. Roper had arranged the meeting with the American for nine in the morning the following Wednesday. Lynch was to go to the Park Lane Inter-Continental and browse in the news-stand until he was contacted.

'How will your man recognise me?' Lynch asked.

'He's already seen your picture,' Roper answered.

Lynch whistled softly. 'Naughty, naughty,' he said.

'That's what happens when you're on the street,' Roper said. 'Nobody taking care of you any more.'

'Will you be there?'

Roper nodded. 'You won't see me till you get into the room. Any questions?'

'Is all this cloak-and-dagger stuff absolutely necessary?'

Roper stood up to leave. 'We have to protect ourselves,' he said. He turned to go but Lynch stopped him. 'Just one more question,' he said. 'Is it illegal?'

'Not in this country,' Roper said.

The following Wednesday, Lynch finished his morning run along the Embankment, showered, ate a light breakfast of tea and toast, put on jeans, sneakers, a casual check shirt and light windcheater. He caught the tube to Hyde Park and when he surfaced at Hyde Park Corner walked along Rotten Row for a few minutes, taking care to avoid the early morning gallopers. Then he cut abruptly through the park and jogged across the lanes of honking traffic streaming along Park Lane. Safely on the pavement on the other side he looked around but no-one was trying to follow him through the traffic. No-one seemed at all interested in him. He continued towards the bottom end of Park Lane then looped back around to Berkeley Square, spent a few minutes browsing among some of the most expensive car showrooms in the world, then checked his watch and walked quickly around to Park Lane again and the Inter-Continental. He still hadn't seen anyone tailing him but all that meant, he knew, was that Porter had heeded his warning and sent somebody better.

He strolled into the lobby of the big American-owned hotel and threaded his way towards the news-stand between the knots of gossiping tourists. He had just picked up a copy of that day's *Independent* when a tall, tanned man with thinning blond hair and a faint moustache appeared silently beside him, smiled pleasantly and said: 'Hi. You're the guy in 826, aren't you?' Without waiting for an answer, he continued in the same easy manner as if he had recently become acquainted with Lynch. 'Hope you enjoy the conference,' he said. 'Gotta go. Catch you later.' Lynch smiled back at the total stranger, put down the paper, walked across to the battery of lifts in the lobby and chose one going up. As he disappeared from view the man in the brown suit sitting watching from a British Rail parcel delivery van outside spoke into the microphone of a two-way radio.

Lynch got out at the eighth floor. Nobody followed. He walked down the hotel corridor until he found room 826, then knocked on the door. He looked both ways down the corridor but saw no-one. A youngish man in neat white shirt, tie and blue suit pants opened the door, looked at Lynch and stepped aside with-

62

out a word to let him in. Lynch walked into the room which was empty except for the two of them. Before he had time to say anything the young business type stepped past him with a courteous 'Excuse me, please,' and rapped his knuckles on a connecting door. The door was opened by Roper. Lynch stepped into the much larger room—a suite with a lounge and glass-topped dining table in one corner. The connecting door closed behind him and Lynch heard the sound of the radio being switched to loud rock music.

'Cheerful buggers these Americans,' Lynch remarked. Roper stepped aside and Lynch glimpsed a beefy man sitting on the edge of the bed in the adjoining bedroom, wearing glasses and apparently studying a sheaf of business papers. He looked up when Lynch was ushered into the room, and took off his glasses.

'This is Jack Halloran,' Roper said. 'The man I wanted you to meet.'

Halloran stood up, walked over to Lynch and shook hands with a grip that was hard and raspy—unexpectedly work-hardened hands for a businessman. He looked to be in his late fifties, or early sixties, though it was difficult to tell with Americans because they courted the sun and it aged them early. He had a bit of a belly but looked strong, and he wore cowboy boots which made him a shade taller than Lynch. His complexion showed years of weather and whisky but his sharp blue eyes glittered like stones. He wore a white, western-cut shirt with tan pants and a leather belt with a silver rodeo buckle. His thick hair was grey and cut short so that it looked like a bed of iron filings. There was another business-suited man in the room, sitting on a chair between the door and the TV, watching silently. Halloran gestured to him but said nothing and the man leaned forward and switched on the TV, turning the volume up loud.

'Glad to meet you,' Halloran said and he looked at Lynch hard. The voice went with the image. Powerful, rough at the edges, used to being obeyed. Had to be ex-military, Lynch decided, by the aggression in his stance probably once a marine. A little fleshy with time and money perhaps, but still tough.

'Have a seat,' Halloran said, nodding at some chairs around the glass table. The three men sat down. Lynch could hear loud music from the rooms on either side as well as the sound from the TV near them, putting up a barrier of noise in case anybody wanted to listen in.

'Sorry about this,' Halloran said and shrugged as if he expected Lynch to understand.

'It's all right,' Lynch said. 'Everybody knows Americans are noisy bastards.' He looked across the table at Roper and wondered what his former comrade-in-arms had gotten him into. Whatever it was, Lynch had the feeling it wasn't going to be as easy to get out of as he had first thought.

Halloran didn't waste time getting to the point.

'Captain Roper has agreed to undertake an assignment on behalf of a group of people whom I represent,' he began. 'He didn't give your name to us. We already knew of your existence before we recruited him. We asked him to make the initial contact on our behalf because you are well known to each other. When you get to know me better, Lieutenant Lynch, as I trust you will, you will come to understand that one of the things I am very good at is finding the right man for the right job. You have skills and experience we believe are essential to the success of this operation. I can assure you the operation is not contrary to the laws of either of our countries . . .'

'Recruiting mercenaries is contrary to the laws of the United Kingdom,' Lynch interrupted.

'Correction, Lieutenant, recruitment isn't. Payment is. Besides we're not offering you any contract which would be recognized by any court of law anywhere. At this time we would be satisfied with an expression of interest from you. All other transactions will be conducted outside the borders and territo-

64

ries of the United Kingdom and the United States ... as will be the operation. However, have no illusions, Lieutenant Lynch, it is your considerable military expertise we want and the consequences of you accepting this assignment would be such that it would be highly unlikely you would ever be able to take up residence in the United Kingdom again.'

'Who are you, Mr Halloran?' Lynch asked politely but firmly. 'And what is it exactly that you want me to do?'

Halloran didn't blink. 'I represent a group of very wealthy, very influential and very tired Americans,' he said and Lynch noticed that the tenor of his voice had hardened considerably. 'I am a very wealthy, very influential and very tired American,' he continued.

'Tired of my country getting its nose rubbed in the dirt by every ass-hole dictator in the world who gets some raggedy-assed army behind him armed with a couple of billion dollars in military hardware from the Soviet Union and decides he's going to tell America what it can and cannot do, where Americans can and cannot go. I'm tired of ordinary, decent Americans being terrified to leave the borders of their own country in case they are murdered at the whim of fanatics who go unpunished by any law. I'm talking about the greatest threat to the democracies since Nazism was permitted to go unchecked until it was nearly too damn late. Oh sure, our governments will get tough eventually, just like in the Second World War, and the bad guys will probably take a shit-kicking. But the last time, it took us so goddam long to get off our asses that six million innocent people were slaughtered in concentration camps and 50 million people died around the world before the Nazis were stopped. I'm not the first guy to suggest that it would never have got to that point if our governments had had the guts to stand up to Hitler when it counted. Any time from 1933 to 1939 would have done. He gave them plenty of excuses. But the governments of Britain and America at that time did nothing

65

... and they are making precisely the same fucking mistake all over again today with this new generation of tyrant. These people stick their ugly faces up again and again through history and we've got to slap 'em down again and again or we're destined to repeat all the same expensive mistakes.

'Now, I never fought in the Second World War, Lynch.' Lynch noticed that the American had dropped his rank as he warmed to his subject. 'I was too young. I fought in Korea with the United States Marines. I saw first hand what happens when you let the other guys push and push. It took us a while to get rolling but when we did we rolled those bastards right back over the 49th parallel and, if you ask me, we should have kept going to the gates of goddam Peking. We should have reminded the Chinese and the rest of the world exactly what we're capable of when we get pissed-off because they seem to forget real quick.

'When I came back from Korea I went into business, bought a nothing little supermarket in Albuquerque, New Mexico, my home state. Never really expected to get rich. Just wanted to be comfortable. Pretty soon I could buy another store and then I had a little chain and it just kinda grew into a string of supermarkets right across the southwest. From there it was shopping centres, then interstate trucking, cattle, real estate. Christ, what a time that was for America, the 1950s. If a man was willing to sweat a little he couldn't help but get rich. By the time we hit the 1960s I was a very wealthy man, Lynch. Then, it all started to turn to shit. It started right after Jack got shot in Dallas. LBJ was okay but ... all those operations, I think somebody took his balls out by mistake. He went to water over Vietnam. I never would have believed it. Americans demonstrating in the streets against their own troops. Then we had Watergate. Shit, I've been Republican all my life and I didn't vote for Nixon. Anybody who knew Nixon knew he couldn't organise a fuck-up in a whorehouse. I don't mind telling you, Lynch, I wept for my country during those years. We tore ourselves apart over Vietnam and it never would have happened if we hadn't had Curly, Larry and Mo in the White House. I knew a lot of our military commanders at the time and we could have won that war in a year. Instead we let the world dump shit all over us and a bunch of little guys in black pyjamas kick our asses out of south-east Asia. Crisis of leadership, Lynch, that's what I'm talking about. For the past 20 years we have been governed by people who have been afraid to take the big decisions, the tough decisions. Where are the Roosevelts, the Trumans, the new Churchills? The democracies are under siege, the bad guys are winning, too many lunatics out there are getting away with murder and it's about time somebody put an end to their party.

'Let me give you an historic parallel using your own country,' Halloran added. 'Your own Winston Churchill. Before the war he was the only man in the British Parliament to consistently speak out against Hitler ... and he was crucified for it. For years it looked like Churchill was the only guy who really understood what the Nazis were about. Other politicians were whining about appeasement while Hitler was building bombs to blow the fuck out of London. But Churchill wasn't alone. There were others who agreed with him. Wealthy, influential figures with the will and the resources to do something about Hitler. For years they ran their own clandestine operations against the Nazis, gathering intelligence, assessing Nazi Germany's true capabilities and plans. By the time war broke out, Britain was still poorly prepared but nowhere near as poorly as the rest of the world thought at the time. Churchill and his group had contingency plans for the war effort the moment he acceded to the leadership of Britain. That's the kind of group I represent, Lynch. A group of patriotic Americans who believe the civilised world is facing a threat as evil and as insidious as Nazism, the erosion of national will and the destruction of order by terrorism. Terrorists are the enemies of civilisation, Lynch, and our

67

group has resolved to oppose them, to seek out and destroy them wherever they hide. Sure, it's vigilantism on a global scale. Sure, it's against all the principles of international law. Sure, our governments will express their outrage. Sure, it's getting down to the same level as the terrorist and fighting them on their terms. And it's about fucking time. Our government can't or won't do what's needed, despite the clear and express wishes of the people, so we will. Using good oldfashioned private enterprise. That's why we want you, Lynch. We want you to take part in an operation against the greatest source of terrorism in the world today. It is an operation involving the assassination of another country's leader. Let me make myself indelibly plain, Lynch. We want you to go after that rug-biter, Gaddafi, and blow his fucking head right off.'

There was a loud and inane quiz show on the television. It invaded the sudden silence between them and gave Lynch time to think. He knew what he should do. He should ignore Halloran's feverish rhetoric, get up, walk out of that hotel room and go back to the selfish, soothing emptiness of his new life. But it wasn't that easy. Something else told him that as desperate, as unreal and as slightly mad as it all seemed, Halloran and his anonymous group of highpowered American backers offered the one and only chance he would ever have to make the kind of gesture he believed had to be made. To roll terrorist violence right back up the pipeline to its source and ram it down the throat of the man behind it. He looked over to Roper but, as usual, he wasn't giving anything away. Halloran sat quietly, watching, waiting.

'Private ventures of this nature historically don't have a high success rate,' Lynch said, buying more time. 'Remember the Bay of Pigs?'

'I remember,' Halloran said. 'The problem with that operation was that the people behind it trusted the US Government. Kennedy had his hands tied by Congress. The same with private

68

groups supporting the Contras in Nicaragua. You can't depend on the government because it's hampered by the committee process and there are too many bleeding hearts sitting on those committees. Our group has no ties with government at all and, because we are operating outside the jurisdiction of the United States, it matters not at all whether the President, the National Security Council or Congress approves or disapproves of what we're doing. Let me add, we're not talking about invasion here. Just a short, surgical military operation using a small, highly-trained team of private individuals. And,' he added with a wry grin, '*our* funds can't be cut off by Congress.'

Lynch looked hard at Halloran. If he was all he claimed to be, if he represented the kind of people he claimed to represent, he might just have the weight and the resources to launch an operation of this nature.

If managed properly, it stood a chance, a small chance of success. But to maximise that chance, he had to be involved. He thought about the hilly paddocks of west Scotland, the croft he had already visualised on some quiet, windswept shore and the years of peaceful solitude that stretched ahead.

'I'll do it,' he said.

Halloran smiled.

'Only one question,' Lynch added.

'Go ahead.'

'Why do you need me and Roper at all? Why not keep it an all-American operation? Fewer security risks that way.'

'Because,' Halloran replied, 'you are the one man who has had precisely the experience of the type of operation we envisage. A night-time water-borne penetration of Tripoli to secure one of Gaddafi's safe houses and prepare an ambush.'

'South Georgia,' said Lynch.

'South Georgia,' Halloran repeated. 'A very sweet little operation. If you can navigate from submarine to shore underwater, at night in the South Atlantic in winter, get ashore undetected, penetrate a well-laid minefield and capture an enemy stronghold without losing a man, you have the experience we require. Commander Finn says it's one of the neatest operations he's ever seen.'

'Who's Commander Finn?'

'Commander Jerry Finn,' Halloran said. 'The first man recruited for this operation when we started planning it two years ago. Former US Navy SEAL. No jokes about his name please, he heard 'em all in the SEALs. He's a good man and experienced with the kind of hardware we've developed for the operation but we need somebody who's been through the real thing. As somebody once said—there's no substitute for experience.' Lynch knew all about the SEALs, the acronym for Sea, Air, Land Capability which covered the American navy's commandos.

'Good enough,' he said.

'Finn answers directly to me but you will co-operate closely with him. Everybody recruited for this mission is a big boy. They all know how to behave. Each man is a specialist in his field. I suspect we've got a couple of guys coming along who can teach you a thing or two, Lieutenant.'

It did not escape Lynch's attention that now Halloran was relaxed his rank had been restored.

'Each man recruited for this operation is dedicated to its success,' Halloran added. 'Whatever the cost.'

'Which is?'

Halloran affected an expression of pure nonchalance. 'You could all die,' he said. 'But you already know that. The overall financial and material costs of the operation are of no concern to you. Be assured we have unlimited funds to ensure its success. Your payment will be one million dollars, US. The same as every other man on the team. You can have that converted to whatever currency you like and deposited in any bank in any country you like. We will be happy to assist in relocating you to a country of your choice and provide you with a new identity. After that, if you ever try to cause us any embarrassment or anxiety at all, we'll have you terminated.'

'How many men on the team?'

'Six. You and Roper are the only Brits, the rest are American. You're the last man on the team. Everybody understands one thing. If you don't get Gaddafi, don't bother coming back. Furthermore, we've added a little incentive to ensure no-one gets captured alive.'

Lynch raised an eyebrow.

'Any man too badly wounded to get out will be terminated. That's understood. Each man will also be supplied with cyanide capsules as added insurance. We don't want anybody captured, questioned and then exhibited before the world's press. And I can assure you, Lieutenant, you won't want to be taken prisoner by Gaddafi's men. Because, even if you are alive when they've finished with you, there will be no swaps or deals. It'll be a bullet in the head for you or if you're real unlucky an Arab prison for the rest of your life. More likely Gaddafi will have you taken out to a firing range for target practise. It's one of his funny little ways.'

'So,' Lynch said. 'We get to be heroes and millionaires or we get to be dead.'

'Hey,' Halloran grinned. 'It's the American way.'

'You said the laws of England wouldn't be broken,' Lynch added. 'Where's the springboard for the operation?'

'The Mediterranean island republic of Malta,' Halloran answered. 'It's perfectly located, only 180 nautical miles from the coast of Libya—and Tripoli in particular. We won't be breaking the laws of any countries except, of course, Libya and Malta. But in the overall scheme of things,' he asked genially, 'who gives a fuck if they don't like it?' He paused. 'We won't give you any further information and you will not meet the remainder of the team until you arrive in Malta on 8 September. You

71

need have no further contact with Roper after today, and in fact we would prefer you didn't, to minimise any risk of compromising this operation. Once you are both out of the country it will be difficult for your government to exert much influence in sufficient time to jeopardise your participation. Lynch, we know you are under fairly close surveillance. However, that does not mean you cannot take a vacation out of the country. If you were to fly to Malta on your own it might arouse suspicion in some quarters; therefore we have arranged for you to have a girlfriend who will accompany you. Her name is Janice Street.' He ducked quickly into the bedroom and returned with a photograph which he pushed across the table at Lynch. 'As you can see, she is young and attractive.'

Lynch studied the picture of a strikingly pretty brunette in her mid-twenties. 'She looks very nice,' he said.

'She's a whore,' Halloran answered. 'One of the best. All she knows is that she's been hired to keep some Limey company on a trip to Malta and that she's not to ask too many questions. She's American. She's been hired temporarily to work as a receptionist at the London branch of a company called Excelteq which happens to be owned by a close personal friend of mine. You may have heard of Excelteq; it is one of the world's largest manufacturers of marine electronics.

'Miss Street arrived in London two months ago. It has been arranged for you to meet her at your local bar, the Dove, next Thursday night.'

Lynch smiled. They had done their homework. And they had been confident of his acceptance. Halloran ignored his smile.

'She will be with a girlfriend who will know nothing. All you have to do is find a plausible way to introduce yourself to Janice in case anyone is watching you. Whatever you say doesn't really matter, she'll find you charming, witty and generally irresistible. She's already seen your picture. She thinks you're cute. Afterwards you will see her regularly and you will both cultivate the appearance of a relationship. She'll stay over at your place some nights, you'll stay over at hers. Go to the movies, see a few shows, go for walks in the park, do everything people in love usually do. Fuck her all you want. She's getting well paid. Besides, she's a professional, she'll probably break your back. Before 15 August you will go to the Oxford Street branch of Sunlovers Tours and book a two-week vacation package for the two of you to Malta, departing Luton Airport, 1 September. Don't leave it later than 15 August; we'll make sure a couple of seats are held back. Use your own money to pay for the trip. Pack just as if you were going on vacation. Do not take all your money out of the bank, leave it. Do not make any arrangements for the disposal of your property or personal effects. Just leave it all. Do nothing that would indicate you are doing anything other than going on vacation for a couple of weeks with your girlfriend. Should an emergency come up, tell Janice to phone the man who hired her in the States and tell him she is quitting the company. On receipt of that message someone will contact you. You will not see me again until you arrive in Malta. Everything you need will be provided for you there. You will not receive any payment until you have successfully completed the operation. Any questions?'

Lynch slowly shook his head.

'A few final things. Get in good shape. Join a gun club, get in some small arms practise. How are your underwater skills, night navigation, general fitness?'

'It's like riding a bike,' Lynch answered. 'I'll join a dive club. I was thinking of doing something like that anyway.'

Halloran nodded. 'You'll have time to train with our equipment in Malta,' he said. 'But you better be ready.'

'I'll be ready,' Lynch said. He stood up, and once again Halloran gave him that dry, raspy handshake. He glanced over at Roper. 'See you in Malta,' he said.

'See you in Malta,' the other answered, deadpan.

Lynch was glad to be away from the radio and TV noise which had enveloped their meeting for the past hour. It was beginning to give him a headache. Across the street Brown Suit watched him leave the hotel and walk back towards the subway at Hyde Park Corner. Brown Suit had been onto Control but a check of the guest list on the Inter-Continental's computer revealed only a predictable array of foreign names and addresses; Americans, Germans, Japanese, Arabs. Nothing to trigger an alarm. Brown Suit was convinced Lynch's visit to the hotel was not innocent. He decided to take a closer look at the guest list later.

4

THE DECEPTION

London, summer 1989

The Thursday evening after his meeting with Halloran, Lynch shaved for the second time that day, put on a clean shirt with his smartest jeans and walked over to the pub to meet Janice Street. She wasn't there.

He ordered a half pint of lager and walked out onto the terrace. It was a summer evening of sultry warmth, the kind so rarely associated with London weather but as much a part of the city's summer character as its rain and snow in winter. The tables were all taken and Lynch contented himself with a perch on the wall along the river's edge and passed the time watching the passing traffic on the river and the terrace. He tried to spot the tail for a while but became bored. If Porter was still having him followed tonight it was by a much cleverer team. He wondered if he had been downgraded as a security risk yet. Perhaps Control was only keeping him under electronic surveillance at his flat. He hadn't decided yet whether he should let the woman who was about to become the latest love in his life know about the audience which followed his every move at home. Halloran made it clear she knew nothing of the overall operation but

Lynch suspected she had to know she was involved in some kind of dangerous game.

They arrived soon after eight. Lynch had paced himself and was only on his second lager. He recognised Janice Street immediately but, like every other man in the pub, he would have noticed her anyway. Her thick black hair was longer and cut differently than the photograph but the pretty face and dark, challenging eyes were the same. She wore very little make-up, Lynch noticed, and her face had a healthy, well-scrubbed glow.

She was taller than he expected and lightly tanned with a figure not at all disguised by the loose, white, summer dress she wore. Most of all it was the purposeful, confident way she walked which made men look at her, and the enticing sway of her hips, provocatively close to a female swagger. She was a woman who looked as though she knew exactly where she was going and what she wanted. She was lovely, Lynch thought, and she knew it. As Halloran had promised, she was one of the best. She must be very expensive and Lynch was impressed. He was always impressed by people who knew their worth.

Her companion was a younger woman in red overalls, black tee-shirt and bleached hair cut in a messy shag. They were each carrying a glass of wine and looking for a table. There were still none vacant. Undaunted, Janice Street approached a table where a young couple sat with a copy of *Time Out* spread before them. They looked Scandinavian, early tourists probably. Janice asked if she and her friend could share the table and, judging by the expression on the girl's face, her boyfriend agreed a little too readily. They commandeered a spare chair from another table, sat down and began chatting like any other two young office workers having an evening out. A couple of times Janice looked around but appeared not to see him. Lynch had not wanted to appear too obvious so he bided his time. After a quarter of an hour the Scandinavian couple left. Their chairs had barely been vacated when two smooth young men in

76

suits attempted to move in, only to be discouraged by a shake of the head from Janice. The bottled blonde watched the two young bucks leave and, looking puzzled, leaned over to speak to Janice. Lynch decided he had better wait no longer and walked over.

'You know,' he said, trying not to look as awkward as he felt, 'if I was to sit here for a while I could stop you being pestered by all these rich, good-looking young men.' The blonde looked up at him, then shot Janice a disapproving glance. 'Nobody's had time to pester us,' she complained.

'Come to think of it,' Janice smiled, 'we could probably use a bodyguard for a while.' Her accent was American but had an edge he couldn't quite place.

'You know what you like, don't you?' the blonde muttered pointedly at Janice while looking over her shoulder to see if the two young bucks were still in sight. She saw them inside at the bar talking to another couple of women and frowned. When she turned back Lynch was sitting at their table.

'I'll have a white wine, thanks,' she said, setting her empty glass in front of him. Lynch smiled. 'And you?' he asked Janice.

'Spritzer,' she said.

'Sounds like a big German dog,' he said. 'What is it?'

'Sorry,' she sighed. 'I keep forgetting. White wine and mineral water. I'm a healthy drunk.'

Lynch brought the drinks and they exchanged first names and made small talk for a while. He wasn't sure exactly how fast he should move with Janice. While he accepted Halloran's word that he could proceed as fast as he liked he felt there were certain proprieties to be observed if their relationship for the next three months was to be at all cordial. If they were going to be seeing a lot of each other they may as well be friends, he decided. It would make their little subterfuge a great deal more tolerable for both of them.

The blonde was called Hilary and had been with Excelteq for five years as a switchboard operator.

'Janice is from America,' she told Lynch helpfully. 'She's our new receptionist. She talks American posh. She doesn't seem to like English blokes though.'

Janice accepted the dig but said nothing. Lynch smiled at her and she returned the smile easily but her dark eyes told him nothing.

'I've been trying to place your accent,' he said, before the cockney chatterbox could start again. 'Which part of the States are you from?'

'Portland, Maine,' she said. 'What you're hearing is the Radcliffe in me. It's *the* women's college on the eastern seaboard. It's in Cambridge, Massachusetts. Not far from Boston. If you leave Radcliffe with nothing else you leave knowing how to speak properly.'

Lynch nodded. He had visited the United States often with the navy and he knew about Radcliffe. 'It's more than just a finishing school,' he said.

'Oh yes,' Janice agreed. 'I picked up a degree in business administration while I was there.' He detected a glimmer of interest in her eyes.

'Isn't that a lot of education to waste on being a ...'

'Receptionist?' she smiled.

'Without wishing to be rude ...'

'I'm not ready to commit myself to one corporation yet,' she said. 'I want to see some of the world ... and you wouldn't believe how well Excelteq pays its receptionists.'

'I'm sure, whatever they're paying you isn't enough.'

She tilted her glass in ironic salute and Hilary missed the look that passed between them. However, she hadn't overlooked the increasing evidence of her irrelevance at the table. She excused herself to go to the lavatory and walked past the two bucks at the bar, flashing them a smile as subtle as a billboard.

'I think Hilary is afraid she's not going to get her share of fun tonight,' Lynch remarked.

Janice nodded. 'I know. I've been working on her to keep me company while we do the rounds tonight. She really thinks she's doing me a favour. She's going to be really pissed-off if I just dump her.'

'Let me handle it,' said Lynch.

Hilary returned to the table, hair rearranged in a different tangle, her face freshly made-up, but sullen.

'You know what?' Lynch said to her. 'I think it's time we livened up the party.' He got up and walked inside the pub. Both women watched while he took one of the business suits to one side and spoke briefly to him, then nodded over at their table.

He returned in a moment. 'Better find another chair,' he said, 'we'll be having company in a minute.' Hilary swivelled around to look into the pub while Lynch found another chair. Janice seized the moment to whisper at him.

'What did you say?'

Lynch widened his eyes with mock innocence. 'Nothing much,' he said. 'Just relying on the natural conviviality of the English pub.'

A few minutes later the business suit Lynch had spoken to peeled himself away from the bar and came over to join them. Hilary was thrilled and her mood changed as suddenly as if someone had thrown a switch. Lynch bought another round of drinks and after half an hour decided he and Janice would not be missed if they slipped away for a meal. The other two seemed more than happy to stay and pursue their sudden friendship.

'Like curry?' Lynch asked, as they left the noisy pub.

'As long as I know what's in it.'

'Good. I know a place five minutes from here, serves the best curries in India.'

'Great,' said Janice. 'This isn't India.'

'This part of town is.'

They had reached the narrow lane leading to the restaurant when Janice asked him: 'What did you say to that guy in the pub to make him leave those other women and join us?'

'Simple. I told him Hilary had fallen in love with him at first sight and if he played his cards right, she could do things to him that would make his ears bleed.'

'And?'

He looked at her, deadpan, then looked away again. 'I told him you were a miserable, stuck-up bitch and I was going to take you home and give you a good spanking.'

'That's nice,' she said dryly.

'Don't worry about it. Those people have no feelings. You know what they do?'

'From the fancy suits I assumed they were in finance or something.'

'Or something,' he echoed. 'Don't be fooled by the suits. This is London. A hundred quid will buy any Flash Harry a suit here. Those two are in the pre-owned prestige automobile retail profession.'

She looked at him and began to laugh: 'Used car salesmen?'

'You really are a Radcliffe girl,' he smiled and pushed open the restaurant door for her.

They didn't go to bed together that first night. By the time they had talked their way through dinner and discovered they liked each other it was late and, ironically, she still had a front to maintain and be at work in the morning. They made a date for the weekend and then he saw her into a taxi, kissing her lightly on the cheek.

That Saturday morning he picked her up in front of her flat at Lancaster Gate and they drove to Hastings for the day. They stopped on the way for lunch at a 200-year-old country pub and ate in the beer garden surrounded by noisy families. At Hastings they strolled along the sea front and through the narrow back streets, examining the work of the town's numerous artists. She told him it reminded her of New England where she grew up, except the dates went a little further back. They talked as easily as they had on their first meeting and the day passed in a rush. When he dropped her off at her flat that night it was late. She didn't ask him inside and he didn't press her for an invitation.

During the days he stepped up his exercise routine, working out each morning at the dingy gym full of Rastafarians who liked to sweat and spar to the best reggae tapes. He joined a pistol club and went target shooting two afternoons a week at an indoor range in Southall. He joined a scuba club operating out of a dive shop and school at Richmond. When the owners learned he was an ex-navy diver they had offered him an instructor's job.

'Not a lot of money in it,' one of them had said. 'But all the crumpet you can eat.'

Lynch had rather reluctantly declined.

A couple of weeks after his first meeting with Janice he took her for a Sunday afternoon stroll across Hampstead Heath. They sat on a grassy hillside and made up farfetched stories about the Hampstead personalities who passed by: the intense, balding man with the black, poloneck sweater and decomposing suede jacket was an unacclaimed producer of obscure late-night TV arts shows. The shrill, heavily made-up, elderly woman dragging a yapping wire terrier was an exiled Rumanian aristocrat. After a while they fell silent and watched the young courting couples passing by, hanging onto each other with the kind of public intimacy only the young can manage. It seemed to highlight the lack of spontaneous intimacy between the two of them.

'So,' Janice announced abruptly. 'When are we going to bed?'

He tried not to look surprised but she saw she had caught him off guard.

'Hey,' she arched her eyebrows. 'It's not compulsory.' She paused then added: 'I just assumed it would happen somewhere along the way. It usually does in my line of business. They did tell you what I do, didn't they?'

She was right. Lynch was surprised. Surprised at how much he had been enjoying their counterfeit romance. There were aspects of his fraudulent new lifestyle he found satisfying and her remark had brought him back to earth.

'With a bang,' he said, turning his thoughts into a lame joke.

She gave him a wry look. 'I don't know about you but it's nearly four months since I got laid,' she said. 'And I miss it.'

'That's what I like about you Americans,' he said. 'You're so shy and withdrawn.'

'Look, mister,' she added, digging him gently in the ribs. 'It's time we stopped kidding each other. I'm very comfortable about what I do and how much I do it. When I'm working I get laid three or four times a week and that's plenty for me. I never have to worry about my libido. Now, I may be getting well paid for keeping you company but my libido has been trying to tell me something ... four months is a long time between fucks and I'm horny. I've been saving myself for you, and it's time you appreciated it.'

Lynch couldn't suppress the laugh that erupted out of him. He lay back and closed his eyes and laughed in a relaxed kind of way that hadn't happened for years. 'There's only one thing that puzzles me,' he said, opening his eyes and looking up at her. 'Only three or four times a week ... is that because you're so ugly?'

'Jesus,' she sighed. 'I could make book on the questions guys ask. Look, it costs $500 to spend a night with me in New York and I never spend the whole night. For that you get not only a great body but you get the mind that goes with it. You get philosophy if you want it, opinions on everything from Mayan architecture to French literary classics of the nineteenth century. I speak English, French, Italian and Spanish, play chess and ride competition dressage. In other words when you get me you get to fuck a real live Radcliffe girl, and there are plenty of rich guys in New York who'll pay good money for that. I'm choosy too. I have a restricted client list and some of the guys on it don't even want to fuck me. They just want to go places with me, make their pals jealous, talk to me. Some guys are just weird, they have a class fetish. When I talk dirty and sound like a Kennedy it gives 'em a hard-on. I don't do raunch or kink, I don't do shows, I don't do groups or other women. I fuck nice guys. Some of 'em are pathetic in the sack, some are terrific and, yes, sometimes they make me come. Even with a degree in business administration I can't think of an easier way to make $500 a night. I'm time efficient, I only do two, three nights a week maximum. I'm AIDS safe, there's very little wear and tear and I never, absolutely never, suffer from stress.

'I could work more if I wanted to but I don't. I like my time to myself. I own a terrific apartment in Manhattan and I take vacations anywhere in the world I like. I have a great bunch of friends who know what I do. A lot of them are Radcliffe alumni who have been giving it away for years and don't have as much to show for it as I do. In five years I'll be rich enough to retire on my investments. And the next question is: do I really like what I do? And the answer is: fucking-right I do.'

'Well,' Lynch smiled. 'All that and you're still so romantic.'

There was a long pause before he spoke again. He brushed her bare arm lightly with his fingertips. 'I thought you might appreciate a little time.'

She looked at him. 'In case you hadn't noticed, we don't have a lot of time. Besides, I know what kind of men I like. I've been able to take my pick since I was 14 ... and I like you.'

Lynch reached up, slid his fingers between the thick strands of black hair and drew her face gently towards him. They kissed for a long time and luxuriated in the anticipation that soon they would be making love. He could feel the heat of her through the pretty summer dress she wore.

'These pants are starting to get a little tight,' he murmured. 'Why don't we go back to your place before I break something important?'

They drove back to her flat and stayed in bed till she left for work the next morning.

In the main computer room at Control, Brown Suit cross-checked the Inter-Continental guest list again. He still could find nothing suspicious. Even the queries he had run through Interpol, the CIA, FBI and MI5 had drawn blanks in the weeks following Lynch's visit to the hotel.

Surveillance of Lynch this far had produced a picture of a man gradually trying to build a new life. There was nothing unusual about him exercising every day, joining a pistol club and a dive club. Many ex-servicemen took pride in maintaining fitness and continued the same interests and hobbies they had cultivated while in the forces. There was nothing yet to give substance to the nagging suspicion Brown Suit had about Lynch. He discounted the way Lynch had insulted him by slinging garbage on his lap when he had been sprung. It wasn't only that. He had a hunch about Lynch and he would like to see his face when he learned he was intended to find out he was being followed. Ever since Porter's order to drop out of sight Lynch hadn't sprung any of the new tails. Though Brown Suit was puzzled by Porter's handling of Lynch's case. He especially couldn't understand the need for strangers to participate in what should have been exclusively a CTC operation. He had no idea which department the new team of surveillance people came from but he didn't like the way he had to play second fiddle to them. And he didn't like the way they had access to his information but he did not have access to theirs. If Lynch was a security risk Brown Suit wanted a fair crack at nailing him instead of letting all the glory go to some other department within the security services.

The bugs in Lynch's flat and on his phone had turned up nothing except the irritation of a man who was aware he was being bugged. His flirtation with drink, which seemed to have passed, was normal under the circumstances. Contact with former colleagues at CTC had fallen off. It was all quite normal. The most interesting development yet was the girl. He knew she was American and worked for an American electronics company, with offices in London, called Excelteq. He had put a trace on her through Washington. Brown Suit was convinced there was a link between her and Lynch's visit to the Inter-Continental and if he could just find a little more he was sure he could persuade Porter to extend surveillance and phone taps to the girl.

He summoned up the hotel's guest list on his computer screen again. It showed 227 bookings by individuals, 104 bookings by corporations and official government departments from a number of countries and eight block bookings by travel organisations from various countries. A total of 749 people had been guests at the hotel on the day of Lynch's visit and whoever Lynch met probably hadn't been registered under his or her real name anyway. Instead of processing the names and backgrounds of every individual on the list he decided to isolate every name with a corporate connection, however tenuous. Then he culled the list further to those corporations with American links. He already knew neither Excelteq nor any of its employees appeared on the list. He tried a fresh tack. For the next few hours he went patiently through every company name on the list, cross-checking subsidiaries and examining every corporate shareholder. It was almost midnight when he keyed in the name Standard Transport Charter of California. The company had booked three rooms for visiting executives for a period of five days, one of which had been the day of Lynch's visit. He referred the name to the US companies register in the CTC computer library and watched yet again as a fresh list of subsidiaries filled the screen. It told him nothing. He keyed up the list of shareholders in Standard Transport. When he read the fifth name from the top he stopped. It was Excelteq (California) Ltd, and it had a 17 per cent holding in Standard Transport.

'Bingo,' he breathed softly. It wasn't a lot. Just a link. But perhaps the link he needed. He would start a closer examination of the officers and directors of both companies in the morning. He realised he was going to be late for his turn on the midnight shift. When he checked with Control he was amused to hear where Lynch was spending the night. Half an hour later he was in the back of a van painted in the same livery as the gas board, looking up at the darkened window of Janice Street's flat in Lancaster Gate.

'Soon,' he told himself, as he settled down for a long night. 'Soon we'll find out who you really are, Miss Janice-bloody-Street.'

5

THE DEPARTURE

Malta 1989

On the last Monday in July, Lynch caught the tube to Oxford Street and walked to the office of Sunlovers Tours. On the way he found himself rubbing at the small of his back, where he had a nagging ache after the weekend with Janice.

When he asked the young woman behind the counter to book him two seats on a package tour to Malta, leaving 1 September, she told him cheerfully there were no seats left.

'You've left it a bit late, sweetie,' she chirped in bright cockney. 'Malta's always popular, you've got to book before April usually. At this short notice, we can probably get you to Majorca or Malaga or, if you don't mind spending a bit of money, the Seychelles are very nice . . .'

'Would you just check for me please . . . sweetie,' Lynch persisted.

The girl shrugged and called up the Malta flight on her computer screen. 'Here,' she said, looking surprised. 'That's funny, there are two seats. I was sure that flight filled up weeks ago. Well, half your luck.'

Lynch paid cash; the girl made the reservations and wrote

out the tickets. When she handed them over they came with an armful of accommodation vouchers, pamphlets, luggage stickers, a red plastic travel wallet bearing the Sunlovers crest and complimentary Sunlovers shoulder bag. Lynch thanked the girl and left the office without noticing the overweight, middle-aged man in sports jacket, grey trousers and white shirt who had followed him in and was inspecting the brochures offering Sunlovers packages to Asia.

He followed Lynch back to Hammersmith and when he was satisfied his target had settled safely inside, disappeared down a near by lane and radioed in this latest piece of intelligence. It went first to his own controller and from there, two hours later, into the computer file on Lynch at CTC. Later that same day Brown Suit had poached the same information from that file and added it to the case he was compiling to present to Sir Malcolm Porter. It was the final piece of evidence he believed they needed to pull Lynch in. He suspected Lynch was deeply embroiled in some act of American adventurism. That Lynch had bought tickets to Malta only steeled his suspicion. Malta was the perfect springboard to any one of a dozen countries in the Middle East and North Africa, but most notably Libya.

He had no theories yet about what kind of American plot Lynch was involved in but he suspected it had something to do with the billions of US oil-industry dollars in Libya. He had found out precious little about Janice Street except that she came from a respectable, middle-class home in New England, had attended Radcliffe College in Cambridge, Massachusetts and had been a minor figure on the New York social circuit before going to work for Excelteq and getting a posting to London. However, he believed she had been instrumental in Lynch's recruitment. He was reluctant to push the CIA in Langley and the FBI in Washington for any more information about one of their citizens, in case it aroused their curiosity too much. He had spent hours at the computer playing with Excelteq and

Standard Transport Charter's corporate connections but had failed to find anything which tied either of the giant corporations into any of the big American oil companies. Brown Suit decided he would put in a little more time at the terminal before requesting a meeting with Porter and unloading all his suspicions. He tapped in Sunlovers Tours and discovered that its corporate parent was a holding company called the Brighton Group which was in turn was owned, through a majority shareholding, by a company called Bright Investments Ltd.

The chairman of Bright Investments was Sir William Bright, one of Britain's most prominent financiers, a knight of the realm, die-hard Tory and outspoken critic of what he considered the Prime Minister's soft line on terrorism. He found nothing to tie Bright in with Lynch or with the girl, Excelteq, Standard Transport or any US oil company either. He had drawn a blank. Using the same code he had used earlier to poach Lynch's file, Brown Suit relayed himself through CTC's computer to MI6 and keyed in Sir William Bright's name. It showed him a long list of Sir William's interests but nothing he didn't already know. He picked out the name of Sir William's personal brokers—Bowen, Hindmarsh & Hogg—and keyed them into the MI6 computer. The screen promptly scrolled up the broker's overseas client list. And there it was, in alphabetical order, Standard Transport Charter.

It could be just a coincidence, Brown Suit realised, but this looked like one coincidence too many. And there had to be an explanation. He could now tie Lynch in to a meeting at a London hotel, a relationship with a girl and the purchase of air tickets from a company all of which had one thing in common. The same corporate American names kept cropping up. He already had the name John Halloran, president and founding chairman of Standard Transport Charter, in his file. Halloran was closely associated with Excelteq and, knowing Halloran's politics, it was more than possible that he and William Bright were known to each other. Brown Suit had all the evidence he needed to haul Lynch in for questioning now.

'No,' said Sir Malcolm Porter.

Maurice Cassell couldn't believe his ears. He rubbed the palms of his hands on the knees of his shiny brown suit and wished he could stop sweating. He could see all his hours of work, all his labourious detective work at the computer terminal, all his initiative, disappearing down the Whitehall drain without a trace.

'You've done a remarkable job of work, Maurice,' Sir Malcolm continued. He was standing in the window of his office looking out at the elms. The buff file marked 'Top Secret', with its diagonal red stripe, sat on his desk where he had left it after reading carefully the report inside and listening to Maurice Cassell's theory. He turned back into the room and looked down at the wretched Cassell with eyes which were uncompromising but not unkind.

'What I want you to do now may be very difficult for you to understand after all your efforts but that is part of the business we're in too, Maurice. You are to leave this report with me and do absolutely nothing. All I want you to do now is maintain surveillance on Lynch but I do not want you to hinder the departure of him or his girlfriend, do you understand?'

Brown Suit stared limply back. His face reflected his utter bewilderment so completely that Porter had to make an effort not to smile. 'We'll be keeping an eye on Lynch in Malta,' he offered by way of consolation.

'What about the connection between Halloran and Bright?' Brown Suit protested.

'That's not a matter for you to be concerned with, Maurice, believe me.' Porter was trying to be patient.

Brown Suit knew what had happened. He had just been assisting MI6 all along. Now this file and all his hard work would vanish into MI6 and somebody there would get all the credit for his inspired detective work. Or perhaps—the thought suddenly occurred to him—perhaps it was even worse. Perhaps Porter and Bright and Halloran were somehow connected and he had stumbled on something much bigger.

It was entirely possible. It wouldn't be the first time in the history of the British secret services that a department head, a product of the privileged upper class, had been guilty of treachery. He fought to regain control of himself and got up to go. 'Very well, sir,' he said, and put the notebook containing all his scribblings of the past two months back in his jacket pocket. He would have to find a way to go around Sir Malcolm Porter, he decided. A way of bringing his suspicions to the attention of someone who might be prepared to act. He was more convinced than ever that he had stumbled onto something that could be directly prejudicial to British interests in North Africa and the Arab world.

'By the way, Maurice,' Sir Malcolm added. 'If you leak this to anyone, anyone at all, I'll have you transferred to customs and excise and you'll be doing body searches of Russian trawlermen in the Outer Hebrides for the next 20 years.'

Brown Suit winced.

Sir Malcolm turned to look back out the window and Brown Suit had just reached the door when he heard Porter call to him.

'One last thing, Maurice,' he said. 'Leave your notebook on my desk too, there's a good chap.'

Lynch stood in the doorway of his flat and took one last look. There hadn't been much room for sentiment in his life. There were no family photographs on the dresser, no pictures of children or former sweethearts, not even souvenirs of other times and places to clutter up his life. It was the home of a man whose clothes and possessions were simply tools and accessories to help him get through life efficiently. He had followed Halloran's instructions and left everything as he would if he were going on holiday.

His diving gear was stacked in a corner of the bathroom, there was food left in the fridge, the bed was unmade and the wardrobe contained clothes he could live without. The only exception had been the Colt .45 automatic he had bought years earlier from an old navy hand and which he had been using for shooting practise. He had dismantled it and dropped the pieces in different parts of the Thames. He flicked off the light and carried his bags outside. He was just about to shut the door when he stopped, walked back into the room, fiddled with the radio tuner till he found some Chinese opera on an international waveband, then turned it up as loud as it would go.

'So long, you bastards,' he said to the eavesdropping devices he knew were planted somewhere in the walls of his flat. He would have been disappointed had he known that the only listener back at Control merely took off his earphones, yawned, noted the time of Lynch's departure and gratefully wound up what had been, for him, a tedious assignment.

Lynch drove the Escort in the direction of Lancaster Gate. It was shortly after seven in the evening on the last day of August and traffic was bad. As he nosed his way slowly across town his mind wandered back over the past three months. Ironically, they had been among the happiest in his life and he realised this said something poignant about his life. He wondered if Janice had enjoyed herself as much as she had appeared, or if it was all a skilled performance. Whatever the truth he was grateful to her for one thing above all else. She had been just the distraction he needed to stop the nightmares.

He parked the car a short walk down the street from her apartment building. On the way inside he stopped for a moment by the kerb, fished the front door key to his flat from a jacket pocket and dropped it down the drain. Janice had made dinner and opened a bottle of good claret but her mood was subdued and they ate in silence.

When they went to bed she made love tenderly but was more restrained than usual and, afterwards, lay back and stared moodily at the ceiling. He lay on his side, one hand propping up his head, the other delicately tracing patterns on her belly. Even when he wasn't making love to her he liked looking at her. Knowing time was running out for them both only made him hungrier. His fingers drew a meandering line to the soft, black hair between her legs and he began to caress her but she gently moved his hand away. He said nothing and waited. After a while she looked at him and asked: 'Are you some kind of hit man, professional assassin or something?'

He lay back and let the question pass.

'Are you planning some sort of job for Jack?'

He shot her a warning glance. 'Don't even think about it,' he said quietly.

'This place isn't bugged,' she said. 'It's been swept by a couple of goons from Excelteq once a week, every week since I moved in. This is one of the company's executive apartments. They have to keep it clean in case of industrial espionage, apart from whatever little caper Jack has got you involved in.'

There was a long silence before she spoke again.

'You going to take a crack at Gaddafi?' she asked.

Lynch kept the shock off his face but she read him anyway.

'I thought it was something like that,' she said. 'You didn't show it in your face but your body turned to rock,' and she scratched his rigid stomach muscles with a fingernail. 'It's all right,' she added. 'I won't let Jack know I figured out his little scam.'

'That might be prudent.'

'Why?' she asked brightly. 'You going to snuff me for knowing too much?'

He shook his head and smiled. 'I might,' he said. 'If you don't shut up.'

'Better check with Jack first,' she said. 'He likes having me around.'

Lynch said nothing.

'Look,' she tried again. 'It's just my way of dealing with what's going on here. It wasn't hard to figure out what Jack was up to. I've known him for six years. You don't spend much time with Jack before you discover how he thinks the world ought to be run. The difference between Jack and other men is that he can make it happen. Christ, he's had more dinners at the White House than the President. He knows all the right people, all the generals and admirals and security chiefs going back to Eisenhower's time. He knows how to get what he wants. What puzzles me is you. You've got a mind of your own. You're not the kind of guy who usually gets mixed up with Jack.'

Lynch hesitated. 'He's supposed to be good at finding the right people for the right job.'

She looked at him with what appeared to be resignation. 'We all have our price, huh?'

'You sleep with Halloran?' he asked.

'Uh-huh,' she admitted. 'In the beginning. It was Jack who set me up in Manhattan. I'd be just another pushy bimbo on Wall Street if it wasn't for Jack. He offered me something a little more exciting, a little more rewarding. He introduced me to the people he knew. I discovered I enjoyed being close to the power. I like powerful men. You know what I like about them the most? They aren't afraid to fuck with history.'

'You like fucking with history?'

'It's better than being fucked by history,' she smiled thinly.

'How much is Halloran paying you to keep me company?'

'$60,000 a month plus expenses,' she answered. 'Oh, and my receptionist's pay.'

He smiled. 'What happens to you after Malta?'

'Back to the States, I suppose. It depends on Jack.'

'Does Jack own you?'

'Jack owns both of us, honey. There's no difference between you and me. He's using us both to get what he wants. The secret is not to mind.'

Lynch rolled onto his back and glanced at the bedside clock. The glowing digital figures said quarter to midnight. It was five to midnight before he spoke again.

'The difference between you and me,' he said, 'is that what Jack Halloran is paying me to do, I'd do for nothing.'

She propped herself up on one elbow and leaned across to look into his eyes, one of her breasts lightly brushing his chest. 'Matter of fact,' she said, 'so would I.' Her voice had softened and for the first time he thought he detected a note of self-doubt behind the hard polish. 'That's the problem,' she added. 'I'm not sure how comfortable I am with this business of fucking some guy who's going off to get himself killed. I don't know how soldiers' wives stand it. It's goddam ghoulish. No wonder most of them hit the bottle or go crazy.'

'That's the price you pay for being a clever girl and figuring everything out,' he said. 'A little knowledge is a dangerous thing and all that.'

'I'm usually so in control,' she sighed. 'I know where I go from here ... what about you? Where you're going there's a chance you won't be coming back at all.'

'The secret,' he smiled, 'is not to mind.'

She gave a short, brittle laugh. 'You're one of the strangest bastards I've ever met, Lynch ... and I've met some. I've been watching you these past weeks and unless you're a better actor than I think you are, you've been having yourself a ball. Yet, here you are, ready to leave it all behind and risk your life

95

taking a pop at this prick, Gaddafi. You're no hit man. I've met them too. They've all got dead eyes. What's in it for you, Lynch? What's really in it for you?'

When he answered her, the words came in a clear, prolonged and intense burst, as though he had put all his motives and frustrations into perspective for the first time. 'I've been on the receiving end of that bastard's terror,' he said. 'I've seen the victims, the faces of innocent people, men, women and children who died and the fear frozen on their faces. I've seen the face of a defenceless child, a little girl whose last emotion on this earth was the purest terror. I want to pick some of that terror up in my hands, to hold it ... and take it all the way back to Gaddafi. I want to see the look on his face when he sees me coming through the door. I want him to know what it's like. I want to see the same expression on his face that I've seen on his victims. That's worth more to me ... than anything else in this life.'

She watched him in silence until she felt his body relax, then slid closer to him and held him. 'That's the real difference between you and me,' she said. 'I can't afford you.'

Long after she had fallen asleep he was still awake, watching the minutes on the digital clock slipping silently forward.

The clock radio woke them at seven and they got ready quickly. Unlike Lynch, Janice didn't give a backwards glance when she closed the door to her apartment. The drive to Luton Airport took almost two hours. Lynch parked the Escort with the keys in the glove compartment and then locked all the doors. They cleared check-in easily and found themselves in the departures lounge with a gaggle of noisy English holidaymakers. While Janice idled the time away with a magazine Lynch browsed through the newspapers, absorbing the mood and flavour of a country he wasn't going to see again for a long time. Most of the stories were depressingly familiar: racial unrest, an increase in street crime, political scandal. The only bright spot was a photograph of Princess Diana arriving at the Leicester Square Odeon for a charity movie premiere. Lynch recalled that he never had got a response to that memo he sent Control.

He was interrupted by the announcement that their British Airways flight to Malta was ready for boarding and he and Janice collected their things. As they followed the stream of passengers towards the exit doors Lynch happened to glance through the glass partition which separated them from the adjacent security area.

Brown Suit was standing with his hands in his pockets watching impassively as Lynch and Janice went to board their plane. It was only pettiness, Brown Suit realised, just a minor point of pride, but he wanted Lynch to know they were leaving only with his tacit approval. Lynch recognised the gesture but it still left him puzzled. How much, he wondered, did Brown Suit really know? More urgently, how much did Porter know?

When they had disappeared Brown Suit turned and walked back out of the busy terminal. He had been doing a lot of thinking since his last meeting with Porter. Everything he had compiled from his surveillance of Lynch and the girl had disappeared. Everything in the computer's memory had been pulled and filed elsewhere. His improper access to MI6 computers had been detected and he had been reprimanded. All that was left was inside his own head. He was more convinced than ever that Porter had deliberately stifled his investigation and he wasn't satisfied that what he had uncovered would be put to good use by MI6. There was a good chance that Porter was playing both departments off, one against the other. Each would think the other had the Lynch affair under control while, for reasons of his own, Porter had elected to let Lynch slip between the two of them. The only logical conclusion was that Porter was involved with a third party, probably the Soviet Union or even the Americans, in a plot which could be contrary to the interests of his own country. The names Burgess, Maclean, Philby and Blunt had floated through his mind many times. Now, Porter's motives, and consequently his loyalties, had to be in doubt. Brown Suit had decided he would take his suspicions about Porter somewhere else later. In the meantime he had to worry about Lynch.

The solution, he realised, was to find a third party of his own. A friendly nation with regional interests similar to those of Britain. A country to whom he could leak just enough information to cause alarm. He had decided on France. He would arrange a discreet tip to French intelligence operatives in London that a former officer in Britain's security services was engaged, with American private citizens, in the clandestine preparation of a mercenary operation in Malta, with the potential to destabilise certain countries in the region, particularly Libya. The French were xenophobic enough about their interests in North Africa to be alarmed at the prospect of armed intervention by mercenaries. He could supply photographs of Lynch and the girl, enough names and leads to persuade the French to launch a spoiling operation of their own. That ought to neutralise Lynch and frustrate Porter's devious little game, he thought. By the time he reached the car park Brown Suit was smiling.

'Shit and corruption,' said Janice as she stepped out of the plane at Valletta and took her first deep breath.

'The twin smells of the tropics,' Lynch grinned, following her into the simmering midday heat. 'I love 'em.'

There was a cursory immigration check and no display of interest by customs. Planeloads of vacationing Britons rarely brought anything of interest into the island republic. It was when they were leaving that their luggage was most likely to contain petty contraband. They had just retrieved their bags in the chaotic arrivals hall when a youngish, clean-cut man tapped Lynch on the shoulder and introduced himself.

'My name's Tim,' he said in an American accent. 'Mr Halloran sent me to meet you both.'

Lynch recognised him as one of the men with Halloran at the Park Lane Inter-Continental. He took Janice's bags and left Lynch to carry his own as he led the way out of the chaotic airport. A smoke-coloured Mercedes waited at the kerb. When Tim had stowed their bags in the trunk and settled them both in the plush back seats he switched on the air conditioning and nosed the car expertly between the clamouring hotel buses and taxis.

'Is Jack Halloran here today?' Janice asked.

'Yes, ma'am,' he answered. 'Mr Halloran is at the house. It's a 90 minute drive so I suggest you relax and enjoy the view. There's a drinks cabinet in front of you, between the front seats, if you'd like something after your trip.'

Janice leaned forward and opened the door of a compact walnut cocktail cabinet and examined its contents. Lynch noticed there was even a small ice tray. Janice poured herself a double Jack Daniels over ice and raised an eyebrow at Lynch but he declined. He watched as Tim took the fork leading away from Valletta and began heading inland, south-west through the rugged heart of the island and towards the south coast which faced Libya. He knew Janice had never seen Malta before but she seemed more absorbed by her own thoughts and her drink than the passing scenery. Lynch had been there several times previously with the navy, and once on a secret exercise with the SBS when the socialist government took power on the island and Britain had been interested in some Soviet naval vessels using Malta's vast dockyards. He had seen little of the island outside Valletta. The countryside looked parched and harsh. He saw jagged mountain ridges, sparsely-grassed pastures for goats and sheep, dusty olive groves, villages of yellow clay houses, women wearing black shawls, children with glossy brown skin, chocolate eyes and tousled hair, men playing cards in the shade and watching as the Mercedes hissed by. After a couple of hours they began to catch glimpses of the Mediterranean again and a few more elabourate houses, the villas of wealthy expatriates from France, Italy, Britain, West Germany and of the occasional oil-rich Arab.

After a while the driver forked onto a narrower, rougher road winding rapidly down towards the coast. Abruptly they came to a gate set in a high chain-link fence topped with new razor wire. The driver climbed out and opened the gate and when he had driven through shut it again and made sure it was locked. On the other side of the gate the road became an unmade track and meandered down a scrubby cliff face until they had almost reached sea level when they drove around a high bluff and Janice gasped.

'I was beginning to wonder,' she said. 'But this is more like Jack.'

Lynch stared through the windshield trying to get a good, comprehensive look at the huge villa which occupied the whole seaward side of a flat, man-made promontory jutting out from the rocky beach into the sea. Palace would have been a better description than villa, Lynch decided. It was obviously only a couple of years old, because they could still see the corrugations of bulldozer tracks in the crushed limestone apron the width of a football field that separated the villa from the mainland. Even so, the walls looked nicely weathered. They rose two storeys on the landward side and three on the blustier, seaward side, climbing almost sheer from the pale green water of the Mediterranean. The house was opulent and Moorish in design with arched windows and balconies studding the seaward walls and the only incongruous touches were the red-tiled, Italianate roofs on several levels which suggested a multitude of rooms. But it was a mix quite in keeping with Malta's Afro-European character. Its most impressive feature, Lynch thought, was that it could not be approached from land or sea without the occupants knowing in plenty of time that they had visitors.

The Merc navigated the last scrubby 'S' turn, leaving a long, milky, dust plume as its signature down the cliff face. The crushed rock beneath their wheels crunched and spat as the car bumped over the wide, open space towards a pair of iron-barred gates set in the landward wall. In an emergency it would be easy for the villa's defenders to rake this entire apron with gunfire, Lynch realised.

The car ground to a stop and the driver waved to a shadowy figure behind the gates. A moment later the gates swung soundlessly inward and they drove through. Lynch noticed the villa's walls were almost half a metre thick and to the right of the gates as they passed was a guard post built from the same stone. It appeared to be manned by two men, one standing outside and watching them as they drove in, the other sitting inside at a computerised panel which probably controlled the perimeter security system. Both guards looked to be very fit, in their late twenties, wearing casual slacks and shirts. What struck Lynch most forcibly was that both were wearing unconcealed shoulder holsters holding baby Uzis.

They drove across the broad tiled courtyard, past an open garage on their left which accommodated a second Merc, a couple of Jeeps and a mini-bus. They drove around a pretty, ornamental pond close to the house and pulled up outside a pair of enormous, polished cedar doors. No-one came out to greet them nor was anyone else to be seen. As Lynch climbed out he looked back towards the main gates and saw that the guards there didn't seem too interested in them either. He walked up the shallow flight of steps leading to the big doors and discovered the landward horizon was defined by the long, undulating line of the cliff tops. Even an ant would be noticed if it poked its head over the cliff for a look at the villa.

'I'll get someone to show you to your rooms.' Tim suddenly interrupted his observations. 'Then I'll tell Mr Halloran you're both here.' He pushed open one of the solid cedar doors and led them both inside. They found themselves in a grand, cavernous entrance hall with blood-coloured tiles on the floor. Corridors led away to the right and left and there was a closed door in one corner of the hall as well as a high arch leading to a vast and deserted lounge. Lynch strolled across to have a closer inspection and was struck by the wide, panoramic windows looking south-west over the sea. A set of double sliding-glass doors were open and he could see they led to a terrace and then to a set of stairs which, in turn, led to a large swimming pool.

The driver had disappeared, leaving their bags in the hall. Janice sighed and sat down in an antique armchair, apparently still preoccupied. Lynch inspected the big lounge and saw it was furnished luxuriously with beige leather sofas and age-blackened antique tables and chests in the solid Moorish style. When he looked through the windows he could see beyond the pool to another flight of wide, white stone steps leading down to a large floating dock where an ocean-going cabin cruiser, the *Junior Endeavor*, swayed in a light swell. Lynch heard his name called and turned to see that Tim, their driver, had returned with a fresh-faced replica of himself in an almost identical uniform of light slacks and cream, short-sleeved shirt. All of Halloran's men had definite similarities, Lynch thought. It seemed all were under 30, fit, polite and obedient. Almost certainly all were ex-US forces. Halloran probably recruited them on personal recommendation soon after discharge and moulded them swiftly and efficiently into his own private, corporate army. Lynch knew there would be no shortage of such men who shared Halloran's views and who would be more than happy to devote their civilian careers, for generous pay, to assisting him in the fulfilment of his aims. Especially when those aims were in America's interests.

'This is Dennis,' the driver introduced the newcomer. 'He's American like the rest of Mr Halloran's staff. He'll show you both to your rooms. Your bags will be sent up in a few minutes.' He stopped and gave a slightly self-conscious smile. 'We're new at this, but I think we run a pretty good hotel here. I'll go tell Mr Halloran you're both settling in.'

They followed Dennis along a wide corridor which ran around the inside of the house. Even the corridor was furnished with expensive exotica, some African, some Arabian. They passed a number of doors until they had almost reached the north-eastern corner of the villa when the young man stopped and opened a solid, arched door leading to Janice's room.

She stepped into the high-ceilinged suite with its huge bed and magnificent furnishings. One door led to a dressing room and bathroom. There was a pretty, dining alcove and a pair of French windows opening onto a tiny balcony with an impressive view of the Mediterranean.

'It'll do,' Janice said, standing in the middle of the room, hands on her hips and looking critically around.

Lynch caught Dennis giving her a long, appraising look. The younger man suddenly realised he'd been caught and flushed, shooting Lynch an apologetic smile. They left Janice and when Dennis had shown Lynch into the suite next door he explained: 'We've been here nearly three months, setting this place up. Mr Halloran says no distractions, so there's no women allowed. Most of us don't even get to go into town.'

Lynch smiled to put the young man at ease and casually inspected his suite, which was a mirror image of Janice's.

'What's the set up here?' he asked mildly.

'It's run like a swell kinda officer's club,' Dennis volunteered. 'We have our own mess, but you guys will probably eat in the house most of the time. If there's anything you want just pick up your room phone. It connects automatically with switch and if you ask for staff there's somebody on duty 24 hours a day. We even do room service if you want to eat in your room. The kitchen is pretty good. We've got two cooks. One is ex-navy and the other is Mr Halloran's personal chef but he only cooks on Mr Halloran's say so.'

'How many others have arrived?' Lynch asked.

'You mean like you?'

'Like me.'

'Well, Commander Finn has been here almost a month and he brought another guy with him. They're both ex-navy SEALs. Another guy got in yesterday. Kind of a rough diamond but okay. Name's Reece, I think. Ex-marine. Says he's never seen anything like this before. Thinks he's died and gone to heaven.'

'Yes,' Lynch agreed. 'Not like any branch of the services I've ever seen.' He paused, then looked directly into Dennis's bland young face and asked: 'Dennis, do you know what we're here for?'

The young man tensed slightly but only hesitated a moment.

'Yes, sir,' he said. 'We all know. And we're under orders to do whatever it takes to make sure you guys get all you need to ensure the success of the operation.'

Lynch nodded. He was satisfied for the moment. Dennis's language had confirmed his service credentials, probably navy or marines, which Halloran clearly favoured. He was satisfied too that Halloran had the total loyalty of Dennis and all the others like him, however many of them there were at the villa. He still wanted to talk to Halloran about the quiet farewell he had received from Brown Suit at Luton but it could wait. He dismissed the young American, closed the door and finished the inspection of his room. He was unable to find any bugs but that didn't mean they weren't there. The view from his small balcony was lovely and when he looked along the seaward wall of the villa he saw half a dozen similar balconies attached to rooms at different levels, giving the occupant of each total privacy. The dusty brown shore was to his right and below the balcony there was a drop of 10 or 12 metres to where the shallow, blue-green water sucked and slapped at the rock foundations. An easy escape, he realised, if he wanted one. He hadn't seen anything yet to suggest that security at the villa was anything other than for the protection of the occupants. He stepped back into his room and pulled a heavy tapestry away from the wall adjoining Janice's room. There was a small connecting door but he decided against trying the handle just yet. Instead, Lynch pulled off his shoes and sprawled backwards on the big bed, stretching all his joints and muscles and luxuriating in the sensation of being alone in peace and quiet for the first time in 24 hours. He closed his eyes and knew he could easily fall asleep. Then he heard the connecting door open and the sound of fingers scrabbling at the heavy wall hanging.

He looked up to see Janice padding across the red tiles in bare feet. She was wearing a white bathrobe and there were tendrils of wet black hair escaping from the white turban she had fashioned from a towel around her head.

'Have you seen Jack?' she asked.

He shook his head but didn't get up. 'Neither have I,' she said and plumped down beside him. She leaned over him and he felt a few tiny droplets of water on his face and hands.

'I hope we get a chance to say goodbye properly,' she said tenderly.

He looked at her. 'Been saving it all up?'

'Something like that,' she smiled faintly. 'I ... I don't want to make my problems yours. I'll deal with it. I've had a hell of a time and I'd like it to end on a ... civilised note.' And she giggled softly.

'Well,' Lynch sighed, glancing around the room. 'Halloran is nothing if not civilised.'

They were interrupted by a flurry of loud banging at the door and Lynch got up reluctantly to open it. When he swung the door open Halloran stood there, grinning hugely, one of Lynch's suitcases in each fist.

'Bellhop,' he bellowed, laughing and enjoying his own joke. 'What have you got in here, all your worldly possessions?' Without waiting for an answer he threw Lynch's bags to one side as if they had ceased to matter and strode into the room.

'Welcome to Malta,' he said, grabbing Lynch's hand and giving it the harsh wrench that passed for a handshake. 'Glad you made it in one piece.' Then he turned to Janice, who still sat on the edge of the bed, and his voice became unexpectedly gentle. 'You too, honey,' he said and bent down to kiss her on the cheek. Janice smiled back with what seemed like genuine affection and Lynch sensed there had been more between them than Halloran's disparaging choice of words had suggested earlier. Halloran straightened up and stepped back to look at them both. 'I understand you two have been getting along real well since we last met,' he said.

His tone suggested it was more an acknowledgement of the success of the relationship rather than implied criticism and Lynch let it pass. 'That's good,' Halloran added. 'Because there ain't going to be much fun after today ... at least not for you, Lieutenant.' He paused and the smug smile of the satisfied matchmaker was replaced by the mask of business.

'Janice,' he said, 'you'll be leaving tomorrow. You'll fly from here to Madrid then on to New York. Lynch, you and I will talk tomorrow but you'll have two days to settle in before we all get down to serious business on Friday.'

'Is Roper here?' Lynch asked.

Halloran shook his head. 'He's coming the long way round. Dublin and Lisbon. Most of the team is here; you'll meet the others tomorrow. Tonight, the three of us will have dinner, you and Janice can say your goodbyes and after that ...' He left the words hanging. They understood what Halloran meant. The rich American turned to leave but he hesitated and did something which surprised Lynch. He walked over to Janice, cupped his hand under her chin and looked down into her eyes. For that moment, Lynch may as well not have existed. This was something intensely personal between Halloran and Janice and all the heat and glare of Halloran's enormous personality was focused on her. 'Thanks, honey,' was all he said. But Lynch could see the depth of the look that passed between them and that Halloran was thanking the girl for nothing less than his own safe delivery. The Briton wondered if Halloran was aware of how much Janice knew or if that too was part of the unspoken understanding between them both.

'It was a pleasure.' She smiled, and the moment passed.

'You're a good kid, Janice,' Halloran said and his cheerfulness returned. 'See you both at dinner,' he added, walking to the open door. 'Nine-o'clock. The evenings are beautiful here this time of year so we'll have dinner on the pool terrace. If you can't find it, Lynch, don't bother reporting for duty on Friday.' Then he laughed again at his own joke and left them alone. They listened to his footsteps fading up the corridor, then Lynch quietly closed the door.

'I'm glad that's over,' said Janice self-consciously. 'Now we can relax.'

'Just how much more of a chaperone than a cover were you?' Lynch asked. He spoke softly but she heard the underlying hardness in his voice. She stood up, walked over to him and slipped her arms around his waist. 'Jack told me you had developed a fondness for the bottle,' she said, looking him in the eye. 'I was supposed to keep your mind off drink and on exercise.'

'That's it?'

'Yes,' she said and he found himself believing her.

'Jack thinks of everything, doesn't he?' Lynch conceded.

107

'The secret is not ...'

'... to mind,' he finished for her. She stood on tiptoe, kissed him on the lips and he held her hard against him. With one hand he untied the sash on her bathrobe, reached inside and felt the burning softness of her skin. 'Bastard,' she whispered, taking the towel from her head and shaking her hair loose so the wet strands fell across her face. 'Ghoul,' he whispered back.

He awoke, alone in his bed, around quarter to nine. His internal alarm had told Lynch to wake up and he was surprised Janice hadn't disturbed him when she left. He had fallen into a deep, restful sleep after they had made love and he awoke feeling refreshed and full of energy. He showered quickly, towelled his hair dry and opened his suitcases. His clothes looked like dish rags. He checked the wardrobe and found clothes his size already hanging there, the same light slacks and short-sleeved shirts worn by Halloran's civilian army. He got dressed then tapped on the connecting door to Janice's room and looked inside but she had already gone. It was a few minutes after nine when he walked briskly down the corridor leading back to the main part of the house.

It was already dark and outside the villa was lit with a soft, yellow glow from discreet electric lighting. The big dining room and lounge were dark and deserted but the sliding glass doors stood wide open. When he stepped through he could see the pool terrace below lit by a necklace of flaming torches set in braziers along the whitewashed balustrade. Halloran and Janice were already seated at a beautifully-set, round dinner table. Janice wore a simple blue linen skirt with a demure white blouse and managed to look both prim and sexy while Halloran was grand in an elegant white dinner jacket. Lynch felt under-dressed but as he walked down the wide stone staircase leading to the terrace he saw Halloran had a can of Budweiser clenched

108

in one hand. The chunky American put the beer down as he got out of his chair to welcome Lynch. 'The tux is in Janice's honour,' he smiled apologetically. 'She's been missing New York so I thought it was the least I could do.'

He gestured Lynch to the only empty chair. 'We were about to send for you,' Janice said. 'We thought you might sleep through till morning.'

'Oh, I'm sure you two found plenty to talk about,' Lynch answered.

'Mostly good, Lieutenant, mostly good,' Halloran said pointedly. 'Drink?' he offered.

Lynch smiled at the subtle vote of confidence. 'No thanks,' he said, 'it interferes with my exercise programme.' Janice smiled and looked away but Halloran let it pass. Halloran ordered another beer and a Perrier from one of two employees hovering obediently near by. It was a pleasant enough meal, the fish they ate was fresh and well prepared, Halloran was a gregarious host and Janice shot several warm glances Lynch's way but he was excluded from most of the conversation because it concerned the latest gossip from New York and Lynch knew none of the people whose names cropped up. Though he did recognise some of the names as prominent American business-men and, in a couple of cases, former White House aides who had once figured prominently in news bulletins.

It was evident too that, however insultingly he had referred earlier to her role in his world, Halloran trusted Janice and valued her judgement. Clearly, she was more than a casual employee. She was Halloran's sometime confidante and ally in the successful manipulation of the useful and influential people who populated their world. When all was said and done, it was a most successful business arrangement. They appreciated each other's talents and, more importantly, they enjoyed each other. For Janice, Lynch suspected, the world she inhabited was the tenderest of traps. Seeing it all, he felt not even a twinge of jealousy. He, in his world, used women the way she used men in hers. In the weeks they had spent together they had forged an understanding. His only regret was that it was ending so soon. There had been elements of their relationship, however mercenary, he had deeply enjoyed. Occasionally it had given him glimpses of the other man in the other life he might have led. But he and Janice were pragmatists. Reality would always drag them back from their fleeting dalliances with romance. Midnight was never far away for either of them. No matter how charming it had been, he understood they were coming to the end of an interlude in the bigger, more dangerous game that had brought them here.

Lynch was relieved when the meal was over. When he and Janice got up to leave Halloran again kissed her on the cheek and gave Lynch a look of amiable envy.

'You're the luckiest man on the island tonight, Lieutenant,' he said and Lynch didn't doubt that he meant it. They said their goodnights and walked back up to the villa, leaving Halloran alone at the table with a cigar and the two forgotten employees waiting patiently in the shadows. Before entering the house Lynch turned to look back. Halloran was on his feet and leaning against the torchlit balustrade, staring out to sea. South by south-east, Lynch reckoned. The direction of Africa. The American was just as obsessed as he was with the thought of murdering the Libyan madman, he realised. Roper made three. Tired, obsessive, emotionally crippled in some way, all three of them. Lynch wondered about the others on the team whom he hadn't yet met and the kind of men they all must be to even consider such a desperate gamble.

They went to Janice's room and made love with an urgency that surprised them both, appetites and senses heightened by the awareness of impending separation. He wasn't sure what woke him up some time later. He guessed it was the sensation that Janice had left the bed. A layer of cloud had moved in

110

from the south, shutting out the moon and stars, and the room was ink-dark. He felt a gust of cool air and saw her shadowy outline in the open doorway leading to the balcony. Janice was standing, quite still, one hand resting lightly on the door jamb. She couldn't see the surf but she could hear it a few metres below, licking coldly at the rocks. He asked if she was all right, but she said nothing, just shivered slightly, then hurried back to bed, pulling the covers over her and pressing her body against him. She must have been there a long time, he realised, because her skin was as cold as alabaster. They made love again but this time, when he came, she held him inside her body as long as she could as though clinging desperately to the single intimacy that held them together, the fragile strand of sexual communication which, for them, replaced all others.

'I'll try,' she said, after a while. 'Believe me, I'll try to forget you.'

He played with her thickly-tousled hair and smiled to himself. 'We've set ourselves apart from other people,' he said, addressing the single thought that had been nagging at them both since leaving London. 'We can't allow ourselves ordinary pleasures like falling in love. It's not part of the game for people like us . . . and we know it.'

In the morning she left without a word.

6

THE TEAM

Malta, September 1989

He heard Janice get up around six, listened to her shower, watched her dress, pack her few things and carry the rest of her unopened bags outside into the corridor. He saw her turn in the doorway to look back at him. Because she was silhouetted against the outside electric light he couldn't see the expression on her face. He wondered if she could see that his eyes were open and that he was looking back at her, but the room was still so dark that he guessed not. She blew him a quick kiss and closed the door. He listened to her footsteps as they echoed down the hard, polished tiles of the long corridor till they were gone. A moment later he heard someone collect her bags then it was silent again. He got up, went to his own room and climbed into his own bed with its cold, pristine sheets, as if he needed to get away from the warmth of her body which still clung to her side of the bed and the perfume which lingered on her pillow. He couldn't get back to sleep and, irritably, got up again, deciding he might feel better after some hard exercise. He knew he needed to start putting her out of his mind immediately. He pulled on his swimsuit and the white bathrobe behind his bathroom door and walked barefoot through the house and down to the pool. It was almost seven and a pink dawn was reaching over the eastern horizon. There were a few people about. He looked out of a window down the length of the courtyard and saw a guard stretching and yawning inside the main gates. One of Halloran's people was sweeping the corridor and he heard noises from the kitchen as he passed. When he reached the pool there were already two men there, doggedly swimming laps. They might be fellow team members, Lynch thought, but they could just as easily have been on Halloran's staff.

He guessed the pool was a good 25 metres long with six lanes. Built more for serious swimming than playing, he surmised, though there was a deep end opposite with a springboard. Lynch knew he had maintained a high level of fitness in the past three months but had no illusions about the degree of stamina he would need for the job which lay ahead. He decided on 40 laps to warm up and then a few sprints to see how he felt. He threw his bathrobe onto a near by sun chair, picked an empty lane, dived in and began a strong rhythmic crawl. The pool was filled with salt water and unheated, though it couldn't be considered cold by any means. Lynch had learned to swim as a boy in the chill Scottish waters of the Solway Firth and anything else usually felt like bathwater by comparison. Lynch pushed himself and when he checked his watch at the end of 40 laps saw he'd swum the kilometre in 15½ minutes. It was a good time but he was breathing a little more heavily than he would have liked. He also felt he could shave his time in a bigger pool without the distraction of frequent turns. Swimming in the sea would be better, he knew, but he would wait until he learned what kind of training they would be doing first. He suspected that for the seaborne operation Halloran had in mind, they would be spending much of their time ahead in the sea anyway. Lynch spent the next

114

20 minutes doing fast sprints and then finished with another kilometre, this one a full minute slower than the first. Gradually, the accumulated *angst* of the past few days began to seep from his body and when he pulled himself, panting and streaming water, from the pool, he felt considerably better. He noticed there was only one swimmer left in the pool, persistently swimming laps. The other man had climbed out just ahead of Lynch and was drying himself near by.

'Speed's okay,' said the man as he caught Lynch's eye. 'Stamina's what counts.'

Lynch had heard the accent before and guessed it was southern California. He noticed the authority in the man's voice and bearing and realised he was used to giving orders.

'Speed kills,' Lynch answered amiably, falling back on an old SAS joke he'd heard during counter-terrorist training.

The man smiled faintly and continued getting dressed. Lynch estimated his age in the early forties but he was very fit and deeply tanned. By comparison Lynch knew he looked pale and pasty despite his obvious fitness—a legacy of the years in Britain's insipid sunshine. The man also had the powerful neck and shoulders of the longtime swimmer. Like Lynch he scraped in at a shade over six feet and his sun-bleached light-brown hair was cut short. He pulled on a worn, navy-blue tracksuit with a faded, illegible insignia on the left breast, then walked over to Lynch and offered his hand.

'Jerry Finn,' he introduced himself. 'Commander, US Navy.' Then he added as an afterthought: 'Retired.'

They shook hands and Lynch said: 'Colin James Lynch, Royal Navy . . . also retired.'

'Some retirement home, huh?' Finn offered, as though trying to get off on a better footing.

Lynch nodded, finished drying himself and put on his robe. So this was his opposite number from the SEALs, he thought. These élite American underwater units, like the SBS, speci-

115

alised in clandestine coastal surveillance, infiltration, reconnaissance, sabotage and, when necessary, assassination. Lynch
had visited the US often, seen many American naval installa-
tions, enjoyed the company of American officers during shared
naval exercises and exchanges of hospitality. But that had all
stopped when he joined the SBS. Officers of élite units rarely
had the opportunity to fraternise quite so much with their
opposite numbers from other countries and there were far
stricter controls on exchanges of information on new weapons
and tactics. Consequently, Lynch and Finn eyed each other
with undisguised professional interest.

'Looks as though we're going to be spending a bit of time
together,' Lynch said eventually.

'Looks that way,' Finn agreed. Again there was that hint of
authority in the voice as though Finn were bidding to estab-
lish seniority right from the start. Lynch had noticed Finn had
seen fit to announce his rank when they introduced themselves
although rank carried no weight here. He let it pass.

'See you when school starts,' he said lightly and turned to
go back up to the house. He had only walked a couple of steps
when Finn called after him. 'I've heard a lot about you, Lieutenant,' he said. Lynch turned and saw there was just a suggestion of awkwardness in Finn's manner and perhaps a note
of concession in his voice. 'I like what I've heard,' Finn added.
Lynch gave him a courteous nod and continued on his way up
the stone staircase. Perhaps that was it, he thought. Good
man. Poor officer. It was a snap judgement but he'd seen the
type. He didn't intend to let it get in the way.

Back in his room Lynch showered and, in deference to the
athletic atmosphere of the place, put on his grey tracksuit with
the 'Everlast' insignia, over shorts and tee-shirt. He picked up
the phone, noting that there was no dial. A male voice came
on the other end and said simply: 'Staff.'

'What's on the breakfast menu?' Lynch asked.

116

'What do you want?' the voice answered.

Lynch took the voice at its word and ordered orange juice, bacon with four scrambled eggs, toast, orange marmalade and the biggest pot of tea they had. He had chosen to eat alone instead of in the dining room because he didn't feel in the mood for socialising just yet. Dennis arrived in a few minutes with a breakfast tray including a metal teapot that must have held at least a quart. He set it on the small coffee table on the balcony where Lynch had decided to eat, then handed the impressed Briton a newspaper. Lynch opened it. It was that day's edition of the *International Herald-Tribune* from Paris. Obviously somebody from the villa went to the airport early each day.

Lynch ate in peace. No-one called. There was no indication that Halloran wanted to see him yet.

After breakfast he read the newspaper cover to cover. Then he put his bare feet up on the balcony and considered how superior the view was to that of his little Hammersmith flat. This was the lull before the storm, he knew, and he savoured it. When the big meal had settled he decided to take a walk and examine his surroundings a little more thoroughly. He laced on a pair of running shoes and walked back down the corridor to the entrance hall. There were a few more people about but no-one he recognised, and it was impossible to tell who was staff and who might be on his team because everyone was dressed similarly in casual slacks and shirts or tracksuits. The whole villa had the ambience of an exclusive health club. Everyone he passed gave him a friendly 'Hi' but otherwise seemed disinterested in him. He glanced around the big lounge. The dining table had already been cleared and a couple of men sat separately on the big leather sofas, reading. Through the enormous windows facing west over the Mediterranean he could see nothing but a clear expanse of sky and water. The swimming pool was deserted and the *Junior En-*

deavor still bobbed at the dock-side. There was no sign of Halloran. As he walked around Lynch was struck suddenly by the realisation that there was no music anywhere in the villa and no radio or TV in any room. No piped music. No electronic distractions at all. Consequently the whole complex was suffused with a kind of peace, punctuated only by the natural sounds of gulls calling above the constant wash of the sea. He strolled across the open courtyard and the only people in sight were the two guards at the main gate, one leaning against the door to the guard post, the other a shadow, just visible inside. They were still the only men Lynch had seen openly wearing weapons. He did an easy circuit of the courtyard, looked over the vehicles in the open garage and saw that one of the Mercs was missing, probably the one used to deliver Janice to the airport. At the side of the garage there was a flight of stone steps leading to a row of rooms, with a matching set on the wall across the courtyard. On the ground floor of the opposite wall was a heavily-barred door, possibly leading to the armoury Lynch knew existed.

He poked his nose into several of the rooms and no-one tried to stop him. There were a couple of well-equipped workshops and a series of bedrooms, each furnished with army bunks. He found a pump room and the generator room which apparently supplied the villa's power and water. He found the kitchen with a huge pantry and walk-in coldroom bulging with frozen carcasses. The villa seemed entirely self-sufficient. He didn't yet know how many men were quartered here but he had seen enough supplies to provision a small army for months. It all reminded him of a luxuriously-appointed desert fort, an outpost of the Foreign Legion perhaps or, more appropriately, a bastion of Americana on the edge of twentieth-century civilisation, with the savages lurking just beyond the horizon.

He decided it was time to discover exactly how much a

volunteer or how much a captive he was in Fort America, and casually strolled up to the guard at the main gate.

'Can I go outside for a run?' he asked.

'Sure,' the guard grinned. He was taller than Lynch and heavily-built with swarthy Arabic features, though his accent was American. 'Just use the inside gate here,' he said and pointed to a one-man entrance set within the framework of the main gate. 'It's open all the time. No problem. If you want to run, stick to the track you came in on. The other track leads to those cliffs.' He pointed to the crumbly cliff tops curving around to the south-east. 'It gets pretty rough going up there,' he added. 'You could turn an ankle.'

'Thanks,' Lynch said as the guard pushed the gate open for him and stood aside. He stepped out and walked for a few minutes across the broad apron of crushed grey rock and dirt before turning round to look back at the villa. It might look like something from the *Arabian Nights*, Lynch thought, but it was ideally situated for defensive purposes. Nobody could enter from this side without crossing a hundred metres of open space. It would be impossible to reach the gates without the goodwill of the guards inside. The other three sides of the villa could be approached only from the sea.

Lynch walked on until he reached the bottom of the bluff where the two tracks led in opposite directions. The one to the left wound back seven or eight kilometres between scrubby hills towards the road leading inland to Valletta. The one on the right was steeper and narrower and led up to the crest of the bluff which ended in the series of sheer cliffs reaching around this southern corner of the coastline for several kilometres. He went through a few stretches and warm-up exercises before breaking into a comfortable trot. He ignored the guard's advice and pointedly took the track leading to the cliff tops. After a few minutes he had gained some height and looked back at the villa but if anyone there was concerned about his departure there was no sign of it. Eventually the track dissipated into treacherous scree studded with tufts of coarse, burnt grass and he was forced to take a more careful pace. As the guard had said, it would be easy to turn an ankle. He went on till he reached the shoulder of the bluff where the land began its headlong rush to the cliffs and their dangerous, fragmented edges. From this crest he could see no sign of the villa at all. It was obscured completely by the contours of the coast and anyone approaching this way would not know it was there until they literally fell upon it. He looked inland at the dry, undulating country with its ancient olive trees, bent and stunted by the prevailing hot breath of Africa. The wind coursed through a network of stony gullies and whipped his hair, grown longer in the months with Janice. He breathed the warm clean air deeply for several minutes and then he suddenly caught a scent of something different. It was only there for a second but it was enough to trigger an alarm. He turned his back away from the wind and strolled further up the bluff for a few minutes, sniffing discreetly. He caught it again and this time there was no mistaking it. He was careful not to display any reaction to his discovery. Instead he started back down towards the path leading to the villa and filed this unexpected piece of intelligence away for use later, if need be.

When he got back to the villa it was almost two in the afternoon and the same guard welcomed him back with a big grin.

'I tell 'em all,' he said. 'And they all ignore me and go their own way. They have to go see for themselves I'm not lyin'. You're the third one in a week to do the same thing. Christ knows how Halloran is goin' to get you guys to take orders. We wouldn't last five minutes on his staff if we behaved like you.'

'It's reassuring to know there are a few pros left,' Lynch joked as he stepped through the gate. The guard watched him go and, when he had disappeared inside the house, turned and nodded to the man inside the guard post. The man pushed a button on the keyboard in front of him and spoke into a small microphone: 'Come in pickets one, two and three,' he called. 'Any of you guys make him?' There was a short pause, then another voice responded clearly over the two-way. 'Picket one here,' it said. 'I saw him. He just looked round a bit. Seemed satisfied and left.'

'Thank you, picket one,' the guard said and punched a prominent white button on the keyboard. A small video unit slid silently out of the panel mounted over his desk and the guard tapped in a short entry which would show up on the VDU in Halloran's office when Halloran wanted a security check. Up on the bluff, in a foxhole expertly hidden among the scrubby gullies, picket one put down his radio and shoved the Armalite AR18 with its cumbersome snipperscope to one side before making himself comfortable and checking his watch again to see how many hours were left before dark when his relief would arrive.

Lynch went back to his room and lay on the bed, a few intriguing thoughts circulating through his mind about Halloran, Finn, the villa and what he had detected up on the bluff. He began to form a plan and, after a while, he smiled and drifted into sleep. A few minutes later he was disturbed by the shrill ringing of his bedside phone. When he picked it up Halloran was on the other end.

'Come to my quarters for dinner tonight and meet some of the guys you're going to be working with,' he said abruptly. 'Nothing formal. I'm in the wing on the opposite side of the house from you. See you at nine.' Lynch hung up and wondered why he felt so groggy. He looked at the clock and saw that many more than a few minutes had slipped by. It was almost seven. He had slept more than four hours. Still feeling sluggish, he decided another swim would wake him up. This time he had the pool to himself and, instead of counting laps, thrashed up and down for half an hour till he felt the familiar surge of juice through his veins again. When he had showered and shaved, he discovered his clothes had been neatly pressed for him and put on smart, sober black slacks and shirt. He felt better equipped now to deal with Halloran, Finn and the other men who would soon be his team-mates.

As he crossed the villa a few minutes before nine he noticed the lounge was dark and deserted. The house, he suspected, was reserved exclusively for the use of Halloran and his guests. The ony staff allowed here were Halloran's most senior personal aides, or bodyguards and kitchen staff, cleaners and domestics. When not working, they kept to their own quarters in the rooms around the courtyard. The south wing of the house, where Halloran resided, was similar to the north, where Lynch had his room, and had an almost identical corridor running its entire length. The only difference was that there were fewer doors. The guard floor was deserted and it was the sound of voices which led Lynch up a short flight of stairs to the second floor.

Lynch suspected that the entire south wing constituted Hallorin's private quarters. He found his way to a pair of arched double doors, one of which was open and led into a room many times bigger than Lynch's suite. It was one vast reception room, appointed even more lavishly than the downstairs lounge. The furniture was grander, more ornate, more Turkish in design. The walls were hung with silks and tapestries of breathtaking opulence. Several closed doors only suggested other, more private rooms of equal decadence. It wasn't the kind of place a man like Halloran would normally occupy, Lynch knew. It had the look and feel of a sultan's palace. Lynch was convinced the villa was the borrowed residence of some Middle-Eastern magnate, almost certainly an arms dealer, over whom Halloran had some considerable influence. On the far side of the room, a series of open French windows led on to an enormous balcony where a table big enough to seat 20 had been set at one end for five. The same two employees from the previous night were serving drinks to a group of men gathered at one end of the balcony. As usual, Halloran was doing most of the talking though when he saw Lynch he interrupted his own monologue to welcome him and make the introductions. Lynch looked at the other three men on the balcony and recognised only Finn. He was the only man wearing a jacket. The other two looked very young and ill at ease. At most they could only have been in their late twenties. One was tall and fair, the other dark and muscular. They were casually dressed, the taller of the two wearing jeans. Lynch noticed even Halloran was wearing chinos and a western-cut blue shirt.

'I believe you and Commander Finn met this morning,' Halloran said as he drew Lynch into the group. 'This is Commander Finn's partner, Emmet Tuckey, formerly Ensign Tuckey, US Navy,' he went on, presenting the taller man. 'He and Commander Finn were in the same SEALs unit before joining us.' Lynch shook hands with the young man, who seemed to be struggling to grow his first moustache. 'And this is Henry Reece,' Halloran continued, introducing the tougher-looking man with cropped black hair. 'Formerly Sergeant Reece, US Marine Corps.'

Reece's handshake was like iron and even though his manner was deferential in the company of senior officers and he was, no doubt, a little intimidated by his surroundings, Lynch caught the suggestion of swagger in him. 'Sergeant Reece is one of two demolitions experts on the team. His partner, Private First Class Bono, also ex-Marine Corps, will be getting in tomorrow. That makes Sergeant Reece and myself the only two non-coms here this evening, gentlemen. I hope you won't hold that against us.'

Having made his point Halloran went back to what was obviously a favourite subject, the ineptitude of American foreign policy. They all listened dutifully and when Halloran had finished he gestured to them to sit down for dinner. Half way through the first course Halloran leaned over to Lynch for a quiet word. 'Roper will be getting in tomorrow with Reece's pal,' he said. 'You'll have gathered already that the team is designed to operate in pairs. Guys with a long track record of working together successfully. We figure it gives us the best chance of success because that way, the team breaks down into three components, any one of which can do the job if the others should fail. We'll be having our first full briefing tomorrow night when the whole team is here but if, at any time, you see anything you don't like, anything that can stand improvement, anything that worries you at all, I want you to speak up. We'll be going over it again and again in the next few weeks and there will be plenty of opportunity for you to give us the benefit of your experience and expertise. We expect the same from every man in the team. Anything we've missed, we want to know.'

'Who devised your plan?' Lynch asked.

'Commander Finn,' Halloran answered and Lynch saw Finn take sudden interest in their conversation at the mention of his name. 'We've done our homework,' Halloran added. 'The plan is good and we're utilising some of the most advanced equipment in the world, stuff even the SEALs haven't fully tested yet. You're joining us a full two years into our timetable, Lieutenant.

'All that remains is for the team to synchronise with the equipment and the plan ... and we've got eight weeks to do that. It should be enough. Commander Finn and I have no worries about you, Roper or Tuckey but in that time we have to teach Reece and Bono to dive and turn them from novices into experts in submarine warfare without killing them in between.

'Before that,' he added, leaning back to include the others in their conversation, 'we have to make sure you're all fit and strong enough for the job—and that's where Commander Finn comes in.'

Finn took his cue and the others listened carefully.

'For the next two weeks we'll be spending a lot of time in the ocean,' he said, 'swimming and doing other exercises designed to increase our stamina.' At the use of that last word, he paused momentarily and glanced at Lynch. 'Now, I know most of us recruited for this task are already far above average fitness levels but that may not be enough. Getting to the Libyan coastline will be demanding in the extreme. We'll be spending many hours in the water in total darkness and the combination of sustained stress and high exertion will take a toll. We cannot afford to arrive at our destination exhausted. As Lieutenant Lynch knows, navigating safely to enemy-held coastline is only the beginning. Once ashore we will be required to perform many hours of difficult physical labour before we have any chance to rest.

'And,' he added, 'there is the high probability that we could be engaged in hostilities soon after arrival. We simply do not know. Therefore we have to be ready. For these reasons I ask you all to enter into the next few weeks' training in the right spirit. It will be hard, deliberately so, and there will be a few unpleasant surprises along the way to test stamina and stretch each man's personal resources. There will be no drop-outs,' he said. 'We are all locked into this mission. From the moment of each man's arrival here he is committed totally to the mission's success.' He paused for emphasis and added: 'I hope you all understand my meaning.'

Lynch was the first to speak. There was just a shade too

much rigidity in Finn's attitude and it concerned him. That and a few other things.

'Just one point,' he said, directing his words at Finn. 'I'm sure you're aware, Commander, that even the best plans go wrong, the best equipment breaks down and the best preparation in the world often fails to anticipate realities in the field. We should be careful not to overlook the importance of individual initiative. When confronted by the unexpected initiative usually makes the difference between success or failure.'

'Quite so,' Finn acknowledged. Then he added: 'Equally, there are times when discipline and good planning are all that hold a mission together under pressure.'

Halloran looked from one man to the other, faintly amused. 'Good,' he said. 'I like competition. It sharpens a man's combative edge.'

Neither Lynch nor Finn felt like arguing the subtleties of their opposing philosophies further and the conversation drifted into less sensitive areas. Reece, it transpired, was 28 and originally from New Jersey. He had served with the Marine Corps for 11 years, he said, and had been recruited to this operation by no less a figure than his old major-general, another friend of Halloran's. He had been discharged from the marines only three weeks earlier, on the strength of a fake medical certificate which said he had developed diabetes. Tuckey was 26, originally from Florida. Like Lynch he had joined the navy and found himself drafted to an élite unit because of specialist skills, which in his case were marksmanship and an aptitude for diving. He had been recruited by Finn, his unit commander, six months earlier. Finn had resigned his command and simply disappeared into Halloran's business empire. Tuckey had followed after purchasing his discharge, with Halloran's money, on compassionate grounds.

After dinner Halloran produced a flask of port and a box of cigars for those who smoked, with the warning that it would be their last till training was completed.

All but Finn took the offered port though only Reece joined Halloran in smoking one of his cigars. Lynch noticed that the brawny young American inhaled the strong tobacco smoke easily and, he decided, with lungs like that Reece would have little difficulty learning to dive.

Halloran led them away from the dining table on the balcony and back inside the huge reception room to an arrangement of sofas covered in heavy silk damask. Lynch was sure he heard the cushions sigh as he sat down and they enveloped him in sensual softness. Halloran watched him as he sipped his port and gazed around the room and its overwhelming richness.

'This will remind you of what you'll be missing if you don't come back,' Halloran smiled.

'A million dollars wouldn't buy this room,' Lynch answered. 'I can appreciate why you chose Malta—but isn't this all rather ostentatious for our purposes? Won't we attract attention just by being here?'

'On the contrary,' Halloran said, as the others switched their eyes to him. 'This corner of the island is reserved for VIPs and their villas. The Maltese leave its residents alone because there's an understanding that the people who live here want to be left in peace and security and that they bring plenty of foreign exchange with them. As far as the government of Malta is aware this villa is occupied by its owner, Prince Hassan, from the United Arab Emirates. The Prime Minister of Malta and the government would shit if they knew we were here. But they don't. They allow the prince, his family and his guests pretty well to come and go as he pleases, either by private jet or aboard his yacht. Just as long as he spends a few million American dollars each year in refitting and refurbishing in the Maltese shipyards and on provisions for this residence. If any Maltese officials were to come snooping around, you've seen our set-up, we'd have plenty of warning to get you guys under cover and make things presentable.

'That's the beautiful thing about Malta,' he continued. 'The Maltese understand the art of diplomatic compromise and they still play the same old game. This place has been a crossroads for four thousand years. It's where Europe meets Africa. It has a long history of occupation, colonisation, conquest and re-conquest and through it all the Maltese have practised business as usual. Servicing everybody who passed through, making money, providing a haven with no questions asked for a lot of rich people who appreciate a cosy little island retreat in the Mediterranean. Having a house in Malta is a little like having a Swiss bank account. You can fall back on it when things get too hot at home ... and the locals won't bother you. Malta gets a lot of Arabs, Libyans too. They come here for R & R away from the prying eyes of Colonel Gaddafi. It's a kind of neutral zone that suits everybody. The Libyans come to play and make deals. Arabs from the oil states come to berth their yachts or keep homes here. There are plenty of villas as decadent as this one hidden around the coast. As long as the occupants keep spending plenty of money the locals won't stick their noses in. This is a dangerous place, it's a dirty place ... and it's the right place for us. Just as long as we keep a low profile. Make no mistakes, the Maltese would do more than object if they knew this place was crawling with Americans who've come to burn their meal ticket. But they don't. Our cover is as damn near perfect as it can get. I have a few Arabic-speaking people on my staff. Lebanese-Americans all of 'em. They look Arab and they speak Arab but they were born in the States. We even have one guy who can speak

Maltese. He keeps the cover up by making sure we stick to the same buying patterns as the prince when he's in residence. He does all the deals with local suppliers. As far as the Maltese are concerned the prince and a few of his playboy pals are in residence at the moment. The prince has guards, so do we. In truth, the prince hasn't been near here in months.'

'What happens if he decides to drop in?' Lynch asked.

'He won't.'

'Why not?'

'Let's just say he knows enough to stay away. Prince Hassan is one of many pro-Western Arabs in the Middle East. People forget we have a lot of friends in the region as well as enemies. He doesn't know our precise objective but he is sympathetic to our cause.'

Lynch put his empty glass on a near by table. 'Isn't the prince going to be a trifle embarrassed when it becomes known how important an asset his residence was in the mounting of this operation?' he asked.

'Not half as much as the government of Malta,' Halloran answered. 'Though we have taken steps to protect the prince. Steps which suggest he was fooled into lending his Maltese villa to a friend of a friend. The fact is, when this mission succeeds there's going to be so much dust nobody is going to see clearly. Nobody will suspect a non-governmental agency was instrumental in Gaddafi's removal. The Soviets will claim it's a Western plot and our governments will be able to deny it with full integrity. When both sides have finished their disinformation campaigns nobody will know what happened . . . and events will have taken place which will make the nature of Gaddafi's departure irrelevant anyway. All that will matter is that he's gone. The worst that can happen is that Malta will break off diplomatic ties with Washington and the prince will lose his villa. I suspect Washington can survive Malta's anger.

The prince has approved another residence I have offered him in Hawaii. He already owns other houses in Monaco and Spain so he won't be denied port facilities in the Mediterranean.' He held his hands up to indicate that further explanation was unnecessary and they politely accepted the hint. Halloran stood up and nodded in the direction of a large and elegant clock which told them it was nearly midnight. 'If you'll excuse me, gentlemen, I still have some work to do.'

Lynch made sure he hung back after the others left the room and then turned to Halloran.

'There's something important I think you need to know,' he said. Halloran showed no surprise but gestured Lynch back into the room. At that moment, Tim, the big blond man who had driven Lynch and Janice from the airport, stepped into the room through a far door. He first ensured that the two employees who had served dinner had left and then closed the door leading to the corridor. Lynch realised Tim was one of Halloran's closest aides as well as a bodyguard and felt reassured that they had rated such a highranking chauffeur. Halloran signalled Tim to continue what he was about, then faced Lynch and waited for him to speak.

'I was watched until the moment I left London,' Lynch said.

'I know,' Halloran answered.

'That isn't what bothers me,' Lynch added. 'I got the impression they knew I was up to something but they let me go anyway.'

'Why do you say that?' Halloran asked and Lynch saw a wary glimmer in the American's eye.

'I'm not really sure. Just a gut feeling about the bloke who saw me off. I'd sprung him following me weeks earlier. I got the distinct impression he was telling me something ... that I hadn't seen the last of him, something like that.'

130

Halloran nodded. 'Okay,' he said. 'Leave it with me. I'll look into it.'

'How?' Lynch asked.

Halloran smiled but Lynch detected a twitch of annoyance there too. 'Keep your mind on the job ahead, Lieutenant,' he said. 'You ought to know by now I know how to look after the details. Nothing will be allowed to jeopardise the success of this mission, be assured of that.'

He walked Lynch to the door. 'Enjoy your little run today?' he asked.

Lynch winked. 'Stamina's what counts,' he said and strolled off down the corridor. Halloran closed the door and crossed the big room to where his aide had opened a pair of double doors.

'Trouble?' the blond man asked.

Halloran shook his head. 'Lynch is okay,' he said. 'But he thinks something might be wrong at the British end. If he's worried, I'm worried.'

His aide secured the double doors and disappeared into the dimly-lit room beyond, emerging a few minutes later, pushing a trolley carrying a large, folded-metal dish. He manhandled the trolley onto the balcony, then lifted the apparatus off, set it on the empty dining table and unfolded its leaves until it was revealed as a microwave satellite receiving and transmitting dish. When he had plugged it in and hooked it up to the communications console in the temporary electronic office he had set up for his boss they were ready to bypass the Maltese telephone system and tune in direct to the ITT telecommunications satellite suspended 27,000 kilometres overhead. Tim sat at his keyboard and awaited Halloran's instructions. At his desk near by Halloran looked at his watch and saw it was almost half past midnight.

'We'll do New York first, then LA,' he ordered and his

aide obediently tapped the international access code to the satellite followed by the code for New York and then the first of a series of phone numbers his boss wanted. Halloran swung his feet onto the desk and pulled the speaker closer to him. 'Then get me London,' he said. 'We'll wake those bastards up and find out what the hell's going on over there.'

The next day Lynch woke early and swam a couple of kilometres in the pool before deciding to have breakfast in the main dining room to see what the set-up there was like. Reece and Tuckey were already seated, eating pancakes and bacon brought by Dennis who was lounging near by acting as a waiter. Finn had already eaten and left, apparently on some errand of his own. Lynch asked Dennis for scrambled eggs on toast, then used the informality of breakfast to probe Tuckey a little about Finn.

'He's okay,' Tuckey volunteered in a voice surprisingly deep for a man who looked so young. 'He likes to think he's a bad ass. Likes to keep a little distant from his men, but I'd trust him anywhere. I've done some hairy stuff with him, man: the Persian Gulf, Philippines, even Cuba. Went into Havana harbour at night to look at some stuff the Russians shipped in. He always gets the job done. I heard what you said last night and I know what you did against the Argentinians—but the commander knows what he's doing. He's always the last one to eat, the last one to get tired, the last one to get to sleep and the first one up the next day. I'd never have picked him for something like this, but the fact that he thinks it's the only way convinced me. He's about as tough and as smart as you can get.'

'Hey,' Reece interjected and directed his attention at Lynch.

'Were you in that little business between the Limeys and the spics? Tell me about it, I want to hear about that.'

Lynch smiled and was about to deliver his own shortened history of the Falklands conflict when they heard the outside door open and they all looked up. Roper walked in first, followed by one of the ugliest men Lynch had ever seen. The newcomers looked lost for a moment until they caught a glimpse of the men at the dining table through the archway leading down from the entrance hall. Lynch hadn't seen Roper since the meeting at the Inter-Continental and, taciturn though he might be, Lynch was glad to see a familiar face, in the oasis of Americana.

Roper strolled down the short flight of steps into the big room, nodded to everyone and slung his kit bag onto a near by chair. It would be just like him to bring everything he owned in a single kit bag, Lynch thought. He got up and offered his hand and as they shook, Reece brushed past them in the direction of the newcomer who stood, glowering, at the top of the stairs.

'Bono, you magnificent bastard,' Reece grinned. 'Get in here and sit down before you break something.'

The big, ugly man stood his ground and squinted at the faces turned his way, then slowly took in the plush interior of the villa.

'Where the fuck are we this time, Reece?' he asked finally. 'Some kind of dago whorehouse?'

A faint smile crossed Roper's face, something Lynch hadn't seen in two years on the same counter-terrorist squad. 'He was on the same flight as me from Lisbon,' Roper said. 'Sat in the rear of the plane. I think the hostesses were afraid of him. He didn't say much on the ride here. Seems harmless enough.'

Lynch looked at Roper. It was impossible to tell if he was joking.

133

The big man hadn't moved even though Reece was endeavoring to relax him and introduce him to the others. It wasn't just his bulk that was impressive. There were plenty of big men in the services and he would have been no more than 190 centimetres at most. It was his compelling ugliness. He was a redhead but his hair was thinning and clung patchily to his big, sunburned head in greasy red wisps. Like a lot of men with too much testosterone he may have been losing the hair on his scalp but his body hair was abundant. It crawled down his thick neck like coils of barbed wire, covered his massive forearms with brassy curls and bristled through the weave in his sweat-stained olivedrab tee-shirt. His skin was badly pock-marked from childhood acne and his slitted eyes regarded the world with the same wary malevolence the world reserved for him.

He had a squashed, puggish nose, and thick tufts of red hair jutted from each nostril. His mouth was a wet gash and when he spoke it sounded as if he needed to clear a quantity of phlegm from his throat. Because of his ugliness it was difficult to guess his age but he already had heavy jowls and a gut spilling over the dirty green army pants he wore with sneakers which had once been white and were now a leprous grey.

'Jesus Christ,' said Tuckey, still seated at the table, hypnotised. 'Do we throw him a bone or just shoot him now and get it over with?'

Lynch glanced down. 'Got any silver bullets?' he whispered back.

Eventually the big man relaxed enough to let Reece lead him down the stairs, into the big room and to introduce him to the others as Samuel Jackson Bono, Private First Class, US Marine Corps. AWOL. When Lynch shook hands with him he felt as though his hand had been ground in sandpaper. As Bono passed he felt a rancid vapour trail and Lynch

134

made a point of stepping away. He had hoped to finish his breakfast. When the introductions had been made Bono picked a chair at the table and sat down with a grunt. His eyes finally settled on Dennis. 'Any chance a man can get a decent steak around here?' he asked in the same low, slushy growl.

'Sure,' Dennis shrugged, standing up. 'How do you like it?'

'Just clip its horns and wipe its ass,' the big man said.

7

THE PLAN

Malta, September-October 1989

On the afternoon of his third day at the villa, Lynch was sunbathing by the pool after an hour-long swim when one of Halloran's clean-cut employees told him he was expected, with the others, in the conference room at six sharp. The conference room, he was told, was upstairs from the main lounge.

Lynch arrived a few minutes early. The room reminded him of a plush lecture theatre, only much smaller, with six descending tiers of reclining red seats, each tier accommodating only eight seats with an aisle down the middle. On the floor below was a small platform where a desk and two chairs had been set up, occupied by Halloran and Finn, both in deep conversation. Above and behind them, on the wall facing the empty seats, was a movie screen. Lynch looked around and saw the wall slots which identified the projection room. It was, he realised, Prince Hassan's private cinema. In his absence it made a perfect conference room. Lynch picked an aisle seat near the back and sat down. A minute later Roper arrived and sat near by. He was followed closely by Tuckey, then Reece and Bono together. Wherever Bono went, Lynch thought, he had a way of regarding his environment as though he suspected it might turn on him at any moment and he might have to neutralise it quickly, preferably with explosives.

When they were all seated Finn asked the last man in to close the door but either Bono didn't hear or he ignored the commander and it was Reece who got up and pulled the door shut. Finn frowned but let it pass as Halloran stood up to speak to the men. His manner was still calm but Lynch sensed an undercurrent of tension, that same controlled energy he had first encountered in London.

Halloran was brief and to the point. 'Gentlemen,' he began, 'I have spoken with all of you, individually, and you know why you are here. The six of you represent the most capable private force assembled in the world today. You have been selected to launch a swift, incisive strike into the capital city of a hostile nation with the objective of applying maximum violence against that nation's leadership. You are the men who will rid the world of Colonel Gaddafi and his terrorist regime ... and this is how you are going to do it.'

With that he turned the meeting over to Finn and sat down. The commander began by reaffirming what Lynch already knew, that the six of them would operate in two-men units; Finn with Tuckey, Reece with Bono and Roper with Lynch. Because of Reece and Bono's lack of diving experience, Finn said, they would be split up and paired with the most experienced divers during the water-borne penetration of the Libyan coast. Then he picked up a remote control, darkened the theatre lights and punched up a slide picture onto the screen. It was a map of the eastern Mediterranean showing the southern boot of Italy, Sicily, Malta and the coast of North Africa with Libya flanked by Tunisia in the west and Egypt in the east. After delivering a short geography lesson Finn punched up a second map, this one giving a more detailed picture of Malta and the Libyan coastline, with Tripoli clearly delineated, and arrows showing prevailing ocean currents in the Gulf of Sidra. A red line had been drawn from the south-western tip of the island republic to Tripoli. Finn picked up a marker and pointed it at the red line.

'A distance of 257 kilometres as the seagull flies,' he said. 'Or 136 nautical miles. That's 13½ hours aboard a vessel with a cruising speed of 10 knots. That means we're less than a day's cruise from Tripoli aboard the vessel we'll be using, gentlemen.

'However,' he added, 'we can only approach the coast of Libya to a distance of about 20 nautical miles. That puts us outside the international 12-mile limit and beyond their coastal radar.

'As you will be aware, the Libyans insist on a 200-mile coastal limit, which would put us in their territorial waters the moment we depart Malta. America, among other nations, refuses to recognise the 200-mile limit, as we all know. In fact there is very little the Libyan navy or air force can do to police it but occasionally they try, and they're selective about whom they harass. Small, private vessels belonging to countries the Libyans consider unfriendly are easy prey. Vessels belonging to most other nations make a point of obtaining clearance from Tripoli before cruising the disputed waters, usually *en route* from Suez to Tunis or through the Strait of Sicily. Vessels owned by most Arab nationals are pretty safe but that can depend on which way the political wind is blowing at the time. There have been occasions when the Libyans have acted in a hostile manner towards Saudi-registered vessels, for instance, because they consider the Saudis to be pro-Western.

'The vessel transporting us to the launch zone will be disguised as a private yacht with Liberian registration identifying its owner as a member of the royal family of the Sultanate of Oman. We have decided to give Prince Hassan a break this time. When we get to the launch zone we'll radio Tripoli,

139

giving a false position and requesting permission to cruise just outside the 12-mile limit *en route* to Alexandria on the Egyptian coast. That will give us time to launch and depart, whatever their reaction. There is always a possibility that they will attempt to intercept and board us, either because they want to have a look at us when we've radioed-in or because one of their gunboat patrols has found us by accident. If the first scenario develops our misleading radio message should enable us to evade interception. In the second case, we'll have to allow them on board and see if we can continue the deception. If that fails we'll have to arrange a permanent disappearance for the gunboat and its crew. However, accidental interception is unlikely.

'The Libyans don't have many gunboats. No more than eight. It is to our considerable advantage that the Libyans make lousy sailors and, like their air force pilots, don't like straying too far offshore at night.' He allowed himself a fleeting smile. 'The vessel which will transport us to the launch zone is Mr Halloran's own yacht, *American Endeavor*.' He thumbed the remote control again and a photograph of Halloran's massive private yacht appeared on the screen. Reece jabbed Bono in the ribs but the big man only sniffed to demonstrate his indifference.

'Seventy-six metres long with a 16½ metre beam and displacement of 2200 tonnes,' Finn continued. 'Cruising speed 16 knots, top speed 26 knots. Range without refueling, 4500 nautical miles, stabilisers, satellite navigation, helicopter pad aft, eight-passenger chopper under canopy, permanent crew of twenty-five. Has a dive chamber with exit hatch in the hull.' He paused for effect. 'Concealed armament includes 60 mm cannons fore and aft, Sea Wasp surface-to-surface missiles and Sea Hawk surface-to-air missiles.'

'No nuclear capability,' Halloran added dryly. 'Yet.'

Lynch and Roper exchanged glances.

'The *Endeavor* will call here soon, ostensibly on a pleasure cruise. It will unload special cargo after dark, then proceed to the Adriatic Sea for a few weeks of pleasure cruising. Its presence in the Mediterranean is a regular occurrence and will not arouse undue interest. As our jump-off date approaches— yet to be fixed—the *Endeavor* will return to this region and the crew will effect certain alterations to its profile and paintwork. The captain will keep the vessel away from regular sea lanes but in a position to reach us here in a few hours of fast steaming. We will be on board the *Endeavor* by midnight and at sea before dawn. The following day will be spent establishing an approach consistent with a vessel proceeding from Sardinia to Alexandria. We don't know, but we have to assume the Libyans can refer to the Soviets for checks on shipping movements via Russian spy satellites.

'We will commence our approach to the launch zone off Tripoli at dusk. Should the Libyans refer to the Soviet spy satellite readings for the preceding 24 hours when we make our false radio report on arrival at the zone they will find our route checks out. If they look back further than 24 hours and engage in a little detective work they might get suspicious. However, that would take time and initiative. Plenty of time for us to launch and for the *Endeavor* to leave their waters before they suspect any kind of a threat. The worst that can happen is that we'd have to sink one of their gunboats. Even then, there's a good chance they would consider it an unfortunate encounter with an American spy ship. There would be no reason for them to suspect a team of men was being put ashore from that far out to sea. Thanks to Mr Reagan, they still think their biggest threat is from the air.'

Finn punched the remote control again and the *Endeavor* was replaced by an aerial photograph of Tripoli and its coastline which could only have been taken by an American spy satellite.

'Don't ask how we got this,' said Finn, anticipating their thoughts. 'This is the launch zone,' he added, using the marker to point to a red circle drawn on the photograph far out from the coast. 'On this scale, that represents a circle with a diametre of five nautical miles. When we pass through this zone some time between 22.00 and 23.00 hours we will stop just long enough to execute our launch. That will take 20 minutes, maximum. And this is what we will use to approach the Libyan coastline undetected,' Finn said, punching up another photograph. To a man they sat forward in their plush red seats and stared at the object on the screen.

The photograph had been taken in a corner of a factory or large workshop. It showed a technician in a white coat standing beside a long, black cylindrical object which looked like a cross between a torpedo and a mini-sub.

It was cradled in two mesh slings, suspended from heavy cables and, using the man in the picture as a gauge, looked to be about 10 metres long and a metre wide in the middle. Its nose contained a light and, splitting the light in half, was the serrated edge of a steel blade. There was a propellor at the stern protected by what looked like an adjustable housing. About a third of the distance up from the stern was a pair of handles, like those on a motorbike, and a small, recessed seat moulded into the superstructure. Between the handles, on top of the cylinder, was an instrument panel. About a third of the way along again, towards the nose, there was another pair of handles, only smaller, and another seat. Below and behind each seat were small footrests set into the body. There were a few barely visible rings and clasps around each seat and Lynch could make out a set of flukes in the belly of the beast but that was all.

'Five years in development, $50 million already invested in research and testing, this is the fastest, smallest two-man scooter in the world and absolutely undetectable unless you

142

run into it. The US Navy SEALs know about it. They don't know several have already been tested successfully by Excelteq, the marine electronics company which built them. We will depart the *Endeavor* in two-man teams using three of these scooters. They are powered by batteries of revolutionary design which can propel them through the water at a constant four knots for eight hours before expiring. We expect to make landfall in Tripoli in five hours, assuming there are no mishaps, which gives us a good safety margin. These scooters have been built with brains. They can think. They will look after us. They are fitted with the latest fibreoptic guidance and navigational systems which will enable us to travel the 20 nautical miles to Tripoli at constant speed and depth without deviating from our course. Once understood they are virtually immune from human error. They operate on the same basic principle as the submarine, using compressed air and water ballast to adjust trim. They can achieve a speed of six knots but that drains the batteries quicker and reduces range accordingly.

'Despite the superb aqua-dynamics of these machines, water resistance would make it impossible for any man to stay attached to the scooters, travelling at four knots for five hours, without assistance—no matter how strong that man might be. Therefore, each man will be attached to his scooter by a harness. These harnesses can be released easily in an emergency by pulling a release key similar to the emergency release on a parachute.'

He flicked the remote control again and the scooter vanished to be replaced by something made of deep-blue, non-reflective material and which looked like a designer space helmet with jet pack attached.

'This is our breathing apparatus,' Finn explained. 'The most advanced re-breather ever designed for military application.'

143

Lynch leaned forward. He had only heard about the new generation of re-breathers but never actually seen one until now.

'It weighs 50 pounds or approximately 20 kilos,' Finn added. 'It's non-magnetic, has a thousand foot or 300 metre depth range, if you think you can go that far, but more importantly, for our purposes, it provides 12 hours-plus endurance. And, of course,' he smiled indulgently at Reece and Bono, 'no bubbles.'

'Excelteq is particularly proud of the helmet,' he went on. 'Full night-vision face mask and inside there's a holographic heads-up display which will give you full instrumentation readout on your depth, position and relationship to local geographic features according to maps already imprinted in the helmet's computer memory.' He paused to let the information sink in. 'The helmets and wetsuits fit together and are fully enclosed. No fins. Any man who gets lost or separated from his scooter won't need fins. There will be no pick-up, no rescue. Nowhere to go. However, you will have the comfort of knowing that your helmet's internal display will tell you exactly what deep shit you're in.

'Talking of deep shit,' Finn smiled thinly, 'now we come to the good part. Our access to Tripoli will be via sewer tunnel.' He punched the remote control and a photograph of Tripoli taken from the sea appeared. He waited a moment, then clicked up another photograph, this time a close-up of a sea wall showing buildings behind and the black mouth of an ancient sewer entrance, centre foreground.

Just visible on the left of the photograph was the edge of a long stone jetty, probably the arm of a small harbour. Lynch assumed the photographer had been standing at the end of this jetty when he took the picture. Of the buildings clearly visible behind the sea wall, he recognised a tall, spindly minaret and, to the far right of the picture, an Italianate clock tower.

'This sewer is situated in the eastern sector of the city of Tripoli,' Finn said. 'It's a residential area. Used to be pretty grand before Gaddafi's coup got rid of King Idris. Now it's occupied by what's left of the middle class and a lot of people from Gaddafi's Revolutionary Guards who like the big old houses. Most of these houses were built by Italian administrators and merchants during the days of Italian colonisation at the beginning of this century and they're pretty substantial buildings. They were taken over by the British after the Second World War until the Libyans got their independence in 1951. Since Gaddafi took over, in 1969, the whole city has deteriorated. By all accounts Tripoli is a dismal place now. Until three or four years ago, the better homes were occupied by engineers and executives from US oil companies, then most of them had to get out too. One of these houses has since been taken over by Gaddafi, and is used frequently as a safe house by him when he's in Tripoli. It's one of several places he uses at random following the bombing of his barracks at Aziziya by the US Air Force in the spring of 1986. Seems he's followed some advice from his pal, that other gem of a human being, Yasser Arafat, about the wisdom of sleeping in a different bed every night. We have in our possession detailed plans of the layout of this house and of this part of the city. A branch of this sewer runs right past Gaddafi's safe house.'

There was absolute silence in the theatre as Finn went on.

'We can go from launch zone to within 500 metres of the Tripoli shore, before we have to break the surface to get a precise fix on the sewer entrance. Our dive helmets will also be equipped with night image intensifier lenses—Excelteq calls these aqua-nites—which will enable us to get a precise visual fix from prominent city landmarks, like the minaret and the clock tower you see in this photograph, and to make our final approach.

'Once we have positioned ourselves accurately and locked

145

the final coordinates into the scooter guidance systems we will be able to go from open water right into the tunnel before breaking surface again. Our intelligence tells us the water in the tunnel is three to four metres deep before bottoming out at around two metres once we're 20 to 30 metres inside. As we all know, the Mediterranean has no tides so those depths should remain constant.

'The water will be pretty filthy and visibility will be zero,' Finn added pointedly. 'That is why it is imperative we get our coordinates right when we surface offshore for the final approach. The entrance to the tunnel is a circle, six and a half metres across. The depth of the harbour at that point is only around 10 metres, the same cruise depth we'll have maintained from the launch zone, so we'll have to adjust our depth to only three metres to clear the bottom lip of the sewer mouth. That will still keep about a metre of water over our heads and that should be enough to keep us invisible from the surface because of the dirtiness of the water. You will be pleased to know that this is a main sewer, it's well-used and there ought to be enough natural disturbance of the water surface to conceal our arrival.'

'How good is our intelligence?' Lynch interrupted.

'We have a man on the ground in Tripoli,' Finn answered. 'You'll be hearing more about him later. The moment we are secure in the tunnel we will shut down the scooter engines. They only make a faint, high-pitched whining sound but the three of them together, amplified by the tunnel, might attract attention. The flow of sewage in the tunnel will be running at one to two knots so it is important we anchor the scooters within minutes of penetrating the sewer. Once anchored we will dismount, retrieve gear and weapons then sink the scooters. Each scooter will be armed with high explosives to be detonated by radio signal on the successful completion of the mission. This will destroy all evidence of our arrival and at the same time create a significant distraction to facilitate our escape.

'At no time, while we are in the sewer tunnel system, will we remove our breathing apparatus. This is to protect us against the possibility of sewer gas. That means we'll have to wear the re-breathers and carry our gear through the sewer for a distance of one and a half kilometres. Assuming we launch from the *Endeavor* at 23.00 hours and cruise on a fixed course at a constant four knots we should make landfall in Tripoli around 04.30 hours the following day.

'That will give us an hour and 37 minutes to manhandle our gear through the sewer and to secure the safe house before dawn. Only when we have left the tunnel and secured the safe house will we be able to remove our helmets.

'Now,' he paused and looked around the room. 'You will appreciate the importance of a high level of fitness of this operation.'

Bono's thick slushy voice filled the silence. 'Wait a minute,' he growled. 'Let me get this straight.'

'Yes?' Finn waited.

'You mean we have to swim up a tunnel full of Ay-rab shit?'

'Yes,' Finn said evenly. Then he thumbed the remote control anid flashed another slide up while Bono scowled and looked around. The photograph showed a pair of tall, green, solid wooden gates set in a high wall.

'This is the safe house,' Finn added. 'We can't show you any photographs of the interior, though we have plans and diagrammes furnished by the former occupant—an American oil engineer with a flair for detail—which we will study at length. These gates represent the only way in and out of the villa. They open into a fully-enclosed courtyard, 30 metres by 22 metres. The entrance to the house is inside, opposite these gates. There is a carport inside on the right. The house is in a block comprising similar residences, all very sound construction, walls of brick and clay a couple of feet thick in places, providing considerable protection. It faces a street 22 metres wide called Via Corviale. The block is 120 metres long and the buildings opposite are villas of similar construction, most of which have been converted into cheap apartments for the people, especially Gaddafi supporters. There are a couple of shops and one café but they're rarely open because they've got nothing to sell.'

He flashed up another slide, this one taken at an angle but still showing the green gates from a short distance away.

'The photographer took this standing in the middle of the street on the manhole cover through which we will make our exit and approach the safe house. It's a distance of 37 metres. Our man says the sewers are rarely entered or serviced any more. Fortunately the Romans built their sewers to last and the Italians improved on 'em so the tunnels themselves should be clear. The manhole hasn't been used in years so the cover may take some budging . . . and it will have to be done quietly.

'According to our man in Tripoli, and he risked his life to get these pictures, this is one of about half a dozen safe houses Gaddafi uses when he's in Tripoli now. Our man confirms what we all know, that Gaddafi is erratic and moves around the country on impulse. We expect that when he's in the capital, he will use this house maybe one night in six or seven, though the night and his arrival time are impossible to predict. He has to be in Tripoli in the first two weeks of December for a series of people's congresses he is expected to address. When we get a better idea of when he's expected in Tripoli we'll know when to move. Out aim is to get into the house and neutralise its occupants and wait in ambush for Gadaffi, however long that takes. It could take anything from hours to days, maybe even weeks. The longer it takes the more difficult it will be for us to remain undetected. But the fact remains . . . this is the best crack we're going to get at him—

the best opportunity we're ever going to have to get up close to him, and put a bullet in his head.

'Our man says the villa is occupied permanently by a caretaker and his wife. The guy is ex-army and we must assume a trusted Gaddafi supporter. They don't leave the house much, probably on Gaddafi's orders. The woman occasionally leaves to pick up a few necessities but most of their supplies are delivered by army truck. When Gaddafi intends to stay the night or a few hours his arrival is always preceded by an inspection by two or three of his bodyguards. We have to allow these guards to conduct their inspection without noticing anything suspicious.

'That is why we have to secure the co-operation of the caretaker and his wife without causing them physical harm, if at all possible. Because none of us speaks Arabic we will be assisted on the ground by this man . . .' Finn flashed up another picture, this time a head-and-shoulders colour photograph of a young Arab male.

'This is Mouad Bouraq,' Finn continued. 'He's a Tuareg, one of the Berber tribes of North Africa, not all of whom are warmly disposed towards Gaddafi. Bouraq studied engineering at UCLA on a scholarship provided by the oil industry. On his return to Libya he was one of the few people who could push the right buttons and open the right valves when most American technicians left the country on Reagan's advice, leaving a lot of job vacancies on the oil fields. Bouraq is our man in Tripoli. He is pro-American and violently anti-Gaddafi. He has been of invaluable assistance to us in the preparation of this mission. In return we have promised him safe passage to the United States. He'll be coming back with us.'

There was a sudden chill in the air as some of the men bristled at this unexpected complication but Finn held up his hand.

'Bouraq won't be any part of the action. Once he's got us

149

into the safe house he's to help run whatever deception is necessary for Gaddafi's bodyguards. Then he has to make it to the pick-up zone himself or he stays behind to face the music. He knows that. He won't get in the way.

'Now, the moment Gaddafi has been given the all-clear by his men at the safe house he usually arrives by fast military convoy. He always rides in an armoured Mercedes Benz in the middle of the convoy. The convoy seals the street, Gaddafi's car pulls up beside the gates, he's hustled from the car into the house by his bodyguards. He has 30 to 40 bodyguards with him all the time. Not one of them is Libyan. They are all East German. The Libyans in the rest of the convoy were all trained by East Germans so they are good at what they do. The convoy consists of military jeeps with mounted machine guns and, sometimes, a couple of British-made Ferret scout cars.

'In addition to the bodyguards, who stay in the house with him, there are between 50 and 60 Revolutionary Guards in the convoy who are responsible for securing the immediate area. Gaddafi has relied exclusively on the East Germans and his Revolutionary Guards for protection after the two assassination attempts in the past 18 months by the Libyan Army's officer corps. The Revolutionary Guards are armed with Kalashnikovs, with which most of us will be familiar. Fine weapons, 7.62 mm, rate of fire 600 rpm. More than 35 million made by the Soviets since 1960. The East German bodyguards are armed with something different.' Finn thumbed up another slide, this one a photograph of a stubby submachine-gun with a pistol grip and folding stock, similar to the Israeli Uzi.

'This is the SIG MP-310,' Finn expounded. 'Swiss-made, 9 mm, magazine capacity of 40 rounds, rate of fire, 900 rpm. It's light, compact, easily hidden and every man on Gaddafi's bodyguard will have one, even if you can't see anything. So there's to be no hesitation about shooting unarmed men. Rest

150

assured, if they draw their weapons, a burst from one of these will bring tears to your eyes. We can only speculate about their level of commitment to Gaddafi. They may be prepared to die for him. They may not. We will have the advantage of surprise, position and superior weaponry. If we inflict sufficient casualties on them in the first seconds they may break and desert Gaddafi. Or, they may make us fight for him. Either way, we will be well-equipped to overwhelm their firepower despite their superior numbers.'

Finn punched up another slide. It showed them a weapon none of them had ever seen before.

'This, gentlemen,' Finn announced, 'is the Heckler & Koch G11. Nothing quite like it has ever existed in the world of arms. It is the most devastating assault rifle the world has ever seen.'

The G11 looked like something from science fiction. It bore only the slightest resemblance to conventional assault rifles.

Instead of the usual assault-rifle configuration, the stock, grip and barrel blended into one uniform, rectangular shape, as though all its components flowed into one another. Most startling of all, it had no visible magazine.

'The G11 fires caseless ammunition,' Finn said. '7.62 mm. It has two modes of fire, 600 rpm on auto and 2000 rpm on burst mode, firing three-shot bursts. It's tough, simple, takes a lickin' and comes up kickin'. This one carries a magazine of 80 rounds in the specially adapted stock and it is devastatingly accurate. Gaddafi's boys won't know what hit 'em. More importantly, caseless ammo means no spent cartridges, no clues, so they won't know who hit 'em. If they're smart they'll know they're outclassed and get out fast.'

Lynch leaned forward. 'How did we get our hands on G11s?' he asked. 'Heckler & Koch haven't even released them to friendly governments for testing.'

'Heckler & Koch don't know we have 'em,' Halloran said. 'But we have friends in Bonn.'

'When do we get to try 'em out?' Reece asked.

'Soon,' Finn smiled. 'You have to learn to dive first. Now, we will position ourselves in the house in such a way that once Gaddafi enters he cannot leave alive. Lieutenant Lynch and Captain Roper will lead us into the house and guide us in the preparation of the ambush. Sergeant Reece and PFC Bono will lay explosives in the house, around the gate and in the sewer in the immediate area of the safe house to cover our escape. Reece and Bono will also be in control of the signal device which will detonate the explosives in the scooters when we are clear.

'When the shooting starts, we have only one objective. To kill Gaddafi. Whoever gets the chance takes it. The moment Gaddafi is confirmed dead I will send a signal from a high-powered transmitter I will be carrying. Should I be dead you will have to retrieve the transmitter from my body and send the signal yourselves. Without that signal there is no way out.

'From the moment the signal is sent we have 40 minutes to get to the pick-up zone and be lifted out by chopper. Our escape route will be the same as our route of entry: via the sewer tunnel. We can expect to get out faster than we got in because we will not be carrying the same load of equipment and there will be no need for stealth. Furthermore, there will be considerable confusion and panic caused by explosions deployed to destroy our remaining equipment and cover our escape. When we reach the mouth of the sewer we will access to the sea wall by ladder and make our way to the western arm of the near by harbour.'

He flashed another slide on-screen. This time the photographer, Bouraq, had been standing at the end of a long stone jetty running out at a right angle from the seafront. The mouth of the sewer was visible in the sea wall to the right of the jetty while, to the left, were a cluster of fishing boats inside the small harbour.

'The distance from the sewer to the beginning of the jetty is about 60 metres,' said Finn. 'The jetty is almost 100 metres long. We have to be at the end of this jetty exactly 40 minutes from the time we transmit our rescue signal. The chopper won't wait. The moment the signal is received aboard the *Endeavor*, which will be cruising in international waters, the chopper will be despatched. It will be camouflaged to look like a Libyan military helicopter. The pilot will bring the chopper to the end of the jetty and if we aren't in sight he will leave.' Again Finn paused to let the words sink in.

'Once we are aboard, the chopper will return to the *Endeavor*, which will be travelling north-west at full speed in the direction of Sicily and out of disputed waters. We have to assume that the Libyan forces will act reflexively and that the air force will give pursuit. Therefore, our chopper will not hang around. It will be stripped for speed and loaded only with fuel. Our best chance will be to get out fast, fly low, evade pursuit and make it back to the immediate protection of the *Endeavor*.

'Once there we can seek the further protection of the US Fifth Fleet, if it is in the region, or request cover from the US Air Force at the NATO base in Sicily. Like any other American pleasure craft enduring harassment by hostile planes, we would be entitled to seek the protection of our country's armed forces in the region.' Finn waited a moment, then added: 'I want to stress this point one last time. Any one of us who does not make it to that chopper in time gets to stay in Tripoli . . . permanently.'

He shut the projector off and switched the theatre lights back up. The men shuffled and Bono yawned widely.

'Two more things you need to know,' Finn said. 'After this briefing and before dinner you will all proceed downstairs to

153

be measured for your wetsuits. Tuckey and I already have ours. The suits we will wear on this operation are custom-made from a new synthetic. They will be delivered here in time for us to commence exercises on the scooters.

'Also, starting Monday at 18.00 hours you will all report to the surgery in the south wing for dental work. If any of us winds up dead in Libyan hands the quickest way to identify us as Americans or British is by our dental work. It is imperative that the Libyans are not able to identify our bodies. Therefore, all our dental work will be replaced in the next couple of weeks to resemble Russian dental surgery. It's cruder and they don't use as much gold. We will need time for these new fillings to settle while we are diving because of the discomfort alternating pressures can cause in new fillings. It may cause occasional pain and bleeding in the gums but that's just tough. If the Libyans do get their hands on any of us, anything identifying us as Soviet agents will fuel suspicions that it was the Russians who got tired of Gaddafi first and would almost certainly destabilise Libya's relationship with the Eastern Bloc. It is absolutely vital that not one scrap of evidence is left behind which would enable the Libyans to point to a Western conspiracy.

'We can assume our action will create turmoil in Libya. We can only hope this turmoil will lead ultimately to the restoration of sanity, an end to that country's sponsorship and exportation of terrorism and the installation of a government more sympathetic to the democracies.

'That,' he stressed, 'is why no man left behind on this mission will be left alive. Once Gaddafi is dead we cannot jeopardise the long-term benefits of our operation by leaving anything that will lend credence to those of his supporters who may attempt to succeed him.' Finn stopped and took a deep breath. Every man in the room could tell by the expression on his face that there was more. Instead, he nodded towards Halloran and said: 'Mr Halloran has something he wants to say about that,' and sat down.

Halloran stood up slowly, beefy red hands thrust in his pants pockets, and looked around the room. Then he carefully pulled a small, white capsule out of his pocket with his right hand and held it up between thumb and forefinger for everyone to see.

'The Germans perfected this,' he said. 'It's a cyanide capsule. Causes death in two to three seconds. Relatively painless, so I'm told. Before each of you embarks on this mission you will be given a couple of these to keep safe. A supply of morphine will also be included in your equipment, under Ensign Tuckey's control. However, if any one of you is wounded so badly you cannot be moved under the influence of the morphine you can either take one of these capsules ... or be shot dead by Commander Finn. If Commander Finn is dead one of the others will have to do it.'

Lynch watched Halloran closely. He had seen the heat of the American's powerful personality. Now he was seeing the cold.

'Because,' Halloran continued, 'that's part of the deal. If only a few of you come back, not one gets a red cent until it is established that no survivors were left behind to talk or be paraded before the world's press. If any one of you has a problem with that, speak up now.'

Halloran let his words hang in the air for a full minute but no-one moved, no-one said anything.

'Good,' Halloran said finally and put the cyanide capsule back in his pocket. 'Then sleep well tonight, gentlemen, because training commences tomorrow at 06.00 hours with Commander Finn on the dock. I'll see you all there.'

Lynch glanced around at the others. They all got up quietly and filed downstairs to see one of Halloran's men who was waiting patiently to measure them for their wetsuits. Each one of them was aware that he had just demonstrated his willingness to kill any one of his colleagues.

Lynch had set the alarm but, as usual, his internal alarm woke him a few minutes before 5.45 the next morning. He splashed water on his face and brushed his teeth but skipped the shave and his usual shower. He had an idea what Finn and Halloran had in mind. He put on his swimsuit then a pair of shorts, sweatshirt and sneakers. It was just getting light when he made his way down to the floating dock shortly before six. Roper, Finn and Tuckey were already there. Roper and Tuckey had dressed lightly, like him. Only Finn was wearing long pants. None of them had much to say to each other, saving concentration for the test they knew was just ahead. Looking out to sea Lynch saw the *Junior Endeavor* moored four or five kilometres away in shallow swells. The sea was the colour of slate in the pale light. It looked cold and forbidding but Lynch knew its night temperature would be almost identical to its normal temperature during the days, around 16 degrees Celsius. Cool but not daunting. A moment later, Reece and Bono ambled down the stone steps to the gently-heaving dock. Somehow Bono looked even worse in the mornings. Both had made a big mistake, Lynch realised. Reece was wearing jeans and a thick sweater, Bono his standard baggy army pants, tee-shirt and open army shirt over the top.

'All right,' said Finn, checking his watch, and the men gathered around him in a semi-circle. 'Today we find out how fit or unfit you are. We start with a refreshing morning dip. See the cruiser out there?' He didn't look round but waited till they had all found the *Junior Endeavor*. 'That's three nautical miles away. Five and a half thousand metres or five and a half kilometres, whatever you like. Mr Halloran's on board and he's going to time us while we swim out there.'

'Hey,' Reece interrupted. 'We didn't bring no swimsuits.'

'We all swim in what we're wearing,' Finn said. 'You both know how to swim, don't you?'

'We can swim,' Bono growled.

'It'll be hard,' Finn conceded. 'But it's supposed to be. Just try not to sink because nobody will be in any shape to hold you up and there's no rescue boats out there. This is sink-or-swim time, boys.' With that he walked over to a two-way radio lying on the dock and radioed the boat that they were on their way. They heard Halloran 'roger' the call, then Finn put down the radio, walked back to the edge of the dock, kicked off his shoes and dived in. He was followed almost immediately by Tuckey, then Roper. Lynch hung back until Reece and Bono had leaped in then, like the others, kicked off his sneakers. Then he stripped down to his swimsuit, dived in and began a relaxed crawl in the direction of the cabin cruiser. After the initial shock the water felt tepid and the swells weren't heavy. Finn was already far out in front, swimming strongly, with Tuckey and Roper behind him, then another long gap before Reece and Bono. The two ex-marines were sticking close to each other, maintaining a slow but steady sidestroke. Lynch overtook them after a couple of minutes and they noticed he had removed his sweatshirt and shorts.

'Hey,' Reece called to him. 'Isn't that cheatin'?'

'Yep,' Lynch answered and continued past them both.

Reece and Bono looked at each other, then began treading water while they dumped their clothes until they were both naked.

After an hour they had swum more than half the distance and Lynch had passed Tuckey. If the ex-SEAL noticed that Lynch had defied Finn he was saving his breath. A pattern had begun to emerge with Finn still in the lead, Roper about 50 metres behind in second place, then Lynch and the others. Lynch had paced himself and still felt strong, though he knew the three men still swimming in waterlogged clothing must be

157

feeling some strain now, however fit they were. After another half hour the leaders had almost reached the cruiser and Lynch could see Halloran standing in the stern watching them through binoculars. He recognised Halloran's aide, Tim, at the wheel of the *Junior Endeavor*. When Finn was within easy reach of the cruiser he slowed considerably and as the others caught up, Lynch wondered why. A few minutes later he had his answer. The engine of the big cruiser suddenly roared into life. Lynch stopped swimming and began treading water to see if his suspicions were correct. The swimmers were strung out for a distance of about three hundred metres when Tim gunned the cruiser, described a wide arc away from them all and began heading back to shore at high speed, leaving them all to swim the same distance back.

Lynch trod water for a few more minutes, conserving energy and waiting for Roper and Finn to pass him on the homeward leg. Roper swam doggedly past without appearing to notice him but Finn stopped for a moment, his tanned face darkened even more by exertion, eyes blazing at Lynch.

'You're letting the team down, Lieutenant,' was all he could manage between deep, heaving breaths.

'Stamina's what counts,' Lynch answered and began swimming in leisurely fashion back towards the dock.

The swim back was hard for all the men except Lynch. It meant a total distance of almost 11 kilometres. Lynch doubted Reece and Bono could have made it without dumping their clothes. The others, he knew, would finish the swim, as hard as it was, because they were so superbly fit.

Lynch also knew he was equal to Finn in fitness, and he could have completed the swim wearing clothes. Freed from that handicap he would finish it now with only moderate exertion. The fittest man in the team, whether Finn realised it or not, was Roper. While swimming was not the former SAS man's strongest suit, his overall strength, endurance and toughness put him virtually in a class of his own, which Lynch had witnessed before.

After another hour the men had rearranged themselves into a familiar pattern—once again Finn was leading, with Roper behind, then Tuckey. Lynch could have got back first but that was not his purpose. Instead he hung back between Tuckey and the two ex-marines, making sure they didn't get into trouble. As they were unaccustomed to swimming this kind of distance Lynch expected them to experience more difficulty. Watching them he realised they had their own buddy system. They kept a slow but steady pace together, used a variety of strokes, took the occasional rest and, when they had enough breath, like marine 'grunts' everywhere, they insulted each other.

Finn was the first back to the dock and was helped out of the water by Halloran. It was just after nine and he had made an impressive time for a man swimming in clothing averaging 18 minutes per kilometre. Roper arrived a few minutes after him, then Tuckey and Lynch. Like the others Lynch took Halloran's outstretched hand. He was not even breathing heavily, and he caught the glimmer of disapproval in Halloran's eyes.

'Nice going, Lieutenant,' Halloran said. 'Even if you did give yourself an edge.'

Lynch padded over to where he had left his clothes and used his tee-shirt to dry himself off. The others had climbed out of their sodden clothes and were either lying or standing on the dock, getting their breath back. When Reece and Bono arrived Lynch helped Halloran pull them both in, Halloran looking amused at the sight of both men's nakedness.

'You guys go get some breakfast now,' Halloran ordered them. 'There'll be a de-briefing in the main lounge at 12.00 hours.'

Tim, who had skippered the cruiser, handed out towels. The men dried themselves, picked up their sopping clothing and began to drift away, too tired to talk. All except Finn, who had regained enough breath to confront Lynch before he left the dock. Halloran was standing near by, beside the moored cruiser, apparently checking some figures on a clipboard with his aide.

'Why, Lieutenant?' Finn asked. 'You're an intelligent man. You know what I'm trying to do here. Why try to disrupt it?'

Finn was making an effort to stay calm but Lynch could see he was quietly furious.

'Just making a point, Commander,' Lynch answered. 'A point I think is worth making.'

'And what is that, Lieutenant?'

'That individual enterprise is worth more than teamwork in some situations.'

'You think the men appreciated that?'

'The three of us who broke your rules got back here in condition to fight,' he said. 'The three who didn't could barely lift a towel. Normally, I wouldn't tackle Roper unless I had a tyre iron and he was unarmed. Just now I could have pushed him off the dock with one finger and he couldn't have stopped me.'

'The purpose of the exercise wasn't only to appraise fitness,' Finn said, his voice climbing. 'It was to see how the men performed under duress.'

'That's right,' said Lynch. 'Your way was to tough it out. My way was to anticipate it so it didn't hurt as much.'

'Without discipline, Lieutenant, this team is nothing. Without discipline we can't make any plan work.'

'The problem with your plan,' Lynch argued, 'is that I saw it coming. The problem with your discipline is that it will only work if we want it to work ... and the problem with you is that you think you've got something to prove. Save it for the real thing like the rest of us, Commander. We know why we're here.'

160

The words hit home and Finn remained immobile as Lynch stepped around him and continued up the steps towards the villa. A few minutes later, Finn, grim-faced and still angry, picked up his things and followed.

Standing at the end of the dock beside his cruiser, Halloran turned to his aide and asked: 'Who do you think is right?'

'They're both right,' said the blond man.

'Yeah,' Halloran smiled. 'I think I'll let 'em ride each other a little longer. That's what I love about free enterprise, Tim boy. Competition. Toughens 'em right up.'

Finn had regained his composure by the de-briefing and smartly ran through the fitness programme he'd mapped out for them. Each day would start at 06.00 hours with calisthenics in the courtyard, he said. Then there would be a 10-kilometre run increased by an additional 10 kilometres weekly until they could all complete a 42-kilometre marathon. Afternoons would be set aside for the 10-kilometre swim. Swimsuits only. Record times weren't important, Finn stressed. Reasonable times were. The rest of the men had noticed the tension between Lynch and Finn but none had raised it with either of them directly. Finn had, apparently, decided to proceed with business as usual, assuming Halloran would back him in the final analysis if Lynch continued to be disruptive. But Lynch wasn't disruptive. For the rest of the week he followed Finn's training regime like a model recruit. It was at the end of that week, when they were all exhausted, that Lynch played his surprise hand.

Halloran was among the first to know. He was roused from a deep sleep a little after four on Sunday morning, by Tim.

'We might have some trouble,' his aide said.

'What kind of trouble?' Halloran asked, struggling to get himself fully awake.

'Security can't raise any of the picket guards,' Tim said.

'They've been trying for the past hour. Now they've all missed their second hourly check-in.'

'All of them?' Halloran was instantly awake.

'All of them.'

'That's not possible,' Halloran grumbled, swinging his legs to the floor. 'Get Finn.'

Tim hurried away to pass on the order to the guard from the command post who was waiting in the corridor. A few minutes later Finn arrived wearing army camouflage pants, black sneakers and zipping up a navy-blue windcheater.

'You set those pickets up,' Halloran said, still pulling on a fresh shirt. 'You get up there with a couple of my boys and find out what's going on. Tim, you wake the rest of the guys up. I want everybody awake and armed in case something funny is going on here.'

Finn hurried from the room with the security guard in tow. While the guard started one of the Jeeps, Finn opened the armoury and emerged with an Uzi and a bag filled with clips. The rest of the guards began spilling out of their quarters over the garage and filing into the armoury to collect their weapons. Finn grabbed an extra guard and the two of them joined the man in the Jeep and roared through the open gates of the villa. The Jeep howled across the open apron of dirt, headlights illuminating the onrushing cliffs and instead of taking the track left took the steeper, rougher track to the right. Half way up the driver swerved inland on Finn's instructions, bucking and jumping over the rough, scrubby terrain. When they got to the top Finn ordered the Jeep to a stop. The driver switched off the engine and the lights and the three of them jumped out, Finn taking the lead. If the picket guards had been knocked out there was little point in being cautious, he knew. They needed to find out in a hurry how much trouble they were in. Because the foxholes had been dug and camouflaged on Finn's instructions he knew exactly where all three were.

The two guards fanned out behind Finn, following him across the undulating terrain, made even more treacherous in the dark. They came to a gully which snaked down towards the edge of the cliffs and Finn stopped briefly to look around. He spotted a strand of prickle bushes and hurried over to them. Ignoring the thorns he grabbed the branches with his bare hands and ripped the bushes away. Beneath them was a dirt ledge and when he bent down he was able to get his fingers under a length of corrugated iron and wrench it upwards, spraying them all with a shower of dust and small stones. Underneath was a hole, about the size of a large coffin. Inside was a man, shivering either from cold or shock, arms and legs tied, eyes staring wildly at them above a gag that looked as if it had been ripped from his own underwear ... and the rest of him was naked.

'Take care of him,' Finn ordered the driver of the Jeep and hurried up towards the grassy bluff about a kilometre away with the other guard. When he had almost reached the crest he found a small mound and began kicking away a pile of stones and clumps of grass until he had uncovered the second foxhole. He found the same scene awaiting him. He hiked inland for another two kilometres on his own and found the same thing at foxhole three. Every one of Finn's pickets had been overpowered, stripped and bound but otherwise unharmed. Their guns, clothing, radios, binoculars, all their equipment was gone. Finn radioed Halloran that the pickets had all been found, disarmed but unhurt, and told him to step up security and launch an immediate search for intruders.

Finn stripped off his shirt and gave it to the picket guard to cover himself and they began the slow, painful hike back across the broken ground towards the Jeep. The guard told Finn he had heard nothing except that sometime between two

163

and three someone had dragged him from his foxhole, applied a pressure hold to his neck and rendered him unconscious. He didn't see who or how many there were. There had been no warning. All he knew was that it had been fast and silent and he had regained consciousness a few minutes later, stripped and bound.

They still had a couple of hard kilometres to go when Finn heard the Jeep's engine cough into life. It was followed, a second later, by the voices of the guards shouting to each other across the cliff tops.

'Shit,' Finn swore. The Jeep was parked on the slope beyond the brow of the hill and, in a moment, Finn saw the powerful beams from its headlights sweep the skyline. Then they swung away and he heard the Jeep drive off, leaving them to make their way back to the villa on foot, the guards hobbling as best they could on bare feet.

When Lynch arrived at the gates a few minutes later, the villa looked like an armed camp. There were men with guns everywhere, the area in front of the villa was floodlit, lights blazed from the house and he could hear the noise of a vigorous search in progress. The guards on the gate recognised him, even though it was Finn who had left in the Jeep, and despite the fact that Lynch's face was smeared with black grease. The security man in the guard post opened the gates and at the same time spoke into the mike on his desk. Lynch pulled into the courtyard, parked the Jeep in the garage and climbed out. He was dressed in a long-sleeved navy-blue sweater and pants with black socks over his sneakers. He leaned against the back of the Jeep and wiped the engine grease from his face as Halloran strode up to him. The guards had abandoned their search for an intruder and Lynch saw Reece, Bono, Tuckey and Roper in the expectant, gathering crowd, Roper regarding him with a mixture of curiosity and amusement.

Halloran stopped a couple of feet from Lynch, stared at him hard and, in a voice of lethal softness, asked: 'What the fuck do you think you're playing at?'

'Thought you and Finn liked surprises?' Lynch answered coolly. He noticed Tim had appeared at his boss's shoulder and was watching them both closely. From the tone of his boss's voice, Tim knew Lynch was skating on desperately thin ice.

'You'll find your men's Armalites, complete with sniper-scopes, in the back of the Jeep with their clothes and the rest of their gear,' Lynch added. 'I don't like being on the wrong end of a sniper's rifle.'

'They are there for your protection,' Halloran said flatly. 'To keep people out. Not in.'

'Then why are they facing in the wrong direction?' Lynch asked. Over Halloran's shoulder Lynch saw Reece and Bono exchange uneasy glances. At least he had two allies, he thought.

'What are you trying to prove with this little party trick?' Halloran asked.

The silence in the courtyard was palpable. Lynch looked around. He saw Halloran had at least 30 armed men at the villa.

'I can't speak for anyone else,' Lynch said. 'But I want you and Finn to get something through your heads. I'm here because I want to be here. Not because you frighten me. And not because you can keep me here.'

The two men stared at each other for a long time and it was devastatingly clear that Lynch had no intention of backing down from Halloran. Finally Halloran nodded and the anger in him eased visibly from his body.

'You've made your point, Lynch,' he said. 'Now how about letting us all get some sleep?' The tension between the two of them seemed to evaporate and Lynch offered his hand to Halloran. 'Okay,' he said. 'No more party tricks.'

'No more party tricks,' Halloran agreed and they shook on it.

At his boss's side Tim was quietly incredulous. He had never seen Halloran fold on a confrontation before. He ordered the guards back to their posts and the others back to bed, then turned to Halloran.

'I'll send the Jeep back for Finn and the others,' he said.

'Nah,' Halloran said. 'Let the fuckers walk. It'll do them good.' He started back to the house when the thought struck him and he swivelled back towards Lynch.

'How did you know those men were up there?' he asked.

Lynch shrugged: 'If you're going to blend in with the country, you've got to smell like the country,' he said. 'You should tell those guys to stop putting on cheap after-shave before they go on duty.'

Halloran shook his head and walked back to the house. 'Fuckin' after-shave,' Lynch heard him mutter as he went.

The men had all but dispersed and, as Lynch stretched and stepped away from the Jeep, he spotted Roper in the far corner of the courtyard, going back to his room. He called after him and the other man turned and waited. They walked back along the clean, well-lit corridor together. Outside, the first fingers of dawn were just visible in the east.

'Remember when I first met Halloran in that room at the Inter-Continental?' Lynch asked.

Roper nodded.

'You had it all worked out then, didn't you?'

Roper said nothing.

'You weren't going to let me walk away from that meeting,' Lynch continued. 'Just being there meant I knew too much. If I'd said no, you were going to kill me. Either then or soon after. Weren't you?'

They had reached the door to Roper's room and stood facing each other.

'That's right,' Roper said. Then he opened his door to go in.

'Think you could do it?' Lynch asked.

Roper stopped and looked back at Lynch with eyes as dead as tombstones.

'Oh yes,' he said. And closed the door.

8

THE TOOLS

Malta, October-November 1989

The most beautiful ship Lynch had ever seen arrived on the first weekend in October. *American Endeavor* anchored a kilometre offshore in 10 fathoms just before midnight, only her navigation lights showing. Normally the men would have been asleep, exhausted by their six-days-a-week training schedule, but Halloran wanted them to have a look around his ship while she unloaded her cargo. As they waited on the floating dock for the *Junior Endeavor* to ferry them out Lynch conceded to himself that Finn's training programme had worked. They were all fitter. The daily discipline of exercising, running and swimming had toughened them all. Lynch hadn't felt so good since he first joined the SBS. Even Bono had finished Friday's marathon and lost the kilos to show it. There had been an uneasy truce between Lynch and Finn since the night of Finn's humiliation but Halloran had kept his word and Lynch kept his. There had been no more threats, implied or otherwise, and Lynch had applied himself obediently and diligently to improving his fitness. As far as Lynch was concerned their differences were behind them. He hoped Finn felt the same way but it was impossible to tell behind the American's taciturn mask.

The *Junior Endeavor* arrived back from its mother ship and, after a couple of seamen had manhandled a pile of cargo onto the dock, the men climbed aboard. With Tim at the wheel the cabin cruiser smacked smartly through the low swells and, in a couple of minutes, swung expertly alongside the *Endeavor*. The ship's side cargo hatch was open and a pair of davits extended through the open space while a dozen crewmen manipulated a long, heavy crate into a waiting tender.

Near by, a gangway extended down the side of the ship to the water. They pulled themselves up the heaving metal steps and filed up to the main deck where a crewman dressed in white waited to take them to Halloran, already on the bridge. Behind them, Tim gunned the cabin cruiser and manœuvred it around to the side hatch to take on more crates.

Lynch marvelled at the beauty of the ship as he followed the others. Everything about the *Endeavor*, from its polished teak decks, to its sleek white superstructure, reeked of great wealth. They all knew Halloran was fabulously rich but it was only when they could examine the physical manifestations closely like this that they understood exactly the power money represented. On the bridge, Halloran was talking to a dignified, pink-faced man with wispy hair in a frosty-white captain's uniform. Halloran knew they had arrived, but ignored them while he went over some manifests with his skipper. The men looked around the bridge in silence while they waited. Lynch knew ships. He had served aboard the best in the Royal Navy. Everything he saw on the bridge of the *Endeavor* was state of the art ... and there were a lot of things he hadn't seen before.

'This looks like the fuckin' starship *Enterprise*,' Reece whispered, summing it up for all of them.

170

Halloran finished conferring with his skipper and walked over to the group.

'Four hundred million dollars,' he said, reading their minds. 'That's what she cost.' Then he waved them across to meet the skipper.

'This is Captain Penny,' he said. 'Captain Penny used to be in command of a minesweeper. I think he finds life working for me a little more exciting.'

Penny gave them all a chilly nod of acknowledgement but said nothing.

'You won't be seeing the captain again after tonight,' Halloran said. 'And the next time you see the *Endeavor* she won't look quite the same from the outside. But Captain Penny will get us safely to the launch zone. More importantly, he'll get us out again when it counts.'

Lynch thought Penny did not seem the type to be involved in anything quite so nefarious and he created the distinct impression that he would prefer to do his part without meeting any of them at all. Bono must have sensed the same thing, Lynch realised, because the big ex-marine leaned forward and directed what might have been a smile at Penny. 'Nice boat you got here, skip,' he said amiably.

The captain bristled and gave Bono an icy stare. 'The *Endeavor* is not a ...'

Halloran held up his hand, smiling, and cut the skipper off. 'Come on,' he told the men, 'I'll show you around.'

The *Endeavor* had six state rooms, a dozen double cabins and 22 spacious singles. Each double cabin would comfortably accommodate a family of four, the single cabins would hold two and the state rooms were unlike anything the men had ever seen before. The main one comprised six separate rooms and its bathroom had a sunken tub with views over the open ocean. What impressed the men most, however, was the solid

171

marble fireplace in the drawing room. Before they left his stateroom Halloran made a point of calling the men together.

'When all this is over,' he said, 'whatever happens ... I want you to know that every one of you is welcome to be my guest aboard the *Endeavor* at any time. Every one of you.' Lynch didn't doubt that he meant it.

From the luxurious staterooms of the afterdeck Halloran led the men far below decks to the dive chamber. There were two chambers, adjoining each other. The first containing all the pressure controls, the second, the exit chamber with a sliding hatch in the hull of the ship.

'We're 12 to 15 metres below the waterline here,' said Finn, back in familiar surroundings. 'When the exit chamber is pressurised, we step through the hatch and swim underneath the vessel to the port side where the scooters will have been lowered from the side hatch. There will be other divers in the water, from the crew of the *Endeavor*, to assist us. We'll hand our fins to them, then harness ourselves onto the scooters. It's a tricky manœuvre at first but now the scooters and the rest of our gear are here, we're going to get all the practise we need.'

Lynch watched Reece and Bono examining the dimly-lit interior of the dive chamber, its eeriness accentuated by the hollow slap and thud of the sea echoing through the hull. This was already hostile territory to the two of them, Lynch realised. Neither of them had learned to dive yet.

'These scooters as smart as you say, Commander?' Reece asked. 'Can they really find their way in the dark?'

'Yes they can,' Finn answered. 'But Lieutenant Lynch, Ensign Tuckey and myself will be the scooter pilots. The other three will be passengers. Tuckey and I have already put in hours of practise on these things in the States and we all know how smart Lieutenant Lynch is, so he'll pick it up in no time. We can't say for sure but we expect Roper will go with me,

172

Reece with Tuckey and Bono with Lynch. All those three have to do is hang on, be cool, breathe normally and try not to be afraid of the dark.'

Reece seemed satisfied. Bono, apparently, had no questions. It wasn't lack of curiosity that prevented him asking. It seemed the thought never occurred to him that he wasn't up to it. The longer Lynch knew the big, ugly American, the more he liked him.

'Okay,' Halloran interrupted from the control chamber. 'Time you guys were going ashore. You're going to get your first look at those scooters at 10.00 hours and,' he glanced at his watch, 'that's only seven hours from now.'

The next morning the sea was empty. The *Endeavor* had unloaded her cargo and slipped anchor before dawn. Captain Penny would now be *en route* to the Adriatic and four weeks of conspicuous cruising before disappearing off all known sea lanes to disguise his vessel's identity.

A temporary floathouse had been anchored next to the dock to shelter the scooters. A blue canvas canopy was stretched across a metal frame attached to four large, oval floats and the three scooters wallowed in the spaces between the floats. Each float was big enough to support a dozen men. From the air and out to sea the canopy would be indistinguishable from the surrounding water. Inside, the whole scene was suffused with a sickly blue-green light. As they followed Finn down to the dock that morning they noticed the floathouse was guarded by half a dozen armed men and two light tenders offshore each carried two more. From now until departure, Finn said, the scooters would be guarded around the clock. Finn was wearing wetsuit long johns. He led the men onto the first float and when they had lined up alongside the adjacent scooter he dropped neatly into its rear seat. Lynch saw the scooter was

173

tethered to the floats on each side and cradled nose and stern on a couple of slings suspended from the floats so it sat much higher in the water. From this position they could see clearly the controls, the opaque outline of a circular instrumentation panel and the footrests.

'Ignition is this button,' Finn said, rapping a rubber-covered knob set in a recession beside the instrument panel. 'It's deliberately difficult to press to avoid accidental ignition or engine cut-off, so it requires a good, hard punch to activate.' He gave the button a heavy thump and the scooter began to whine softly. At the same moment the characters on the instrument panel began to glow a dull red. 'These characters are light-sensitive,' Finn explained. 'That means the darker it gets, the brighter they glow. Even in zero visibility, when the pilot uses the aqua-nite visor on his helmet on this panel he will be able to read these figures.

'However, the amount of sediment we can expect in the water as we approach the sewer will make even that impossible. Which is why the read-out inside the helmet visor is so important and why it is vital to surface offshore to get precise bearings before homing in. Once those bearings are locked into the scooter's compass the electronic guidance system will take us in. The other dials are depth gauge, speedo and clock. That's all the pilot needs. Once the coordinates are locked in, the guidance system maintains depth and bearing automatically. If we get jolted or pushed off course by, say, collision with a large sea creature or unexpectedly strong current fluctuations, the figures will register the difference and flash yellow, alerting the pilot to compensate. Once the pilot regains the correct depth and heading the figures will stabilise and return to red.'

He tapped the starboard handle. 'Throttle,' he said. 'Works just like a motorbike.' He gave the handle a quick turn and the whine of the engine went up a couple of notes, the screw

174

churned and the scooter obediently tried to surge out of its cradle. Finn turned the throttle back to neutral and the scooter settled. 'It has a couple of refinements,' he added. 'You can lock the throttle in at any speed but, because the ideal speed for our purposes is four knots, it is programmed to lock at that speed. You unlock it by pressing the button set in the end of the grip.' He switched his attention to the handle on the port side. 'The port grip is the rudder,' he explained. 'It controls ascent, descent, pitch and yaw. It also has a couple of refinements.' He grabbed the rudder and pushed it through a couple of figure eights. Then he twisted the grip and yanked it up so it moved out a fraction and rotated back and forth a few degrees, independent of the rudder. 'This controls trim,' Finn added. 'In its normal operating state the scooter is balanced to float on the surface. To descend you draw sea water into the side ballast tanks by rotating the rudder grip backwards. To ascend you rotate it forwards and compressed air will eject the sea water and enable you to surface.

'The grip also has two buttons set at the end of the handle. When the pilot reaches his correct depth he locks that in by pushing the round, white button. When he's got his heading right he locks that in by pushing the square, black button. That way the scooter does most of the work. All the pilot has to do is to keep monitoring the instruments for warning flashes.' Finn punched off the ignition and the whine stopped abruptly, leaving only the amplified sloshing of the water under the blue canvas. He braced himself against the floats bobbing on either side and swung himself back up beside the others.

'It's like learning to drive a car,' he added. 'There seems like a lot of remember and co-ordinate at the same time ... and there is. But with practise you get the hang of it. The tricky bit is doing it all with the extra displacement of two guys on board. That's why we better get Ensign Tuckey to teach you two guys to dive in the next couple of days,' he said, turning to Reece and Bono. 'Lieutenant Lynch, Captain Roper and I will play around with these babes until you're ready to join us.' Finn looked ready to go but Reece had something on his mind.

'What happens if we run into any fishing nets out there?' he asked. 'Or sharks . . . or whales or something?'

The others smiled but Finn took the question and led them to the front of the scooter. 'The blade across the nose will cut through any netting,' he said. 'Rope or synthetic. The best tactic is to manœuvre the scooter head on into the net and thrust through. It may take some pushing but these things carry a lot of weight, about two tonnes with cargo hatches fully loaded, and the net will give.

'As for the bigger sea animals, some of them may be dangerous but the odds of you encountering any are remote. Besides, they don't want to die any more than you do. And remember, these scooters are big, 12½ metres long with two guys aboard, whining along at four knots . . . very few things in the ocean will tackle anything like that.

'In fact you probably won't meet anything at all. You might hear something, like the sound of engines from passing vessels, but your biggest threat will be boredom. The pilot does all the work. All you have to do is sit there in the dark and hang on. Maybe use the time to grab a little sleep,' he smiled, then patted Reece on the shoulder and walked away.

The following morning Reece and Bono were in the salt-water pool with Tuckey, taking their first diving lesson. Finn took Lynch and Roper out into the shallows with one of the scooters and Lynch spent the rest of the day trying to master the controls, with Roper as the passenger and Finn supervising. The sea was still warm enough, so they didn't need full wetsuits but the October days were growing shorter and the nights cooler. The northern winter wasn't far away and soon even the southern Mediterranean would feel its chilly breath.

The next day they wore the re-breathers and helmets over wetsuit long johns and Lynch attempted to take the scooter for a run out from the shallows to slightly deeper water. The first difficulty he noticed was the added distraction of the read-out inside his visor. A steady stream of blinking red figures just above his eyes telling him his depth and heading. On his first break out of the shallows he lost trim and buried the scooter's nose deep into bottom sand, enveloping them all in a billowing white cloud. Lynch was struck by the subtlety of the scooter's controls. He had expected it to be awkward and clumsy in the water but, on the contrary, he found it so responsive he constantly had to exercise restraint. One morning he lost control completely and crashed the scooter into a reef, hearing it grind sickeningly across the jagged rock. When the sand and debris had cleared he saw a couple of large chunks of rock had been gouged from the reef while only the faintest scratches were visible on the scooter.

The week passed, with the *Junior Endeavor* and two other tenders standing sentry duty close by. Lynch built on his hard-won experience and he became more adept at handling the scooter. Even his relationship with Finn improved as they put in hour after dogged hour, starting each day in the water at seven, breaking briefly for lunch and finishing only when it grew dark.

Midway through the second week they were joined by Reece and Bono. That was the day Finn produced their individually-tailored wetsuits. They were already laid out on the dock with their dive gear when the men trooped down for their first day of exercises as a full team. With each wetsuit was a blue, skin-tight undersuit.

'Gortex fabric,' explained Finn. 'With the wetsuit, it will

177

maintain a comfortable body temperature of 29 degrees Celsius for a minimum eight hours.'

Immediately Lynch slipped his wetsuit over the Gortex undersuit he was impressed by the radical improvement over other protective garments he had worn during prolonged exposure to cold water. The new suit was surprisingly thin—no more than three millimetres, he estimated. He was also impressed by the lightness of the material and the freedom of movement it gave him.

'What is this stuff?' he asked Finn.

'One of the spin-offs from the space industry, my friend,' Finn answered. 'Adapted by Excelteq from the suits used by astronauts for space walks. It's an acrylo-nitrile compound with a flexible thermal active laminate. Very tough. Very light. Oh, and one more thing,' he added, almost as an afterthought. 'Bulletproof.'

The others stopped and looked at Finn.

'Bullshit,' Bono said.

Finn shook his head. 'Space suits have to be meteorite-proof. Like small meteorities, bullets won't go through 'em.' Then he added. 'They don't make *you* bulletproof though. What it really means is that if you get nicked by a bullet, it won't cause a massive wound with possibly fatal accompanying trauma, or blood loss. You'll have a fine bruise, of course, and a good hit will break bone. But your probability of survival is much greater if you get creased while wearing one of these.'

'What about a direct hit?' asked Reece.

'A direct hit with a bullet fired from a modern weapon will probably still kill you,' Finn smiled. 'The suit would minimise shock, and prevent actual penetration, but there would still be massive radiated trauma beneath the point of impact.

'The difference is: if you're wearing one of these and you

178

get hit in the arm—it won't take your arm off. You'll feel like you were kicked by a horse but you might live.'

'Sure,' Reece shrugged. 'Long enough to take your pill.' As they finished gearing-up Lynch realised he hadn't seen Halloran for days and speculated that their patron had left the villa, and perhaps the island, for a few days on more pressing business. His aide, Tim, was still around though. His blond, balding head was visible from the deck of the *Junior Endeavor*, or watching from the dock as they took the scooters out each morning for another day of bruising, exhausting exercises.

As promised, Finn divided them into new pairs for their first day's exercise as a complete team with all three scooters. Finn took Reece, Tuckey took Roper and Lynch got Bono. Immediately, he noticed the difference Bono's weight made to the scooter's behaviour. It took another week before the three pilots had again mastered the scooters with their new passengers, but by then Lynch really believed he had developed an affinity with the extraordinary underwater machine. By the last week of October they were all operating proficiently in deep water. By the beginning of November, Finn decided it was time for their first night exercises in deep water. As tricky as it had been to master the scooters in daytime with good visibility, Finn knew it was child's play compared to trying the same manœuvres in the dark. At night there were no standard references: no sun shining through the waves to illuminate the sandy ripples on the bottom, to point out the weed and the rocks, to show which way was up and which was down; no 40 or 50 metres of visibility in the pellucid blue water, with its friendly fish and pretty shadows. At night the water was as black as coffee. The moment the flashlight was switched off, the blackness rushed in. As impenetrable as a cloak. Cold, claustrophobic, terrifying. Stirring up all the basic human fears of the dark unknown. Lynch and Roper, Finn

179

knew, were competent beyond doubt. He had difficulty concealing his admiration of their incredible skills. His greatest fear was that Reece and Bono might not have the psychological strength to hold up under the horrific strains of navigating through the open ocean, underwater at night.

He had deliberately picked a night when there would be no moon. They left aboard the *Junior Endeavor* an hour after dark and headed out to sea, towing the scooters in a line behind them. An hour later, with Tim at the wheel, they had anchored 15 kilometres offshore in a sloppy, rolling swell. A half-dozen armed guards rode atop the cruiser and the two tenders bobbed near by in the dark. A cool, blustery wind lapped at the sea. The water was the colour of ink except for the occasional flash of phosphorescence in the breaking waves and a metallic glimmer of reflected starlight in the troughs. Finn had ordered a full-dress rehearsal and it took them a while to gear-up with re-breather packs and helmets. The objective simply was to take the scooters down to 10 metres, and cruise to within one kilometre of the villa before ascending and completing the run on the surface. From where they were anchored, the lights of the villa were invisible and even the land was barely discernible as a slightly darker series of humps on the horizon. Finn checked the cruiser's position with Tim and calculated the heading back to the villa. As a matter of courtesy, when he had finished, he had Lynch check his figures. The last thing they all heard before fastening on their dive helmets was the coordinates to get them back to shore.

Tuckey and Roper left first, followed by Lynch and Bono, then Finn and Reece. Once astride their scooters the three pilots switched on the nose lights and three powerful beams of light carved tracks across the sea. One at a time they manoeuvred around to the cruiser's port side but even with willing hands the men found it difficult getting into their harnesses. When it came to his turn Lynch accidentally jammed his gloved fingers between the scooter and the hull of the *Junior Endeavor*, adding to the list of small bruises, scrapes, strains and injuries he had collected in the previous weeks. He swore as he used up his air while fastening his harness. The sound of his own breathing inside the helmet was unnaturally loud and he was anxious to get underwater where it would be muffled to a familiar rattle.

He waited until Tuckey was ready and watched as the young diver pulled away, keeping an eye on the nose light while it rose and fell with the waves until it flickered briefly and vanished. The beam disappeared first, like a sliver of light shut off by the sudden closing of a door, followed by the light itself as Tuckey dipped his nose down and slipped beneath the waves. Lynch watched four minutes wink past on the scooter's dial, then throttled away from the cruiser. When he was clear, he checked the readings on his instruments and manipulated his scooter through 180 degrees till he found the coordinates he wanted, then locked them in. He took one last look at Bono's substantial hump a couple of metres in front of him, then yanked the port grip to draw extra ballast and pushed the rudder down. The scooter obediently dived beneath the waves with a whine that was barely audible through his helmet. Lynch glided down to 10 metres, locked the number into the depth gauge and a few minutes later locked the throttle in at four knots. When he was satisfied the scooter's electronic sensors were behaving he punched a white button on his instrument panel and the light went out. One moment there had been a radiant blue pathway through the sea punctuated by pieces of weed and swirling sand particles. The next, there was total blackness. Lynch blinked and tried to focus on his instruments. The characters were just a faint red glow. He saw the outline of the distant coast take shape inside the compass dial, then reached up to his helmet with his free hand, searching for the aqua-nites visor. He pulled it down over his mask.

Instantly the figures on his instrument panel took on a vivid white glow. The aqua-nites leached the colour out but gave much sharper definition. He decided to leave the visor down. He confirmed that the readings inside his helmet matched the scooter's heading. Then Lynch began to relax. He was much happier beneath the slop on the surface. There was no more pitching and rolling. At a steady four knots all he could feel was the undulating pressure of the water slipping over him.

He settled down for the two-and-a-quarter-hour run back to shore, careful to keep an eye on the clock as it ticked away the minutes and the window in the speedo which added up the metres. It was far, far easier, he knew, than finning three kilometres through freezing heavy seas in the South Atlantic. After what felt like an hour he checked the clock again. Only 20 minutes had gone by and the gauge in the speedo registered barely 2500 metres. Monotony, he realised, was the biggest problem. Finn was right. For the man up front, the boredom would be excruciating. Roper was used to waiting. So was Lynch. He wondered about Reece and Bono. Gradually Lynch slipped into that peculiar psychological limbo that comes with monotonous labour, a kind of half-wakefulness wherein he was aware of his surroundings and part of him still kept an eye on the figures, but the rest of him tended to drift off into dreams and reminiscences and sometimes to places where there was nothing at all.

A couple of times the figures vanished altogether, even under the scan of the aqua-nites, but reappeared a few seconds later after they passed through a cloud of sediment, drifting sewage or oil. He had to wipe greasy streaks from his visor once or twice but he was helped by his momentum in the water and the scouring action of the sea. They had just clocked up an hour and a quarter's easy running when something hit him in the face and chest, jerking him back in his harness and pulling the scooter to starboard. The readings inside his helmet spun crazily. He sensed something slimy and blubbery clinging to his arms and shoulders. He clawed at his mask and felt fat, gelatinous handfuls of whatever it was coming away in his hands. He caught a glimpse of the ghostly figures of the instrument panel flashing at him through the mess and he saw the figures on the compass and the depth gauge fluctuating wildly. He pulled away more quivering lumps of tissue until, as suddenly as it had come, it had gone. He held his hand up in front of his visor and saw greyish lumps of jelly shivering between his fingers before they were snatched away by the current.

He had just collected a jellyfish, he realised—probably a Portuguese man-of-war, one of the biggest jellyfish in the sea, whose stinging tentacles trailed three to four metres behind its bulbous, blue-grey head. For the next few minutes Lynch concentrated on bringing the scooter back to its proper heading. The impact of the jellyfish had swung them more than 90 degrees off course. If he could not correct it the scooter would run out of juice some 15 or 16 nautical miles south of Malta. He was pleased to see the scooter had almost corrected its depth itself. When the jellyfish first hit, it had jolted him up and back and that had pushed the stern of the scooter down and tipped its nose up. He had come up to within two or three metres of the surface before clearing himself of the creature's fragmented flesh and stabilising the scooter enough to allow its sensors to bring it back to its programmed depth. Now Lynch swung the scooter back into line with the map reading and recommenced their run to shore. When his heartbeat had settled he wondered how Bono had reacted to their sudden bout of turbulence. Perhaps, he thought, the big, ugly bastard had slept through it all. After another hour Lynch saw they had completed 14000 meters, or just over eight nautical miles—the point at which he was due to surface. As arranged, he switched on the light again to warn their tracking craft he was about to ascend. A couple of minutes later he broke surface smoothly and looked around. The scooter's nose was pointed directly at the villa, slightly more than a thousand metres away. Instead of being in front of the villa, they were about a hundred metres to its south, due to their encounter with the jellyfish. Apart from that they were pointed in exactly the right direction, and the only consequence of their minor diversion was that they would be a few minutes late and their approach angle would be slightly different. Lynch felt elated. For the first time since he had agreed to be part of the mission he believed they had more than an even chance of pulling it off.

The next two weeks were spent on night exercises. Usually, they practised precision navigation through the shallows, but each weekend they did a long run into the villa and each time Finn increased the distance by 10 kilometres. When the sun came up each morning, the exhausted and bedraggled men showered, ate like zombies in the dining room with hardly a word to each other then went to bed and slept the day away before getting up again for that night's exercises. When he was satisfied that they all had complete control of their scooters and there had been no complications with Reece or Bono, Finn called a three-day break. It was barely enough for them to recover from their extreme fatigue and the assorted superficial wounds and bruises they had all collected. Then, on the morning of the third Tuesday in November, Finn introduced them to the G11s.

He announced to the men over breakfast that the week would be devoted to weapons practise and, when they had finished eating, led them through the house, through the kitchen and downstairs to a room none of them had known existed until now. It was shaped like a thermometer. The bulb was situated at the bottom of the stairs and contained a wide, metal bench with six of the G11s laid neatly in a row. Beside each weapon was a pair of ear guards. Beneath the table were four cases full of the G11's caseless ammo. The neck of the thermometer stretched in front of them, a long, narrow chamber lined with silver-foil baffles to absorb sound, flash and ricochet. At the far end of the room was the silhouette of a cardboard target. Either Prince Hassan maintained his own shooting gallery, Lynch realized, or Halloran had had it installed with his compliments. Finn went over to the wall and threw a light switch. The far end of the gallery lit up and the men grinned when they saw the paper image attached to the target silhouette. It was none other than Colonel Gaddafi, complete with bullseye rings around his head and chest.

'We got them from a guy in Atlanta,' explained Finn. 'They've been very popular with shooters in the US the past couple of years.'

The wall behind the target was stacked with unmarked sandbags and the floor beneath was buried in sand. In front of them was a stable door with a bench for shooters to use as a rest. Finn picked up one of the G11s and pushed the stable door open with his toe. 'We won't be needing this,' he said. He grabbed a pair of ear guards and put them on and the others did the same. When they were ready he slipped the safety off the G11, switched the selector lever to automatic, and fired a long burst from the hip. The paper Gaddafi fluttered and danced as the bullets ripped through it with a roar of sound. Finn adjusted the selector to burst mode and fired off a few rounds. The difference was astounding. The G11's 2000-rounds-per-minute rate of fire was so fast the three shots blurred together into a single, abrupt cough. Each time Finn fired, the target shivered. When he had emptied the clip Finn returned the rifle to the table, took off his ear guards and pressed a button on the wall which activated the target pulley and brought the shredded Gaddafi hissing towards them. They crowded around to inspect the damage. With any modern assault rifle it would be impossible to miss a man-sized target at such short range, and, as Finn had demonstrated with the auto fire, the target was peppered with holes. What impressed them most were the slightly larger holes in the head and heart area which looked as though they had been caused by a larger calibre bullet. These were where three shots from the G11 had all connected, virtually on top of one another. From the automatic example they saw that the G11 performed the same as any machine gun, delivering a spray that was either as accurate or as haphazard as the man behind the gun. The burst mode, however, seemed to deliver it all. Speed, accuracy and unstoppable punch. And, as Finn had promised, there wasn't a cartridge on the floor. Once the caseless ammunition had been fed from its clip into the G11's stock it left no further clues.

Finn gestured to the others to each pick up a gun. When he took his, Lynch was amazed by its lightness. It took only a couple of minutes for Finn to run through the G11's mechanics.

Every man present was a weapons specialist in his own right. When each of them had examined the G11 they all had to acknowledge that it was a deceptively simple yet brilliant piece of weapons technology. What impressed Lynch most was that even when fully loaded with 80 rounds, the G11 was still light for an assault rifle. At a shade under two kilos it weighed even less than the American Armalite but offered greater range, versatility and punch. With 80 rounds, and set on burst mode, the G11 offered more sustained combat performance than any other weapon. For combat at close quarters, it was an advantage that would make the difference. Every other combat rifle or submachine-gun in the world, from the Armalite to the Kalashnikov, from the Swiss SIG to the Israeli Uzi, had a magazine capacity of 30 to 32 rounds. Which meant the user had to stop and re-load far more frequently than the man carrying the G11. When running out of ammo in a close-in gun battle meant instant death, the man with the G11 had extraordinary superiority.

'Let me try it,' Bono grunted and stepped forward, the G11 looking like a toy in his big, scarred hands. Finn pulled a fresh sheet of paper from a shelf near by and pinned a brand new Gaddafi to the pulley then sent it winging back to the end of the gallery. They all slipped their ear guards on again while Bono took aim. He set the rifle to burst mode, squinted down the barrel and squeezed the trigger. For the next few minutes he fired one burst after another and the black hole in Gaddafi's head grew bigger and bigger until there was nothing more left of his face. The rest of the target was un-marked. Bono had concentrated his marksmanship entirely on the head area and every burst had connected. When the magazine was empty he turned back and took a deep breath of the lingering gunsmoke.

'That feels better,' he growled and gave the rifle an approving nod. 'Nice gun,' was all he added.

The men spent the rest of the day in the gallery, shredding Gaddafi targets and getting used to the G11. Lynch thought both Reece and Bono looked happier than at any time since they had arrived at the villa. This, he knew, was their element. Not the water. Not careering around the dark ocean for hour after cold, bloody hour in the night. After weeks of exhausting exercises it was therapeutic for them to play with guns again. It was therapeutic for them all. That night, around the dinner table, the mood between the six of them was more convivial than it had ever been. Even Finn seemed to decide it was safe to unbend a little.

They spent most of that week on weapons practise. Reece and Bono inspected the explosives, timers, fuses and radio

187

transmission equipment they would be using. Lynch, Fletcher, Tuckey and Finn went over the plan again and again, looking for loopholes, devising tactics. Lynch and Roper spent hours studying the maps and diagrammes of the safe house, estimating distances, construction and thickness of walls, location of doors, windows, parapets and balconies while they mapped out their ambush plan. The days passed in a blur, the blue skies had been replaced by interminable milky clouds, the sea grew sullen and unpredictable and the weather forecasts became crucial. It was almost the end of November when Finn announced there would be a final, full-dress rehearsal. First, he took them on a short ride along the corrugated coastline in the *Junior Endeavor*. After a few minutes he found what he was looking for. A crooked finger of black rock reached out from a small headland like a witch's claw and in the middle knuckle was the arch of a sea cave.

'That,' announced Finn, 'is about the same size as the sewer tunnel we have to penetrate. That is where we have to score a bullseye.'

He brought the cruiser in for a closer look and the men examined the cave. There was a strong current running around the narrow, rocky promontory and from the necklace of foam around the cave walls there was a permanent and powerful surge. On both sides of the cave mouth there were jagged rocks and the nearest soft landing was a hundred metres away on a small crescent of white sand at the bottom of a steep, scrubby hill.

'You sure about this?' Lynch asked. It was the first time he had questioned Finn through all the weeks of sea trials and training.

'This is the closest we can get to the real thing,' Finn replied.

'It could fuck the scooters,' said Lynch.

'They're built to take a beating,' Finn said. 'Besides, if we can't do this, there's no point in going to Tripoli. We won't make it.'

Lynch turned to look back at the cave. Finn had a point. But losing a scooter would be a disaster. They returned to the villa and Lynch spent most of the next day wondering if Halloran approved, or was even aware of Finn's plan.

The rehearsal was called for the following night. The last Saturday in November. Lynch's question was answered when Halloran appeared without warning aboard the *Junior Endeavor* as they stowed their gear. It took more than an hour to reach the launch zone 40 kilometres, or 20 sea miles, off the Maltese coast. There was no sign of land and the sea was much rougher than they had experienced. Finn, Lynch and Tuckey checked the craft's position with the coordinates for the sea cave. They were to approach it exactly as they would approach the Tripoli tunnel—running underwater till they were 500 meters offshore then surfacing to take pinpoint bearings before heading into the cave. Once inside the cave, which belled out to a diameter of 30 metres, they would ascend and motor out on the surface to minimise the risk of collision with an incoming scooter.

They were about to gear-up when Halloran gathered them together on the after-deck. He had one more surprise for them.

'Until now,' he announced, 'you've just been practising. Tonight is as close to the real thing as we can make it. If you hear any engines near the cave it'll be some of my boys in the tenders harassing you a little.'

Lynch waited with folded arms. There was more, he guessed. The others sensed it too and regarded Halloran with expectant hostility.

'Until now the scooters have only been carrying ballast, to approximate the weight of the equipment you'll have to carry into Tripoli. Tonight, we removed the ballast and put everything in the cargo holds that you'll have to carry through the sewers of Tripoli. Weapons, explosives, rations, everything. After you exit from the cave, you beach your scooters on that little beach to the north-west, retrieve all your gear and make your way overland to the house. It's about 80 metres up the hill overlooking the beach, then 2.1 kilometres back to the house. You have to make it from the beach to the house in one hour, wearing all your gear and each man carrying his share of the equipment. When you reach the house you will proceed to the firing range and put 80 rounds into Gaddafi. Then you can go to bed.'

There was a pause then Bono growled.

'Fuck it,' he said. 'Can I just take the fuckin' pill now.'

There was a ripple of laughter and then they got on with the business of gearing-up.

Finn's weeks of hard training had paid off. Even though the sea was rougher, colder and murkier, they boarded the scooters, harnessed themselves in and pushed off with confidence. This time the run in went without incident for Lynch until he reached the first re-surface zone. When he broke surface 500 metres from the cave, the swells were much deeper and he could see through the aqua-nites there was a lot of spray flying around the cave mouth. He also saw one of the two tenders a couple of hundred metres away but he had surfaced with his light shut off and they hadn't seen him. Lynch fed the new coordinates into the scooter's computerised brain and descended to a shallower depth of six metres, throttling back to only two knots. The closer in he got the stronger the current became and he had to struggle to keep the scooter's right heading. The current was relentless and kept trying to push him away from the cave and around the tip of the promontory. At the same time he was catching turbulence from the breaking waves overhead and the clouds of sand churned up by the wave action kept blotting out his instruments.

He had no idea where the other two scooters might be. The

figures above his eyes flickered madly, uselessly. Despite the aqua-nites he was running the last few metres of his approach completely blind and he could easily have been on a collision course with one of the other scooters making its approach. It took every ounce of strength and control he possessed to maintain stability and keep the scooter's nose pointed in the right direction. At the last minute he throttled back to neutral and lifted the nose to climb with the sea floor and catch the surge into the cave, praying his momentum wouldn't carry him headlong into a wall of rock. Lynch held his breath. He knew he had done everything right but he felt as though he were trying to navigate through a washing machine filled with sand. The temptation to surface was compelling but he hung on. A moment later there was a deafening whoosh and the scooter leaped forward on a violent surge of wave power. The sound in his helmet changed abruptly from a steady wash to a deep, echoing roar and he realised he had made it. He switched on his nose light and the beam picked up a maelstrom of swirling sand. Inside the cave the surge wasn't quite so violent, just a powerful tugging motion which pulled the scooter backwards and forwards. Lynch vented the scooter's water ballast and took her up. It was worse on the surface inside the cave. For a moment he felt like a bug inside a gigantic, booming dishwasher. Through the aqua-nites the water surface looked like a churning sea of foam, and the air was filled with a blizzard of spray. He could still see Bono crouched up front and decided the two of them ought to get out fast. He throttled up again and swung the big scooter's nose around to point out through the cave mouth where the night sky looked like daylight. A moment later he heard the sound of a resounding clang from below and the whole cave seemed to vibrate with the impact of another scooter crashing into its walls. Lynch gunned the engine but for a second it was like trying to break through a sea of jelly. Then the surge caught him again and they leaped out of the cave like a missile.

An involuntary yell of triumph filled the inside of his helmet as they surfed free of the violent, sucking tide in the mouth of the cave and he headed the scooter around towards the near by beach. A moment later he ran her aground on the white sand and shut down the engine. Apart from the gentle rocking by the waves in the shallows, the scooter could only be moved now with a tow rope to the *Junior Endeavor*.

Lynch punched his harness release and stepped free. After five hours, capped by the exhausting run in and out of the cave, every muscle in his arms, chest and shoulders ached. Despite the protective wetsuit he knew there would be fresh welts from the harness straps around his thighs and shoulders. Bono joined him on the beach and both of them took off their helmets and breathed deeply at the fresh night air. The breeze felt like a balm on their faces and, after five and a half hours of canned air, the open air tasted like wine. They looked around and saw they were the first on the beach, even though they had been second away from the *Junior Endeavor*. Lynch looked out to sea and spotted the cabin cruiser and one of the tenders a moment later. Then the two of them set to work retrieving their gear from the scooter's hold. It only took a few minutes to get everything on the beach, still in their waterproof wrappings. The cargo holds were waterproof too but every item of their equipment had been sealed separately as insurance. The rifles were easy enough to carry but the packs of ammunitions and plastic explosive weren't. Added to that were a couple of belts containing glucose tablets, protein cubes and water purification tablets in case they had to spend a week or more in hiding at the safe house and the food and water were not reliable. Once they were out of the water their backpacks added to the burden. Lynch checked his air gauge. He had enough left for five hours. Enough to see them back to

192

the house. They were supposed to wear their helmets and breath the air from their backpacks for the run to the house, to duplicate conditions they could expect in the tunnel at Tripoli, but neither Lynch nor Bono were in a hurry to put the helmets back on.

A moment later the second scooter arrived with Roper and Tuckey aboard. There was a long, ragged scrape down its starboard side where it had slammed into the cave wall. The scooter wasn't damaged otherwise, but when Tuckey climbed off he limped. His right leg must have been caught between the wall and the scooter when they connected. Lynch walked over thinking Tuckey was fortunate his leg hadn't been broken.

'How is it?' Lynch asked when Tuckey had removed his helmet.

'Could be worse, I guess,' Tuckey grimaced. 'It was a glancing blow. Just got caught by the surge and hit 'er sideways. Took it mostly on the thigh.'

Roper and Bono joined them.

'Can you walk?' Roper asked. Tuckey tried a few steps but it was obvious he was in pain and wouldn't be able to make the run. Lynch walked back to his scooter and flashed the nose light a couple of times. A minute later they saw a tender speeding towards them with Halloran and two of his men on board. They waited till it swung around and stopped just behind the surf line and Halloran called to them.

'Tuckey's hurt,' Lynch yelled back. 'He can't walk.'

'Carry him.' Halloran's words floated back to them over the thud of the surf. The three of them looked at each other, then Roper walked back to his scooter, opened the cargo hatch and pulled out his gun. Before any of them could stop him, he had unwrapped the G11, put it to his shoulder and fired a series of quick bursts at the rear of the tender, riddling it just below the water line. They heard the horrified yells from Halloran and his men as the bullets smacked home and the tender began to fill with water.

'You carry him,' Roper yelled back.

The other three on the beach stared at Roper.

'I like that guy,' Bono said eventually. Tuckey limped up the beach and sat down as the other three unloaded the second scooter.

They had just finished when Halloran and his two men waded ashore. Halloran was furious but the shock of being shot at, and the exertion of having to abandon the boat and swim through the cold surf had robbed him temporarily of his speech. His two men stood by, dripping and panting, glaring at Roper and waiting for their boss to regain his breath. Roper went about his business, seemingly unconcerned.

A second later the last scooter arrived, carrying Finn and Reece. When Finn learned what happened he looked dumbstruck.

'You shot at Mr Halloran?' he asked Roper. 'You sank his boat and forced him to swim ashore?'

'Yep,' Roper said. He had finished loading his gear and was about to replace his helmet. 'He and his two goons can carry Tuckey and the rest of us will carry Tuckey's gear amongst us.'

Finn looked around. From the expression on Tuckey's face it was clear he wasn't moving unless somebody carried him. Finn hesitated. The time Halloran needed to get his breath back had allowed his temper to cool. He nodded at Finn. 'Go on,' he ordered, 'we'll take care of it.' Then he turned his attention to Roper. 'That fucking boat cost money, you stupid Limey bastard,' he yelled. 'And you could have hurt somebody.'

Roper shrugged. 'Take it off my pay,' he said. Then he replaced his helmet, grabbed his gear and set off up the hillside.

The cross-country scramble back to the house was one of the most punishing ordeals Lynch had ever endured. He boiled inside his helmet. The sweat poured down his face, stinging his eyes and irritating his skin, but he was unable to wipe any of it away. His body temperature rose inside the wetsuit and he began to overheat but he couldn't stop to take it off. He wouldn't be able to remove it in the sewer under Tripoli. His mouth was dry and he became badly dehydrated. His arms ached with the weight of the packs he carried and his legs threatened to buckle under the impossible burden. With Tuckey's gear divided between them, each man was carrying almost 70 kilos, and over rough country. Roper had left first and Lynch knew there would be no catching him. Carrying ridiculous loads over rugged country was his idea of enjoyment. Lynch tried to keep him in sight but Roper was soon lost in the dark. Lynch dropped the visor on his aqua-nites and found him again immediately, a small grey ghost bobbing ahead in a black-and-white landscape. Wearing the aqua-nites made it too difficult to see where he was putting his rubber-booted feet, and Lynch gave up on Roper and concentrated on himself.

By the time he reached the bluff and the beginning of the descent down towards the villa, his arms and legs were screaming. All he could do was to try and ignore the pain and keep his eyes on the villa gates. The walk down the steep, broken track was hellish. When he reached the apron of dirt at the bottom his muscles had grown numb, his hands had locked into claws and he had begun to feel nauseated from dehydration. Much more of this and, he knew, he would pass out. The hundred metres to the front gates, which he had jogged across so easily in a few seconds on other days, felt like a kilometre. When he reached the villa the guards opened the gates. He weaved inside and stopped, his fingers locked, unable to release the packs he was carrying. Two guards came forward and eased his fingers open, taking the packs and lowering them to the ground. Next they helped Lynch out of his back-pack, and the moment they lifted it off him he felt as if he might float up into the night sky. His breath came in deep, searing gulps and his mouth felt like sand. When he took off the helmet the relief made him almost dizzy. He struggled to focus on his air gauge and saw that he was almost out. He had gobbled almost five hours of air in the hour it had taken him to carry the gear two kilometres. He tried to speak to the guards, but his mouth and throat were so dry he couldn't utter a sound. Instead, he picked up the G11 and set off towards the house.

On his way across the courtyard he saw Roper slumped on the steps leading into the house, wetsuit open, head bowed, shoulders heaving. Lynch passed him without uttering a sound. He didn't even look up. Lynch walked slowly and deliberately down the corridor to the kitchen. The basement door was open. He picked his way shakily down the steps to the illuminated firing range where one of Halloran's guards waited patiently, and swung the rifle up to his shoulder. A few days ago it had felt like a child's toy. Now it felt like a log and his arms trembled with the effort of holding it up. He lowered it for a moment, took a deep breath and composed himself. When he was ready he swung the rifle back up and focused all his attention on the paper Gaddafi at the far end of the tunnel. He started squeezing. Like Bono. Burst after burst after burst. He couldn't hope to make a head shot but he watched with exhausted satisfaction as one black hole after another appeared in Gaddafi's torso. Suddenly, the magazine was empty. Lynch turned, dropped the rifle with a clatter on the bench near by and walked back upstairs.

When he reached the kitchen he went straight to the sink, turned on the tap and held his head underneath for a long time. He had just finished drinking his fill when he heard someone else arrive and looked up to see Finn. Finn looked terrible, his face almost burgundy with exertion and flecks of salt and dried spittle coagulated at the corners of his mouth. Lynch realised he must have looked much the same a few minutes earlier. He stood up and walked out of the kitchen to join Roper, waiting on the steps. He glanced at his watch. It was almost five in the morning. They had finished under time. A short while later Reece and Bono arrived. None of them told the guards Halloran and two men were walking in carrying Tuckey. They all sat on the steps and talked. After a few minutes, they heard the *Junior Endeavor* motor up on the seaward side of the villa, the scooters retrieved and under tow. Then Tim appeared around the corner, on his way up from the dock.

He read the situation at a glance and ordered one of the guards out in the Jeep to collect Halloran, Tuckey and the other guards. They returned in a few minutes. Halloran climbed out first, clothes still wet, bedraggled, hair plastered to his red face. He ordered the guards to take Tuckey to the surgery where his battered leg could be treated by his personal doctor. Then Halloran walked slowly across to the grand entrance of the house where his five mercenaries lay sprawled on the steps waiting in sullen exhaustion. He looked them up and down for several minutes, saving his closest scrutiny for Roper, who looked back, face impassive.

'You guys are fucking dangerous,' Halloran said and walked past them into the house.

9

THE COUNTDOWN

London, December 1989
Maurice Cassell looked out of the window of his Lambeth flat, past the raindrops streaming down the window pane, at the bleak, grey vista of Battersea Power Station. Winter in London was a miserable time. Tomorrow would be 2 December. Another 23 shopping days till Christmas. Already it looked like being an even worse winter than the one before. That morning's news on the radio had reported heavy snowfalls in Scotland, Wales and the West Country. Maurice found himself wondering again what sort of life he might have in the frozen archipelagos of the Scottish isles if Sir Malcolm ever discovered his treachery. He did not doubt that the old man had been serious when he had threatened exile in the Customs and Excise outposts of the Orkneys, where the only duty was endless searches of stinking trawlers from the Communist bloc and preliminary assessments of defecting Polish drunks. It had been a couple of months since he had mailed a small envelope containing certain information from the post office off Trafalgar Square to the French chargé d'affaires in London. Then there had been nothing. Nor did he really expect to hear anything except by the most circuitous

route. Rumours of a minor diplomatic embarrassment in Malta perhaps, the arrest of a few American and British nationals involved in something shady. At worst the sudden buzz down the grapevine that a former officer in counter terrorism had come to a violent end and there had been repercussions as far. as Whitehall and Washington. That was all he would hear. If he was lucky. If it was anything more dramatic, if Lynch put up a fight and things got messy, as well they might, it could be a different story when he next saw Sir Malcolm.

More likely it would all just blow over, as these things often mysteriously did, and nothing more would be heard of Lynch, his American slut and his suspicious links to influential Americans. Whatever the outcome, it was too late for him to change anything now. He shivered as he looked at the rain spattering against his window. It was still dark outside even though it was after eight in the morning. The street lights outside tried weakly to punctuate the grey with a few puddles of feeble fluorescence. Cassell let the curtain fall and turned back into his room. He wore a frayed bathrobe which had once been white and his bare feet slapped on the linoleum as he negotiated an array of electric heaters struggling against the damp. He had lived in this flat—the top half of a shabby South London terrace house—for eight years though, latterly, he could afford something better. Maurice Cassell was saving for something better, a life far away from cold lino and erratic two-bar electric heaters, retirement to a beach house in Portugal, perhaps. He finished getting ready and selected the least crumpled of the three brown suits in his wardrobe, all virtually identical. Cassell thought himself a master of the English knack of understatement. What he didn't realise was that his uniform drabness only made him seem more eccentric. When he was ready he pulled on an old raincoat and trotted down the stairs to the damp-smelling hallway, past his landlady's door and let himself out. From there it was only a quick run to his blue van. The cold and wet made it harder than usual to start but eventually it grumbled into life and Cassell started in the direction of Chelsea Bridge where he joined the slow, miserable procession of traffic into the city. He had already forgotten about Lynch and Porter, his mind looking ahead at a day on the computer, sifting the names and records of several new appointees to the Soviet trade mission, referred to Counter Terrorism Command by MI5.

'The French . . . why would the French want to poke their noses into this?' Lynch asked.

As Maurice Cassell fought his way through London's winter traffic, 2000 kilometres away Halloran, Lynch and Finn were having a crisis meeting on the balcony of Halloran's private quarters.

'Who knows why the French do anything?' Halloran snorted and leaned against the balcony wall, staring out to sea.

'There wasn't a leak from this end,' Finn said.

'I know,' Halloran answered. He turned and nodded at Lynch who was sitting near by drinking Halloran's breakfast coffee. 'Lieutenant Lynch had certain suspicions which he mentioned to me some time ago and I've learned from our friends in London that those suspicions may be well justified. The leak had to come from London.'

'Now what?' asked Finn.

Halloran shrugged. 'We take care of our end, London has promised to take care of theirs.'

'And just how well placed are our friends in London?' Lynch asked mildly, sipping from his cup.

'Well enough,' Halloran smiled.

'Even if they do have suspicions,' Finn said, 'I'd have thought the French would stand equally to gain from Gaddafi's removal.'

Halloran walked over to the breakfast table and poured himself another cup of coffee. 'On one hand, the French have suffered as much from state-sponsored terrorism as any other European nation. Their own police have been busting their balls to stop terrorism. On the other hand the government goes behind the backs of its own people to make deals with terrorists.'

'Like Irangate?' Lynch remarked.

Halloran shot him an ugly glance then turned away. 'Goddam politicians,' was all he said.

'You'd think even the French would realise they'd have less trouble from Libyan troops in northern Chad with Gaddafi gone,' Lynch added.

'It isn't just Libyans making mischief in Chad,' Halloran said and walked over to the breakfast table to pour himself another coffee. 'The Soviets are there, the East Germans, the Cubans. Maybe the French think that by doing just enough they can contain Gaddafi and keep Chad dependent on them. If Gaddafi goes they're probably afraid the Soviets will install somebody else at the head of a puppet regime, like in Afghanistan. Then the French would find themselves up against the Soviets and they haven't got the guts for that. You've got to remember, the French think they perfected diplomacy. They've become masters at maintaining the status quo until problems just kind of wear themselves out and ... disappear. Gaddafi is the devil the French know and they seem quite prepared to go on living with him, even though his actions might cause the deaths of a dozen innocent French civilians every year. We're not quite so civilised as the French, thank Christ.'

'What are the chances of the Soviets installing their own man as soon as Gaddafi goes?' Finn asked.

'Pretty good, if somebody else doesn't move first,' Halloran replied.

'Somebody else like a military government led by anti-Gaddafi and anti-Soviet officers?' Lynch speculated.

'Were such an event to take place and were such a new

government to request American assistance in restoring stability until democratic elections could be held, then the President of the United States might be inclined to act sympathetically,' Halloran smiled. 'The Fifth Fleet and the US Air Force already know the territory.'

Finn and Lynch swapped glances.

'This all kinda throws a cloud over something I was going to ask you,' Finn said, looking uncomfortable.

Halloran waited.

'The guys could use a bit of R & R before they jump off,' Finn said. 'They've trained hard. They're as ready for this as they could ever be. But they're kinda down. They need a morale booster. They need a night on the town, a few drinks, a few broads.'

Finn had surprised Lynch. The Briton knew he was right. They were all in dire need of a respite and the opportunity to dissipate some of the accumulated tensions of the past two months, but he hadn't expected Finn to be particularly sensitive to their needs.

The two of them watched the cogs turn as Halloran mulled it over. Then he nodded. 'Okay,' he said. 'It's possible. We have friends in Valletta too. I'll have Tim make a few calls, see what we can do. We'll have to be damn careful but I suppose we ought to be able to get 'em drunk and laid in a place like Malta before they go.'

Finn and Lynch stood up. 'What about the French?' Lynch asked, as he returned his coffee cup to the table.

'The French?' Halloran arched an eyebrow. 'Fuck the French.'

Soon after eight that Friday night a convoy of two Jeeps and two Mercedes rolled out of the villa and rumbled up the steep track towards the road to Valletta. The Jeeps were at each end of the convoy and the Mercs in the middle. The lead car held four of Halloran's men, all armed with Uzis. The first Mercedes was driven by Halloran with an armed guard beside him; Lynch and Roper were in the back with Tim, who rested an Uzi on his knee. The second Merc was driven by Finn with an armed guard beside him and Reece, Bono and Tuckey in the back. The last Jeep held another four of Halloran's men and carried extra guns and ammunition.

Darkness fell during the two-hour drive to Valletta and most of the villages *en route* were empty apart from a few nosy Maltese who watched curiously as the convoy sped past in a plume of dust. These were strange times even for a people such as the Maltese, although they were used to seeing carloads of heavily-guarded VIPs moving around the island—an Arab sheik here, an Italian tycoon there, a justifiably-paranoid politician somewhere else.

As they entered the suburbs of Valletta the streets became busier and they were forced to slow down. Malta was preparing for Christmas, a busy time of the year for homecomings—sons and fathers returning from jobs in northern Europe for the holidays—or for wealthy Europeans to trade winter blizzards for a few weeks of comparative warmth in the winter Mediterranean sunshine. As they drove past the city centre, Lynch spotted the sunburnt faces of a few young British servicemen, having a night out from the British communications base on Malta. It was a polyglot crowd which filled the footpaths, bars and restaurants, faces from the Mediterranean and all over the world: Arab, Italian, Greek, Asian, the faces of a hundred merchant nations. And everywhere there were the handsome, hawkish features of young Maltese men looking for fun and profit from the passing stream.

After half an hour negotiating narrow, busy streets the convoy pulled away from the waterfront and the crowds began to thin out. It was almost 11 pm when the lead Jeep swung into a dark, tree-lined street and rolled to a halt a few metres past the doorway to a club with a blue neon sign proclaiming the Tangier Room. The guards in the lead Jeep were already out as Halloran stopped the Merc. All the men were into the club, under escort, in less than a minute. Even Tuckey, limping from his badly-bruised leg protectively bandaged under his jeans, didn't slow the guards down. Once inside, all but Tim and one guard left to park the cars more discreetly and position themselves inconspicuously outside the building.

The owner was waiting for them, a pleasant-looking man with thinning black hair brushed straight back and a sweaty upper lip. He showed them to an upstairs end-booth overlooking a dance floor and a small stage where a youngish combo played watered-down rock for half a dozen couples on the floor. The club was only half-full and the owner assured Tim they were all regulars. Newcomers that night were turned away at the door on the advice that the club had been booked for a private function.

In their booth, the men arranged themselves in a semicircle around a big, square table with Tim and the other guard taking the two end seats. The club had a distinctly fifties look about it, which was probably why Halloran liked it, Lynch thought. There was a faded glamour to its Byzantine excesses, and the thickly-brocaded cushions they sat on and the tapestries hanging on the wood-panelled walls of their booth had a musty smell. From this booth each of them could overlook the dance floor and most of its surrounding tables but very few people could see them. There were even heavy curtains which could be drawn across the entrance if they needed more privacy.

Tim spoke briefly with the owner and a minute later a waiter arrived and took orders for their drinks. Most of the men drank beer, except Roper, who asked for a Coke and Halloran, who drank Scotch. Once their drinks had arrived they were followed by a procession of exotic food dishes: plates of marinated lamb and goat meat, spiced vegetables and some things they had never seen before. None of the men seemed too concerned. For three months they had been starved of exciting food and strong drink and they attacked it all with quiet enthusiasm. Neither Tim nor the guard touched any of the dishes or the drink and Halloran nursed his Scotch and looked on with amusement as the only conversation which passed between the men was the occasional grunt for something new. A few of the other diners glanced their way but apart from initial curiosity quickly lost interest. Malta was full of hard-looking men and it was best not to appear too nosy. It was only when some of the club's patrons wanted to leave that they were met with unexpected inconvenience. The guards at the door wouldn't allow them to leave. It wasn't explained that they would be allowed to leave after the group in the upstairs end booth. Instead the owner skilfully ushered them back inside with glib and profuse apologies and gave them unlimited drinks on the house, to be added to Halloran's tab.

It was midnight before Halloran's mercenaries had eaten their fill. One by one they settled back in the voluptuous cushions to digest the rich food and enjoy their drinks.

The only man still eating, oddly enough, was Reece when the house lights dimmed without warning and the rock combo changed the music. The dancers drifted from the floor as the musicians switched instruments to flutes and bongos and began playing a seductive eastern melody without introduction. They played for a few minutes and then there was a ripple of applause as a belly dancer appeared suddenly in a spotlight on the dance floor. A couple of the men grinned in the gloom and Reece stopped eating. She was fortyish, plump and heavily made-up, but she was an accomplished dancer and every man in the room watched her in silence. In the upstairs booth Halloran's men watched her rotating hips and the undulations of her fleshy belly and were reminded that it had been many,

many weeks since any of them had enjoyed female company. When she finished her dance they joined in the applause and a few of them shuffled uneasily in their seats. Two appetites had been satisfied but a third, more compelling need had just asserted itself. The lights came back up and the musicians took a break. Lynch looked around the table and noticed a frown on Bono's face.

'Don't you approve of this sort of thing, Sam?' he enquired, more out of anthropological curiosity than friendly concern.

Bono looked up at him. 'Don't like them Ay-rab broads, man,' he growled.

'Why? What's the matter with 'em?' Reece joined in and all the others turned their attention to the big, ugly man.

Bono shook his head slowly. 'I know what I'm talking about,' he said, and when he spoke they noticed a glimmer of grease on his red-stubbled chin. 'You ever seen the snatch on one of them Ay-rab broads?' he asked suddenly, looking accusingly at Reece.

Reece shook his head.

'Well, I was fuckin' this Egyptian broad in Jersey City one time,' Bono said. 'She was the wife of a good buddy of mine and I thought she looked pretty fine ...' His voice trailed away as he recalled the distant trauma from his youth. 'Man, when she dropped her pants it was like lookin' at a poodle with its throat cut. Ugliest thing I ever saw.'

They all stared at him and he scowled defiantly back. Then the scowl turned into a slow smile. Halloran suddenly exploded with laughter and the others followed. Even Roper smiled, but Reece only stared at his friend with mute distaste and pushed away the remains of his dinner.

Halloran checked his watch and announced it was time to move on. It was close to 12.30 when they filed out of the Tangier Room under guard. As they appeared the cars rolled up at the door in close precision and they were all whisked away in moments, leaving the dapper owner smiling happily behind on the footpath, his inside pocket bulging with new American dollars.

They drove through more narrow, darkened streets for only five minutes until they entered what looked like an exclusive residential area. The cars stopped outside a house which appeared to be in total darkness and Tim disappeared inside. He reappeared a moment later and signalled it was okay and once again they all hurried inside between two rows of guards. They found themselves in a garishly furnished lobby with ketchup-coloured carpets and gilt mirrors. On the left was an arch leading to an equally violently-decorated room with a small bar and to the right was a drawing room full of young women. Directly ahead was a closed door and beside the door a staircase leading up to a small landing and another hallway lined with doors. Halloran and Tim were already chatting amiably with a tiny, animated woman of about 50 in a chic black cocktail dress. She was flanked by two swarthy thugs who looked relieved when she waved them away into the bar.

'Now *this*,' Bono beamed, 'is a dago whorehouse.'

There were no other clients in sight. Halloran had paid for his men's exclusive use of the brothel. He interrupted his conversation with the madam and nodded in the direction of the drawing room where a dozen girls patiently watched television. 'Help yourselves, boys,' he said and then disappeared with the madam into her office for a quiet drink and a chat about the respective joys of managing the world's two oldest professions—the peddling of flesh and the bearing of arms. The madam had supplied women to Halloran before and he knew he could trust her not to ask too many awkward questions. Tim took up a position outside her office door and the other guard pulled a chair into the front hall and sat down, Uzi cradled on his lap. The six of them dawdled at the door to the drawing room, then Finn peeled away into the bar and ordered a beer.

A few of the girls looked around expectantly, waiting, professional smiles already in place. One of them spotted Tuckey and gave him a hopeful little wave. Tuckey looked around briefly at the others then limped into the room. Bono stepped into the doorway and the girls' faces fell and they looked away. Undaunted the ugly, red-haired man turned to Reece. 'I'm gonna find me a girl with fat lips who can suck my skidmarks down the eye of my dick,' he said and stepped into the room. He stopped in front of a girl no more than 18 or 19 years old with glossy black curls who glanced up at him and shuffled nervously.

'I'm ugly, ain't I?' Bono said with a smile intended to be disarming.

The girl giggled and looked back and forth among her friends, then looked up at Bono and nodded.

'Don't worry about it, honey,' Bono growled. 'The view you're gonna get, I look just like Robert Redford.'

Bono was followed by Reece and then Roper. Lynch was about to follow them but he hesitated then changed direction into the bar.

'Not interested?' he asked Finn.

'Can't.' Finn said, looking embarrassed. 'I'm married. Got three kids.'

The surprise must have shown in Lynch's eyes because Finn went on. 'I know . . . this isn't work for family men. What can I do? I figure if I don't do something the world isn't going to be a fit place for my kids to grow up in anyway. What the hell,' he shrugged. 'One more job. I told my wife I'd retire after this one. That is if I don't get drafted to the National Security Council.'

Lynch smiled. 'Nobody's going to phone your wife.'

'Nah,' Finn insisted. 'I'd know. I guess it's the way I am.' Lynch nodded. He understood. But he understood himself too. Janice already seemed like another world, another time away.

He walked across the hall and into the room full of girls. On the way he passed Reece, going upstairs with a girl on each arm and ordering the barman to bring two bottles of champagne.

It was three in the morning when Halloran emerged from the madam's office and called it a night. Tim dutifully plodded upstairs and began knocking on doors, getting the men out. Finn was already asleep on an easy chair in the bar, the madam's two thugs sitting near by, playing dominoes with the barman. One by one the men began to emerge from their rooms and wander down the stairs, rumpled, mildly hungover, but satisfied. Roper was the only man who appeared refreshed by the whole evening.

Reece and Bono came downstairs at the same time.

'Is yours still alive?' Reece asked.

'Couldn't get enough of me,' Bono sniffed, tucking his tee-shirt into stained and baggy pants. 'Told me how smart I was to pick her because one of yours has the clap.'

The night had a chilly edge as they all filed groggily out of the brothel and into the cars waiting with their engines running. The convoy sped quickly through Valletta's deserted streets, past a police car parked outside an all-night café near the harbour. The two policemen looked up as the cars swished past, took in the fake diplomatic plates and returned to their coffee. Lynch tried to make himself comfortable in the back seat between Roper and Tim and shut his eyes. They made up the same formation. Halloran chose to take the wheel again because he couldn't bear to remain idle for an hour. The drive back seemed longer and when Lynch awoke from an uncomfortable doze he saw they had just entered the foothills and were threading their way up a series of S-bends.

There was a full moon and the coarse mountain slopes were softened and made beautiful by its glow. Roper had his eyes closed and may have been asleep. The only sound in the car was the muted whine of some country and western music from the radio tuned to the US Forces wave band from Europe. Lynch looked past Tim, out the side window at the serpentine outline of the road winding above them towards the pass that would take them to the south-western coastal plains on the other side of the island's corrugated spine. On the left the edge of the two-lane highway ended abruptly with a drop of 70 to 80 metres until it reached the lower loop of the road they had just travelled. The headlights picked out the back of the lead Jeep about 50 metres in front, its rear wheels impudently spitting gravel and small stones in their direction. Lynch estimated there was another half hour to go and squirmed lower in the seat, letting his head fall back onto the cool leather cushion, trying to make himself more comfortable. Then the window on his right exploded inwards with an almighty crack, showering him with broken glass and a fountain of blood. The car swerved wildly and Halloran swore as he tried to keep it on the road. Tim's body fell across Lynch's lap and he felt warm blood soaking into his jeans. The blond man had taken a slug in the right side of the head, and it had passed straight through, blowing out most of the left side of his skull. The spent bullet must have landed in the seat cushion where Lynch's head had been a moment before. He shoved Tim's body roughly back into the corner of the seat and scrabbled on the floor for Tim's Uzi. The Merc stopped fishtailing and the guard in the front seat opened his window and leaned out with his gun. There was a sudden, deafening cascade of metallic bangs down the driver's side of the car and Lynch knew they had just taken another burst of automatic fire. 'I can't see anything,' the guard yelled and ducked back inside as the Merc weaved sickeningly across the road.

A moment later there was a brilliant yellow flash on the road ahead, the lead Jeep bucked crazily, rolled, crashed onto its roof and spun into the hillside amidst a torrent of sparks and flame.

Halloran was racing the engine, struggling to drive out of the ambush, but the last burst of gunfire had crippled the motor. 'I'm pulling over,' Halloran yelled as foul, oily smoke poured into the car. Lynch got his hands on the Uzi and twisted around to get his back against Tim's legs where he could look up with the gun held in front of him. He saw Roper crouched on the floor on his own side of the car, feet braced against the door, one arm on the back seat, the other against the back of the seat in front, readying himself for a roll. Then he had to shut his eyes because of the smoke. He heard the gear box scream as Halloran mashed the gear stick into reverse and the gears disintegrated with a series of loud bangs. A moment later and Merc slammed to a full stop in a cloud of smoke and choking dust.

'Get the fuck outta here,' Halloran yelled above the still-racing engine. Lynch looked up. The door was open and Roper was gone. He propelled himself forward and rolled onto the road. The whole hillside seemed to be alive with gunfire. He got to his feet and sprinted around to the front of the car. The guard was just ahead of him, half-running, half-dragging Halloran into a shallow ditch between the hillside and the road. They hit the ditch and scrambled away from the Merc. A new storm of bullets clanged into the car and smacked into the dirt around them. The guard threw Halloran face down and crouched over him, Uzi up, eyes searching the slopes above for the source of the gunfire. Lynch looked back down the road. The last two vehicles were stopped like them, jammed against the mountainside 60 or 70 metres away and taking at least as much fire as they were. Up the road the lead Jeep was still burning and there was no sign of life. There were two bodies lying in the road but nothing to be seen of the other two. At least five dead in the first hit and no sign of Roper. They were in in lot of trouble, Lynch thought.

Lynch crawled up the ditch past Halloran and the guard. Halloran heard him and looked up. 'Give me a gun,' he grunted. Lynch shook his head.

'Sorry,' he said. 'I'm better with this than you are.' He looked to the guard. 'Got any spare clips?' The guard fished in the pocket of his field jacket and handed Lynch two clips. Another hail of bullets spattered around them, forcing them to crouch further into the ditch. After a minute Lynch looked up. Their attackers must be on the road another hundred metres above them but he hadn't seen any muzzle flashes to tell them where. Lynch realised they had been expertly topped and tailed— ambushed simultaneously by separate groups hitting them front and rear. They couldn't go forward and they couldn't go back. There were hardly any clouds in the sky and the moon lit the countryside like a lamp. He looked at his watch. It was ten after four. Two hours before daylight. Two hours in which Halloran and his men could be annihilated. Lynch looked back at their car. Steam boiled from the radiator and smoke poured from the engine but there was still no sign of fire. Then he noticed the black puddle under the fuel tank and the long, crooked finger reaching down the road towards the other vehicles.

'Get further up,' Lynch ordered. They scrabbled and crawled as best as they could, ripping their clothes and cutting their skin on the sharp rocks, Halloran swearing every inch of the way and the guard struggling to cover him. They were half-way between the Merc and the glare from the still-burning Jeep when Lynch told them to stop. 'It'll have to do,' he said and swivelled round to get a clear shot at the Merc. He lifted the Uzi and angled a couple of bursts at the road under the car, calculated to ricochet up and spark off the car's underside. It worked. On the third or fourth burst there was a dull whooshing sound and the Merc was engulfed by a vivid tulip of fire. The firing stopped for a moment as all attention switched to the burning Mercedes. A moment later Lynch saw a figure sprinting up the road towards them.

He was carrying a gun in one hand and a satchel of ammo clips in the other and running like a cheetah. It had to be Roper. While the other two watched, Lynch tore his eyes away and focused on the road curling up the hillside. Their assailants waited till Roper was illuminated by the flames from the burning car then opened up and Lynch saw the flicker of muzzle flashes from three rifles. The road around Roper seemed to erupt in a spray of fine dust and a second later he thudded into the ditch beside them.

'I've got them,' Lynch said as Roper raised his head. 'Look straight at the road above and count about 70 metres to the right. Keep them busy.' Then he got up, sprinted back across the road and slid over the edge. Behind him Lynch heard the hollow mutter of the two Uzis as Roper and the guard began returning fire. It took him several minutes to pick his way across the steep, scrubby hillside until he passed the next upwards curve in the road and could begin working his way right up the slope. All the time he listened to the sound of firing, estimating the ground he had covered, careful to keep the bulge of the hillside between him and their assailants. When he was satisfied he had made enough height he began working his way back towards the road until he emerged, as he had planned, well above their attackers and could begin getting into a good position behind them. As he picked his way cautiously across the slope he saw there were four men and one car. The men were lying or kneeling on the ground, their rifles trained over the edge of the road at their victims on the next level of highway down. It was a superb ambush position. They could keep their victims pinned down, pick them off at leisure and they themselves were virtually immune. Occasionally one of them would get up, walk back to the car and load a fresh magazine.

From the sound of their weapons they were armed with American Armalites—most commonly used by NATO forces and easily obtainable. Lynch could hear a few odd bursts from the opposing Uzis but they were barely a nuisance to their assailants. He decided he could take no more time and anchored himself into a slight depression in the hillside about 50 metres away.

One of the men got up and hurried back to the car to get a fresh clip off the back seat. Lynch recognised the car as a new black Fiat, almost certainly a rental. The man ejected the spent clip into the floor of the car, slammed in the fresh magazine and was about to turn back when Lynch fired a concentrated. burst aimed at his upper torso. The man flew back and slammed into the ground as if he had been hit with an axe, his rifle clattering to the road beside him. His three companions whirled around in shock and Lynch emptied the rest of the clip in their direction. The 32 rounds were gone in a second and he hurriedly slotted in a new clip. The three men scrambled for their car, two of them firing wild shots up the hillside. Lynch fired another long burst, raking the car, shattering its rear window and catching one of the men in his left knee. He screamed and fell as his companions threw themselves into the car and started the engine. Lynch emptied the second clip and while he fumbled for his spare, it gave the wounded man just enough time to grab the outstretched hand of one of his friends and be pulled onto the back seat as the Fiat slewed away, two doors hanging open, leaving one man dead on the road. Lynch stood up and watched the car race up the hillside. In a few minutes it would pass above and behind but too far away for him to do its occupants any further damage. Then something else caught his attention. On the bottom reaches of the mountain road he saw two pairs of headlights speeding up the valley towards the ambush scene. There was a lull in the firing from below as the others saw them too, then it intensified. Lynch half-slid, half-

215

fell down the rough slope to the road, ignored the dead man sprawled in his path, and ran to the edge. When he looked at the scene below, the Jeep had burnt itself out but the Merc was still smouldering and Halloran was sheltering near by, still in the ditch with his bodyguard. Roper stood in the middle of the road, ignoring the crossfire a hundred metres away, trying to make out the oncoming cars.

Finn, Tuckey, Bono and Reece were strung along the roadside ditch with their guards, using their own vehicles for added cover and exchanging fire with the men clustered behind two more Fiats blocking the road downhill from them. Suddenly, the new cars rounded the bend behind the roadblock, and gunmen leaning from the windows began firing on the men clustered around the Fiats. Lynch heard screams as someone was hit and there was a panic as the ambushers realised they had become the meat in the sandwich. There was a desperate scramble to get into their cars and the first one away lurched into the ditch then bumped out and began accelerating up the hill, past Finn and the others. The second car swung around and tried to follow but it had only gone a few metres when it exploded in flame as its tank ignited under the withering hail of bullets from the men in the newly-arrived cars. The burning car rolled forward into the ditch and stopped and the valley was filled with the screams of the men inside. The men by the side of the road watched motionless, as two figures kicked the car doors open and staggered out, wreathed in flames from head to toe. They only staggered a few steps before they were cut down by a merciful volley of gunfire and their bodies, still burning furiously, crumpled to the roadway.

The explosion had taken everyone's eyes from the escaping car and Lynch switched his attention back to the Fiat as it swerved past its recent ambush victims and up the hill towards Roper. If the car got past him it would turn the corner near Lynch in about half a minute. Lynch checked his last clip in the Uzi and watched. The driver of the Fiat was aiming straight at Roper in a bid to frighten him out of the way or drive right over him. Still in the middle of the road, Roper bent into a slight crouch and began to move. Instead of moving away from the oncoming car and getting into a position where he could rake it with the Uzi he began a slow trot towards the speeding car. Once again Lynch found himself hypnotised by Roper's lethal sense of purpose. This time he wasn't alone.

The driver had his foot to the floor and the car was gathering speed by the second. The gap between Roper and the Fiat closed dramatically and it became only a matter of seconds. Roper appeared to falter and every man watching held his breath but he only seemed to be measuring his own momentum against that of the onrushing car. Then he did the unexpected and burst into a sprint, taking a series of long, fast strides down the road towards the car as it raced up the road towards him. When it looked as if the Fiat had to hit him square in the chest he calculated his last step and leaped high into the air, as high as his own momentum could take him. It only took an instant but it was an instant engraved on the memory of every man who saw it. The tips of Roper's toes cleared the roof of the car by a fraction as it flashed beneath him and as it did he pointed the Uzi down and squeezed the trigger. Every round in the submachine-gun's magazine stitched the car from nose to tail, slicing through the metal roof and everything under it like a can opener. The men inside hadn't a chance. Roper came down and hit the ground with a roll. He hadn't covered much distance at all. He had just gained enough height to let the car pass underneath him and carve itself open on a chainsaw of bullets. The car had already begun to veer off the road as he hit the ground. It ran along the edge of the slope for a few crazy seconds then teetered and rolled out of sight. They all stood and listened as the Fiat smashed and tumbled its way to the road far below and then it was all suddenly very quiet.

Lynch's ears crackled with the echo of gunfire. He looked down at his clothes. They were torn and filthy, the knees had been ripped out of his jeans and both legs were cut and bleeding. He took a deep breath and looked around, then he picked up the dead man's rifle and examined it. As he had thought, it was an AR18. With a gun in each hand he started down the slope towards the road and the others. The scene resembled a battlefield—war in the dying years of the twentieth century, he thought, amused by his own morbid pun.

When he reached the bottom he saw Halloran and his remaining guards talking earnestly with two of the men who had come to their aid. He couldn't hear what they were saying except the newcomers had an unfamiliar accent which he was too tired to try to understand. Roper was sitting on a mound of rubble by the side of the road, the Uzi balanced between his knees. Lynch walked over and sat beside him. They were joined a moment later by the others. It seemed the first two cars in the convoy had taken the worst of the ambush. Neither Finn, Tuckey, Bono nor Reece had been hurt. One of their guards had been clipped on the arm but that was all. As soon as they saw what happened to the two lead vehicles they had stopped, taken cover and been able to stalemate the men at the roadblock. When Roper had come back for an extra gun and ammunition he had assured them they could take care of the assailants to the front. Lynch smiled. Bono looked down at Roper with what seemed like undisguised awe on his great jowly face.

'Where do they teach you guys that kinda stuff?' he asked. 'A fuckin' three-ring circus?'

Halloran had finished talking and the two newcomers set off back down the road to where their own men waited with their cars. He walked over to where his group had gathered and looked at them. His clothes too were dirty and torn and his iron-grey hair was smeared with dust. Lynch thought he looked older but it may just have been his pallor in the bright moonlight. Despite Halloran's confidence, things had gone badly wrong. The whole operation could have ended here on a barren mountainside in Malta, and the puzzled local authorities would have been left to pick up the pieces. The two-way radio in the Mercedes was still working and Halloran had ordered security back at the villa to send out half a dozen men in the mini-bus to retrieve the bodies and remove all clues from the charred remains of the two burnt-out cars. They would collect as many spent cartridges as they could and leave the bodies of their assailants to give the Maltese a time-consuming mystery to solve. Halloran decided to leave his guards with the Mercedes and the rest of them would squeeze into the Jeep and return to the villa before daylight arrived.

'The French?' Lynch asked as he kept pace with Halloran on the walk back down to the Jeep.

'Had to be,' Halloran said.

'I had a look at the guy up there,' Lynch added, jabbing a thumb over his shoulder at the next stretch of road up the mountain. 'I could be wrong but to me he looked and dressed like a Maltese.'

Halloran nodded. 'One of the local gangs might have been paid to do it,' he said. 'But the French will be behind it.' They heard car engines start and saw their rescuers turn back down the winding road.

'What about the Seventh Cavalry?' Lynch asked.

'Seventh Cavalry, Tel Aviv,' Halloran said.

'Israelis . . . Mossad?'

'Something like that,' Halloran said. 'They'll work with anybody who promises to make life hard for the Arabs. Too bad their timing was a little off tonight.' He paused. 'Tim was with me eight years.'

They reached the Jeep and Lynch saw the bullet holes down

the passenger side. 'What's next?' he asked, yanking the door open.

Halloran climbed into the driver's seat and sat down heavily. He switched on the ignition, pumped the gas pedal and the GM engine roared into life despite the rash of bullet holes. He waited while the others climbed over the tailgate into the back then slowly lowered his forehead onto the steering wheel.

'What a fucking mess,' he sighed. 'And,' he looked up at Lynch, 'it could have been a helluva lot worse.' The tailgate slammed shut and Halloran pulled away up the hill, raising a hand to his men still waiting on the road with the Mercedes. 'It's time we got you guys off the island,' he said suddenly, the familiar steel creeping back into his voice. 'The full moon has another two days to go. We go in three.'

Three days later Maurice Cassell was watching the rain beating against the window again. This time it was from the seat of a second-class carriage on the London-to-Edinburgh express. The summons to see Sir Malcolm had come midmorning two days earlier, when he had been deep in a computer analysis of London social events attended both by Arabs from countries with known terrorist links and by the newer representatives of the Soviet trade legation. The meeting had been brief. Maurice was given 48 hours notice of his transfer to CTC, Aberdeen. No explanation. Although, from Sir Malcolm's mood, none was necessary. On leaving the old man's office Brown Suit had allowed himself a smile. Something had obviously gone very wrong in Malta and it had caused Porter immense displeasure. Maurice would bide his time in Aberdeen. Eventually he would have enough information to move against Porter. In the meantime, there was nothing for it but to make frenzied arrangements to leave London for an indefinite period. Very few of his friends and colleagues seemed sorry to see him go, Maurice realised.

Most of them simply expressed their regrets and smiled privately, wondering why it had taken Control so long. His furniture and other belongings would be sent on after him by the department when he had found a flat in Aberdeen. In the meantime he had only a couple of suitcases and a note supplying him with the address of digs already arranged for him in the granite city.

The train was only 90 minutes late into Edinburgh and Maurice had time for a quick lager in the buffet at Waverley Station before catching the next train to Aberdeen. It was after eight in the evening when he finally arrived at the address of the lodgings he had been given, after 12 hours of travelling. His landlady told him it was too late to make him dinner but there was a message waiting for him from a Mr Urquhart with a telephone number to ring. Maurice was surprised. Jeff Urquhart was the Aberdeen head of section and he had not intended to call him until the following morning. Tired and irritable with hunger, Maurice called the number and a few minutes later was connected to Urquhart.

To Maurice's annoyance Urquhart wanted to see him at section's harbourside quarters at ten that night. Urquhart's explanation was that he was leaving on business first thing the next day and he needed to brief Maurice about important matters before then. Maurice swore to himself. No doubt this was all part of Porter's broader instructions to make life miserable for him from the beginning but he wasn't about to resign and lose all his superannuation benefits. He would simply have to wear it for the moment. There was time for another quick drink and some cremated sausages at a pub down the street, then he caught a taxi and asked for the container yards at the harbour. As the taxi drove through Aberdeen's wet, empty streets Maurice was struck by what a mean, ugly city it was. The bottom had fallen out of the oil boom years before and now, like every

221

other major provincial city in Britain, the signs of decay and depression were everywhere.

Angry as he was, Maurice was careful to follow Urquhart's instructions to the letter. He paid the taxi off at the dock gates and walked the rest of the way down the wide, blustery dock-yard past rows of darkened warehouses on his left and a few rust-streaked freighters tethered to the wharves on his right. The temperature was a few degrees below freezing and the air seemed wet and unhealthy. After a few minutes, sleet began to fall and Maurice drew his old raincoat closer around him. About a kilometre away he could see a freighter being loaded, the only scene of activity on the docks that night. As instructed he counted the warehouses on his left until he found number 17, only a few metres away from the busy ship. A rail spur jutted out from between the warehouses and he could see stacks of 44-gallon oil drums being moved by crane from the open rail cars to the deck of the freighter. Maurice found the alley be-tween warehouses 17 and 19, stepped into the shadows and waited, out of sight of the dockers loading the oil drums. He looked back along the docks and down the alley behind him but saw no-one else. He glanced at his watch. He was on time, as ordered. He was always punctual. His feet began to grow numb from the cold and he stamped them to jog up the circu-lation.

A distant clock began ringing the hours and Maurice counted the strokes. The chimes of Aberdeen were the last sounds Mau-rice ever heard. He never heard the man who appeared behind him so quickly out of the shadows. All he heard was the tenth stroke then a wire loop passed over his head, bit deeply into his neck and sliced through his windpipe until it reached the bone. Maurice was unconscious before the blood began over-flowing into his lungs. And he never felt a thing when the man gave a savage twist and jerk to the wooden handles of the garotte, cleanly snapping his spine. The man quickly dragged

Maurice's body back into the alley and heaved it into an empty 44-gallon drum. He covered the body with bricks and sand piled against the warehouse wall and when the drum was full, jammed the specially-constructed lid on top and sealed it. When he was finished he tilted the drum and began manhandling it down towards the dockside where all the other drums were waiting to be loaded. No-one saw him as he rolled his drum into the nearest pile. It matched the others perfectly—painted a deep black except for the yellow and black triangles of the radioactivity warning symbol stamped on the side. Maurice's coffin looked like all the other drums of low-grade radioactive waste transported secretly from the Sellafield Nuclear Power Station in Cumbria to the Aberdeen docks, destined for the deep, cold waters off the North Atlantic shelf a few days later. Satisfied that no-one had seen a thing, the killer melted quietly into the sleet which had begun to fall quite heavily and which was already washing away the few remaining splashes of Maurice's blood in the alley.

The next morning a charming man with a refined Scots accent arrived at Maurice's lodgings to collect his possessions, saying Maurice had been sent away on urgent business on behalf of the same obscure government department which had made the booking. At the same time, a green furniture van arrived at his London flat, picked up all his furniture and delivered it to the East End tip where it was bulldozed into the ground. Maurice Cassell literally disappeared off the face of the earth—though he probably wouldn't have appreciated the irony of his death.

Had he known he was going to his own funeral he might have worn another suit.

10

THE HIT

Tripoli, Christmas 1989

Lynch hardly recognised *American Endeavor* when she returned to Malta, once more under the cover of darkness. An extra funnel had been added. The helipad had been covered with plywood and plastic cabins interlaced with foil strips disguised the ship's radar profile. The paintwork had been altered from all-white to white with green trim. All her American insignia had been removed and, instead of her real name around the stern, there was a necklace of Arab script with the English translation underneath in smaller letters, *Star of Oman*. Captain Penny's crew had been busy during their absence, Lynch thought.

The whole night was spent stripping the villa of everything Halloran had shipped in. His guards and the crew of his ship worked like coolies to remove anything that even smelled of the Americans' presence before first light. Lynch and the others had spent the previous three days checking and rechecking their gear, using whatever spare time they had for light exercise and some extra sleep. They talked little of the ambush on the road from Valletta, trying to keep their minds focused on what was now immediately ahead, the whole reason for their being in Malta, the reason for all the sweat, tension and training of the preceding three months.

The guards had brought back the bodies of Tim and the other men, wrapped in makeshift plastic body-bags. They had been kept in the villa's coldroom and were to be transferred to a freezer aboard the *Endeavor* because Halloran had promised that any fatalities would be given a proper burial in the United States. Finn and the two marine engineers from Excelteq attached to Halloran's private staff had serviced the scooters and ensured all three were fully charged for the mission ahead.

The six of them rode out with the scooters aboard the *Junior Endeavor* around three in the morning and, after stowing their personal gear in the cabins assigned them, spent the next two hours packing their guns, ammunition, explosives and survival equipment into the cargo holds of the scooters. When they were satisfied the scooters were ready, they manhandled their scuba gear below decks to the dive chamber and laid it all out on the aluminum benches of the change room next to the control chamber. Lynch checked the gauge connected to his re-breather to ensure that the helium and oxygen gas-mix he and the others would be breathing was at the maximum level to allow 12 hours' self-contained operation, including the scenic hike once they were ashore. If anything went wrong and the gases weren't purified through the rebreather's crystals he would suffer slow and insidious poisoning and would be forced to take his helmet off in the sewer and risk the equal dangers posed by sewer gas.

They had just finished checking their scuba gear when they heard the deafening rumble of the *Endeavor*'s big diesel engines start up only three or four bulkheads away. When they emerged on deck it was a little after five and dawn was still an hour away. The villa was in complete darkness and Lynch could hardly make it out as the ship slipped gently away in the gloom. The full moon had died and there were a few brush strokes of cloud obscuring the stars. Lynch was tired. There was no sign of Halloran. They had seen little of him since the morning they got back to the villa three days earlier. He had appeared once, briefly, while they were having breakfast in the main dining room the previous morning to confirm that the *Endeavor* would be arriving soon and that they were to be ready. Lynch yawned and decided he was ready for sleep. He left the rail and took the near by hatchway and the stairs leading to the double cabin he had been given. The others followed his example a few minutes later and turned in as the *Endeavor* cruised out to the open sea and set a long, looping course that would take it into the Strait of Sicily and to the start of its approach on Libya.

Lynch woke up in the middle of the afternoon and, for a minute, didn't know where he was. The distant hum of the diesel engines, the shock of sky through the porthole reminded him he was back aboard ship but in all his years at sea with the navy he had never seen such luxurious quarters. He hadn't paid much attention to the appointments of the cabin earlier and when he turned in before dawn, he had been too tired to care. Now he was awake he took in the size of the bed, the bedroom, the rich furniture, the beautifully compact bathroom facilities, the sitting room next door with more leather couches, TV and a small cocktail bar and he knew he was on the *Endeavor*. He shaved, showered, dressed and picked up the phone in the sitting room connecting him to the ship's switchboard. It was after three when a crewmen brought him bacon and eggs from the galley but the crew of the *Endeavor* was used to meals served at all hours. After he had eaten, Lynch went up on deck and took a walk around the beautiful ship as it sliced through the southern Mediterranean. It was a brilliant winter's day for pleasure-cruising off

227

the coast of North Africa. The sky was clear, the sun bright but not at all hot, the breeze had a warm, musky smell to it and the sea glittered like crushed diamonds. From the position of the sun and their speed, Lynch estimated they had completed their diversionary curve and were now cruising south-south-east with the coast of Tunisia over the horizon on the starboard side and Tripoli almost dead ahead. He saw none of the others and decided they must be resting below, preparing for their departure in five or six hours. Lynch didn't feel like sleeping or hiding below decks. Instead he made his way to the after-deck and found a spot overlooking the fantail where he could lie with his hands behind his head and watch the milky wake of the *Endeavor* trailing far behind and the seagulls wheel and dive, looking for scraps. He would be eating enough canned air in the confines of his scuba helmet soon enough, he thought. For the moment Lynch wanted to savour the views of the open sea and its fresh air.

When he next checked his watch it had just gone six. He thought of looking in on the bridge but decided to observe protocol and wait for an invitation from the captain or the owner. The six of them had been urged to eat a good meal and get all the rest they could in their cabins before Halloran called them. Lynch decided to take the advice and returned to his cabin even though he wasn't particularly hungry. He called the galley and ordered a steak with boiled potatoes and ate it in front of the television. The *Endeavor*'s satellite receivers gave him what seemed like a couple of hundred channels to choose from. He settled on an old Jeff Chandler war movie in dubbed Italian because he could watch it without thinking.

The phone rang before he finished his meal. It was an officer on the bridge offering him the captain and Mr Halloran's compliments and inviting him to join them right away. Lynch pushed his dinner tray aside, grateful for something to do.

When he arrived on the bridge a few minutes later he found Halloran, Captain Penny, the first officer, a helmsman, communications officer and one of the guards from the villa.

'You'll be pleased to know the weather forecast is good,' said Halloran, welcoming him onto the bridge. The American nodded through the glass at the approaching night. 'Light winds, seas light to moderate. It's going to be a nice night for a swim.'

Halloran still had bags under his eyes but Lynch thought he looked better than at any time since the ambush. He had probably had less sleep than any of them, considering how much there was to do without the help of his aide, but Lynch noticed the energy had returned, the resilient old bastard had bounced back. Lynch heard the others arrive on the bridge behind him and Halloran waited until they had all gathered around him.

'This is Johnny Haddad,' Halloran said, introducing the guard. Lynch recognised him as the man he had spoken to at the villa gates the day he had gone for his exploratory run. The man nodded to them.

'John speaks fluent Arabic,' Halloran added. 'He's going to talk to the Libyans for us in a few minutes. First, I thought there was something you might all like to see.'

He ushered them over to a big radar scope on the electronic control board where the helmsman sat. They crowded around behind Halloran who pointed at the ragged outline of the coast, with a white smudge at the furthest edge of the scope.

'That's the coast of Libya, gentlemen,' Halloran said. Then he pointed to the white smudge at the side. 'That's Tripoli just coming into view.'

'How close are we?' Lynch asked.

Halloran turned to his captain.

'Between 50 and 60 nautical miles,' Penny answered.

Lynch was impressd. 'Some radar for a pleasure yacht,' he said.

Halloran smiled. 'We made good time despite our circuitous route. We've dropped our speed but we should still be at the launch zone about two hours from now.'

They looked at the clock on the bulkhead. It was just coming up to eight.

'We haven't been challenged this far,' Halloran added, 'by any other craft or shore base. As we expected, most of their attention is directed at the air and the Fifth Fleet is off Lebanon so they're not expecting anything from this direction tonight.' He stepped away from the radar scope and they followed.

'Okay,' he added, looking at Haddad who was waiting patiently beside the communications officer. 'Time for John here to do his thing.' The communications officer already had the right wavelength for the Libyan civil maritime authority. He flicked a switch, handed Haddad a pair of earphones and swivelled the mike his way. Haddad began rattling off a series of call signs in rapid Arabic, waiting, then repeating the message.

'We're giving the genuine ID for all the private vessels owned by the royal family of Oman,' Halloran said. They watched Haddad and waited.

After several minutes Haddad shrugged. 'They're not answering,' he smiled.

'Maybe they're all at a pep rally,' Bono growled.

'Try again,' Halloran ordered. They waited then Haddad's eyes lit up and he nodded. He listened for a few minutes then slipped the earphones back.

'They want to know if we received prior clearance to pass through Libyan waters,' Haddad said. 'And they want to know our precise heading.'

'You know what to tell them,' Halloran answered.

Haddad passed on the information, including their bogus position, then took the headphones off. 'They told us to stand by,' he said. 'Probably going to check with some Revolutionary Guard to see whether the Omani royal family is the flavour of the month or not.'

Halloran nodded. They waited. The minutes ticked past and the *Endeavor* drew closer and closer to the launch zone. It was almost an hour before Tripoli called them back and they were only 20 sea miles from the zone.

Haddad listened, replied in a stream of Arabic, then put the earphones down.

'Permission denied,' he said. 'They said we're not to enter Libyan territorial waters. If we do we'll be intercepted and boarded. Obviously they have no idea where we are.'

'Assholes,' Halloran laughed. 'Give 'em all that business about Prince Faoud being on board with his family, what an insult this is to the royal family of Oman and that you will have to refer to the prince for further instructions.'

Haddad did as he was told then put the earphones down again.

'This guy's a bum,' he said. 'Can't take a shit without asking permission. He's told us to stand by again while he passes all that on.'

'Good,' Halloran said. 'That will give us all the time we need.' He looked at Lynch and Finn and all the others. 'Start getting ready, gentlemen. You're leaving in 90 minutes.'

Lynch walked briskly back to his cabin, an electric tingle running through his body. He threw his clothes on top of his bags in the luggage locker and left them there. Then he pulled on a pair of blue cotton shorts and the Gortex undersuit he would wear under the wetsuit, all unlabelled, all anonymous. When he was ready he looked around the cabin and patted the pockets on his jumpsuit. Then he fingered the hard little nub in the hem of the crew-neck collar where one cyanide capsule had been sewn in. He needed nothing more. He padded down the gangway in bare feet and made his way to the change-room far below. Finn, Tuckey and Roper were already there. Next door two crewmen waited, checking the pressure controls of the exit chamber. They geared up slowly and deliberately, careful to make sure they had every item of equipment and that everything was working. Lynch zipped on the dive boots, pulled on the gloves and then shouldered his backpack. When he stepped into the control chamber Halloran was waiting with the first officer.

'No word yet from our friends in Tripoli,' Halloran said. 'They might be going higher this time. Maybe to Gaddafi.' Lynch nodded, then followed the others through the hatch into the exit chamber. Six pairs of fins had already been set out for them on the gleaming aluminum benches down each side of the chamber. A harsh, white light filled the exit chamber and Lynch blinked. Now they all clumsily perched on the metal benches, fins on, helmets on their knees, waiting to go. Lynch looked around at the faces of the others. No-one had anything to say. They had been rehearsed so often for this moment there was nothing left to question. With their wetsuits, bulky backpacks and futuristic helmets, Lynch thought they looked like celestial stormtroopers waiting to be ejected from a spaceship onto some hostile planet.

There was a sudden change in the engine note and they heard the alternating pitch of the big engines as the *Endeavor* began to slow.

Halloran stuck his head into the chamber. 'Don't forget,' he said. 'Some of our guys will be in the water to help you get started.' Behind him they heard the voice of Captain Penny on the ship's intercom. 'Permission to remain in Libyan territorial waters denied,' he said. 'Repeat. Denied. Tripoli is sending a patrol boat to escort us from their waters.'

'Guess Oman isn't popular with Gaddafi after all,' Finn noted.

'We have plenty of time,' Halloran said. 'They still don't know where the hell we are.' He turned back to the first officer. 'Tell John to inform them we are steering a new course out of Libyan waters now.'

The ship had slowed dramatically and the engines were barely a whisper.

'We're going to have to close this hatch and start pressurising the exit chamber, sir,' one of Halloran's crewmen told him. Halloran nodded. He stuck his head back inside and looked at them all one more time. For once he seemed lost for words.

'Blow the mad bastard away,' he said at last. Then he was gone. The crewman clanged the door shut and spun its locking wheel. The inside of the exit chamber fell silent. Now that the engines had been shut down and the ship appeared to have come to a halt, they could hear nothing but the slap of the waves on the outside of the hull.

'Time to put the helmets on,' Finn ordered. 'See you in Tripoli, boys.'

Lynch secured his dive helmet and his world became even smaller. All he could hear was the sound of his own breathing amplified once more within the confines of the helmet. When they were ready they gave Finn the okay signal and Finn signalled the crewman whose face was visible through the reinforced porthole in the bulkhead. They watched the needle on the pressure gauge inside the chamber and Lynch worked his jaw to equalise the changing pressure in his ears.

It only took a moment for the pressure inside the exit chamber to adjust to two atmospheres, to match the pressure of the water outside the hull. Lynch checked his watch. It was twenty past ten. They waited another ten minutes, then the crewman at the porthole gave another okay signal which was returned

233

by Finn. The hatch in the floor slid open without a sound and water as black as ink slopped in. Finn stood up and was followed by Reece. A moment later Finn stepped forward into the black hole and vanished without a sound. Reece fidgeted for only a second then stepped after him and was gone. There was a brief flurry of turbulence in the hatch, then the water closed over their heads as finally as a grave. Lynch watched a minute go by, then it was his turn. He stood up and took an ungainly, waddling step forward, paused briefly on the edge of the hatch, then stepped forward and plunged into the dark. He was lost in a column of bubbles for an instant and when he looked up saw the brilliantly-lit square of the exit hatch projecting a great beam of light into the dark water. He could even see Bono stepping forward to jump though all that was visible from inside the chamber was the uninviting black surface of the water. Lynch finned gently to one side and hung there for a moment until there was another explosion of bubbles as Bono plunged through the hatch. Then he looked round and saw the beams from the flashlights of the *Endeavor*'s frogmen already in the water around them. Lynch waited for Bono and then the two of them finned slowly down and across to the starboard side of the ship, keeping a respectful distance from the gently-heaving hull of the *Endeavor*. A miscalculation now and a crack from the rising and falling hull of the ship could shatter the aqua-nites on their helmets, or, if it was hard enough, split open the helmets themselves.

A moment later they broke surface about 30 metres away from the *Endeavor* amidst a circle of flashlight beams wielded by the divers who were tending the scooters. Lynch looked up.

The ship was in total darkness. It was not even showing navigation lights and there was no light visible through the hatch from where their scooters and the other frogmen had just been lowered. Still, Lynch thought he recognised the bulky figure of Halloran, watching them.

Finn and Reece were already on board their scooter and had almost finished harnessing in. Lynch swam over to the stern of the next scooter in line and grabbed onto it. There wasn't much of a swell but enough to make movement on the surface of the sea awkward with the cumbersome backpack to manage. He struggled out of his fins and handed them to one of the divers tending his scooter, then slowly climbed on board. When he was securely harnessed in, he helped stabilise the scooter while Bono secured himself amidships. When they were ready Lynch looked around to see how the others were doing. The nose lights were switched off and it took him a moment to find Finn and Reece already drifting 50 to 60 metres away in the current. Slightly to one side and behind him Lynch found Tuckey and Roper. Tuckey's thigh was still bruised and tender but he had given it as much rest as he could in the week since he had injured it and insisted it wouldn't present any problems for him. No one had argued. There was nobody else to pilot the third scooter. Roper, typically, had appeared unconcerned.

Lynch saw the brief wink of the nose light from Finn's scooter. He was clearly anxious to go. Lynch switched on the ignition, eased the throttle forward and began manœuvering around to line up behind Finn. When he was in position he winked his own light briefly and a few minutes later Tuckey fell in a few metres behind him. Lynch switched his attention to Finn in front and a moment later he saw the first scooter glide smoothly forward then dip its nose and slide from sight. Lynch carefully counted another two minutes away and then throttled forward. He locked into four knots then manipulated the rudder and he and Bono slid soundlessly beneath the surface.

The water was as black as death. Even 20 sea miles from Tripoli the sea was turbid and the figures on his instrument panel grew vague in the murk. He glanced up at the readings inside his mask then pulled down the aqua-nites visor and the characters on the scooter's instrument panel assumed a milky glow. They were flashing to show his depth and heading were wrong. Lynch had the coordinates for Tripoli memorised. He took the scooter down to 10 metres and stabilised. Then he manœuvred into the right heading and watched carefully as the luminescent corrugated line that was the distant coast of Libya shimmered into view on the compass dial. He was surprised at how much he had swung off course in so few minutes. The current might be running more strongly than they anticipated. He would need to watch himself. He knew that however carefully they timed their descents, this was never a guarantee of the sequence in which the scooters would surface later. However skilful they may have become in navigating their way to the target they invariably arrived out of synch and from different angles of approach. It is impossible to steer a perfectly straight line through the ocean. The best they could hope for was a meandering arc, sometimes crossing each other's paths, sometimes swinging wildly away. Given the unpredictability of any great mass of water, the oceanic fluctuations, eddies, conflicting currents at different depths and each act of navigational compensation, it was enough that they arrived on target and within half an hour of each other.

The figures on the scooter stopped flashing. Lynch was on course for Tripoli. Next stop was in five hours when he had to surface 500 metres offshore to confirm the coordinates for his final approach on the tunnel mouth. He settled down snug with the lines of the scooter, and felt the water stream over him as the black torpedo sliced menacingly through the sea towards the Libyan coastline.

After three hours, the strain was beginning to tell on his arms and shoulders again as the unrelenting drag of the water tried to pluck him from the scooter's back. The harness straps were beginning to chafe and he shuffled to ease the discomfort. As he squirmed to get more comfortable an immense force slammed into him from the port side. The scooter was thrown into a sickening sideways spin, as if caught by a giant wave rolling them along in its path.

Lynch felt himself thrown around in the harness like a rag in a spin dryer. The straps bit through his wetsuit into his arms and legs and for a moment he feared the release key might spring open under the turbulence and he would be thrown loose into the midst of whatever it was that had engulfed them. A flurry of hard blows pummelled his body and still he spun around in the blackness, unable to see, unable to focus on the digital blur of the panicked readings inside his dive helmet. He became dizzy and nausea threatened to overwhelm him. Suddenly, he realised what had happened. They had been netted by a fishing trawler and were being dragged along with the rest of the catch.

It was perhaps the worst thing that could have happened but the realisation forced Lynch to concentrate. He knew what it was and he had been told how to get out of it. He shut his eyes, tried to ignore the sickening spinning and tumbling and fumbled for the throttle. He found it and his fingers scrabbled desperately for the release button at the end of the grip. He jabbed it hard, the throttled released and he grabbed the handle and twisted it back as far as it would go. He felt the answering surge as the scooter struggled to push forward and free itself from the awful morass. With his left hand he struggled for the rudder but it was like trying to find the loose reins of a rodeo mount. A couple of times it struck his hand, almost breaking his fingers, then jerked away again. He kept trying and the instant he felt it slam into his hand he once more locked his fingers around the pistol-grip handle, ignoring the jabs of pain up his arm. He twisted the throttle back again and pulled the rudder hard to port to try and climb up and out. They were still rolling but he felt something else too.

The controls were answering. The drag was almost unbelievable and Lynch wondered what the breaking strain was on the harness straps and what would happen if he was thrown off the scooter and into the net by himself. He thanked God for the helmet and re-breather pack. If he had been wearing conventional scuba mask and regulator they would have been torn from his face and he would be dead by now.

Gradually, achingly, the scooter pulled around and the spin slowed and then stopped. He was still fighting almost unbearable nausea and had no idea whether he was the right way up or hanging upside down. He could still feel the irresistible pull of the net as it dragged them through the sea inside its great mesh purse but he sensed rather than felt that the serrated blade on the scooter's nose was pointed the right way, against the drag. He felt a sudden shock again as they bit into the furthermost wall of the net and braced himself for another roll. The scooter slowed almost to a dead stop, Lynch jerked desperately back on the throttle willing every ounce of power he had into the scooter's whining motor and as suddenly as it had hit them ... they were free. The knife edge on the nose blades found the net and bit through. The scooter seemed to leap forward through the hole it had made and Lynch felt a great slithering mass of fish rake across his body, then he was through the net and free.

For a long moment all he could do was hang on and let the relief wash over every corner of his body as the scooter glided cleanly through open water. He realised he had better throttle down to save his batteries and then tried to focus on the figures inside his mask. They made no sense. He forced himself to concentrate on the scooter's instrument panel and saw the readings flashing wildly. Lynch singled out the depth gauge and saw they were closer to the surface than he had expected—only 17 metres down. He brought the scooter back up to 10 metres. He looked at the figures inside his helmet but was still so dizzy he couldn't remember the proper bearing. Lynch forced himself to concentrate again and in a minute the figures came back. The net had turned them around almost 180 degrees and they were speeding directly away from the coast of Libya. Lynch brought the machine around and prayed they still had the juice to cover the distance they'd lost. He checked the trim and, though he couldn't see him, Lynch knew he still had Bono on board. He smiled grimly to himself and wondered what the big man had made of their little adventure. One thing Lynch was certain of now. Nothing was going to stop either of them getting to Tripoli.

Lynch looked at the digital clock on the instrument panel. It told him 03.35 hours. He checked the bearings on the scooter against the numerals screened inside his helmet for the millionth time and confirmed they had clocked more than 37,000 metres in five hours. He had added six minutes to his running time to compensate for the time they had lost inside the fishing net. Six minutes was all they had spent trapped in that hellish malestrom and it had felt like six hours at the time. For the past hour Lynch had watched, mesmerised, as the Libyan coastline had grown closer and bigger on the compass dial. He had even been able to make out the waterfront of Tripoli and fancied he had spotted the jetty beside the sewer mouth. Another 10 minutes and he was due to surface to confirm his bearings. Lynch teased the rudder and began a gentle ascent, ears pricked for the tinny jingle of approaching boat engines. He heard nothing but the comforting rattle of his own breathing inside the helmet. He watched the depth gauge and when they reached three metres, throttled down to zero and let the scooter glide smoothly to the surface under its own momentum. A second later his head broke the surface and water streamed from his visor.

He saw nothing. Only the waves and the empty night sky. No city skyline, no harbour lights, no Tripoli. Just ahead of him was Bono's reassuring bulk and, as if to settle any doubts, the big American stirred to indicate he was intact. Lynch frowned and let the scooter drift clockwise a few degrees and the lights of Tripoli gradually slid into view. A little more than a kilometre away. He had lost more distance than he had estimated and his approach angle was off, which was why he had seen nothing when they had surfaced. He was facing east by south-east instead of due south. But he could see the illuminated needle of the minaret on the shoreline now, and then his other markers, the old jetty wall and the clock tower. Lynch had a few more minutes of cruising ahead of him and he was going to be late. But he would be there. He swung the scooter through 360 degrees but saw nothing of the others. Then he took the scooter back down and tracked in on a diagonal path until, after a few more minutes, he surfaced again—exactly where he was supposed to be.

Lynch lined up the markers, did some fast mental arithmetic, then took the scooter back down to 10 metres and steered in on the new heading. He kept the speed around two knots, trying to feel his way in as well as steering by the instruments. After 20 minutes he felt the toes of his boots scrape against the silty harbour bottom. It was shallower than he had been told and he took the scooter up three metres. Even with the aqua-nites it was becoming difficult to see. He pressed his visor almost flat against the instrument panel but saw only the vaguest glimmer of coastline and the accompanying bearings. He was glad of the readings inside his helmet. They told him he was getting close but all they gave him was a blind countdown.

The water was filthy. Trails of grainy sediment formed between his visor and the instrument panel. He scrubbed them away only to have them reappear almost instantly and blot out the figures again. He took the scooter up another three metres and eased the throttle back even more till they were coming in at a snail's pace. He tried desperately to read the compass dial but it was futile. He looked up to try and see something of the sea wall but there was only the foul, thick murk of the cloud of waste which stood permanent guard at the sewer mouth. He tensed up. Any minute he suspected there would be a resounding clang as they crashed head on into the sea wall. He took the scooter up to the two metre mark and struggled vainly to see the figures on the instrument panel again, then the mouth of the tunnel materialised suddenly in front of him as an impenetrable black hole in the greyer mass of the wall. Instinctively he tweaked the throttle and they surged forward and up over the bottom lip of the tunnel. Almost immediately his head and shoulders broke surface and he found himself staring into a great, grey cavern. The water in the tunnel wasn't as high as he had expected but it was running strongly against them and Lynch powered the scooter forward on two knots until he was 20 to 30 metres inside. His eyes had taken a moment to adjust to the ghostly shapes and features defined by the aqua-nites but he thought he saw men moving towards him on a parapet just ahead and to his left.

As they drew closer he discerned the grotesque figures of three space creatures with hunched backs and ugly, swollen heads and he knew they had all made it. He nudged the scooter gently forward until he felt the slimy floor of the tunnel with the toes of his boots but it was too slippery for him to get a hold. He reached down and pulled one of the flukes on the port side and it extended like a long, skeletal claw. Bono struggled up front to keep the scooter steady and two of the three figures on the parapet above reached down to help. Lynch felt along the tunnel wall with his gloved hand until he found what he wanted and jammed the spiked claw into a soft, crumbly crack. It took them a few minutes to do the same with the other three flukes but eventually the scooter was anchored and Lynch could at last switch off the engine.

It was with a sensation of immense relief that he pulled the release key on his harness and felt the straps fall away from his aching shoulders. He couldn't make out the identities of his assistants through the ghostly images of the aqua-nites, but a hand reached down and helped him up to the narrow path on top of the parapet that ran down the side of the tunnel. Two others helped Bono up and then they began the business of retrieving their gear from the scooter cargo holds. By the time they had finished, Lynch was already warming up inside the suit, since they were no longer immersed in the cold sea. He checked his air gauge and saw he still had three hours left. He must have gobbled a lot of air during the encounter with the fishing trawler but he had more than enough to last the hour it would take to negotiate the tunnel to Gaddafi's safe house.

When he was satisfied they had everything, Lynch gave Bono the okay signal and then both sat on the edge of the parapet and kicked the scooter beneath the surface of the foul river until the cargo holds flooded and it sank slowly from view—it was now invisible except for the steel flukes braced immovably in the crevices of the sewer walls. Lynch picked up his gear and walked carefully along the parapet past Bono, who stepped aside for him, and towards the others just ahead.

As arranged, now they had all made landfall safely they would revert to combat teams, with Lynch and Roper leading the penetration of the tunnel. Lynch counted his way past all five men, then turned and gave an exaggerated okay signal. He saw the other fuzzy grey shapes respond and took it to mean they were ready. He began heading deeper into the tunnel and the men followed.

Lynch was impressed by the aqua-nites. A vast leap forward in technology from the nite-sites British chopper pilots had used in the Falklands, they worked even in the confined darkness of a tunnel, concentrating just enough of the minimal light available to enable the wearer to differentiate between various shapes and shades of grey. In the sewage-clogged water there had been too much silt and sediment to allow in any light but in the atmosphere there was always enough. Lynch looked down. He could see his own feet, a lighter grey against the darkness of the stone parapet. To his right there was the undulating flow of the sewer water with its changing swirls and patterns. Lynch looked up at the roof and at the impressive stone arches and became disoriented when he thought he saw a mirrored river over his head. Then he realised it was a river of cockroaches, seething and streaming along the length of the tunnel a metre or so over his head.

He had memorised the route through the tunnel and plodded steadily forward, already feeling the strain of the bags he was carrying. The tunnel angled slightly to the left and carried on for another 60 or 70 metres before splitting into two. Lynch took the tunnel on the left. A few metres further on the parapet ended and he stepped carefully down into the sewage. He wasn't particularly worried about the sewage but the floor of the tunnel was coated in slime and he had to be careful not to fall. The sewage came to mid-thigh level and no longer flowed as quickly as it did near the mouth. The tunnel began to shrink and a couple of times Lynch scraped his helmet against the roof, bringing down a shower of foul algae and cockroaches.

Occasional smaller tunnels reached off to the side like empty arm sockets but Lynch ignored them. Something was beginning to worry him. The tunnel roof had begun a downwards slope. A few steps later it was as he thought. The roof dropped suddenly below the water line. It wasn't on the diagram they had memorised, and their man in Tripoli couldn't know it, but they had come to a dip in the tunnel. There was nothing for it but to duck beneath the water and swim through. First Lynch had to remove his back pack. Part of his SBS training had involved deep penetration dives through nightmarish water-filled caves and fissures under the Yorkshire dales. He knew what to do. He knew Roper, Finn and Tuckey could handle it but if Reece or Bono had any phobias at all, now was the time they would be put to the test.

Lynch turned and gave a deliberate okay signal. He carefully put the waterproof bags down at his feet under the water line, then removed his backpack. There was only half a metre of air hose from his backpack to his helmet and it didn't give him much room to manœuvre when he took the pack off. He laid it carefully on the tunnel floor and his head followed under the water line. Once again even the grey ghosts disappeared and there was utter blackness. The water was moving sluggishly so there wasn't the complication of current to contend with. Pushing his gear and rebreather pack ahead of him Lynch carefully felt his way forward until he found the mouth of a small tunnel. It seemed to be less than a metre across— certainly not wide enough for any of them to crawl through wearing backpacks. They would all have to remove their packs and push them through first. Slowly, carefully, Lynch pushed further and further into the tunnel, bumping his gear ahead of him, feeling the roof of the tunnel with his gloved fingers for the point where it opened out again. He estimated he had crawled six or seven metres and still it hadn't opened. Lynch began to worry. Perhaps the diagrammes had been wrong. Perhaps this smaller, water-filled tunnel went much further.

He knew they still had enough air. It was time that worried him. It would be dawn in another 90 minutes. Lynch crawled on another three metres and his fingers suddenly found the outside lip of the smaller sewer. He pushed his gear ahead of him, pulled himself up and out ... and waited. There was nothing else he could do for his colleagues. He looked around.

He had emerged into a tunnel about the same size as the one on the other side of the barrier and it seemed to lead off in a long, shallow curve but it was hard to see. He wiped the smears of filth from the visor of his aqua-nites and waited. A few minutes late he felt something bump his toe. He reached down and pulled out Roper's pack. A moment later Roper's re-breather scraped into view and he reached down again and lifted it up gently, so as not to stretch the short air hose. Roper's vague grey shape emerged a minute later. Then the two of them waited. Lynch hoped Bono wouldn't be last. Bono was the biggest man and he was inexperienced. The tunnel would be hardest for him. It would be even worse if he came last.

Lynch wasn't sure who came next, it was impossible to tell, but from the size it wasn't Bono. The next man took a desperately long time to emerge. Lynch had made the crawl in about five minutes. Fifteen minutes passed and then Lynch felt that nudge again at the toe of his boot. This time it was Bono. Lynch sighed. Finn and Tuckey had pushed the two novices ahead of them. Lynch could only wonder at the blind courage of the two ex-marines for navigating the tunnel. He wanted to clap them both on the back. Instead, he waited. Tuckey and finally Finn appeared and gave him the okay. They geared up again and plodded on.

The tunnel described a long curl and then widened out. The water level began to drop. Instead of mid-thigh it was only ankle deep. Lynch looked around him carefully as he walked. Finally, he was satisfied. He waited until they had all caught up, then jabbed a finger upwards. The clear outline of a metal ladder could be seen in the wall. It led up to small circular hatch. This was their way out.

He lowered his gear to the tunnel floor beside the ladder, unzipped one of the bags, felt inside and pulled out a small oblong package sealed in waterproof plastic. He tore open the plastic and inside was a rubber sheath. Even through the aqua-nites the men saw the outline of a wicked-looking knife which Lynch pulled from its sheath. Then he climbed up the steel rungs of the ladder. Behind him Roper had pulled a second knife from the bag and was waiting at the bottom.

Lynch braced his elbows against the sides of the manhole wall, ignoring the crackling sensation of squashing cock-roaches against his arms and hands. He pushed gently against the manhole cover, then harder, but it wouldn't move. He inserted the tip of the knife and began working it around the rim, sending a fine rain of dirt and crushed insects cascading below. Then he tried again, but it still wouldn't budge. It took Lynch another 20 minutes of digging and prying at the jammed manhole cover before he sensed the first movement. Clearly it hadn't been used for years and had been sealed harder and harder into the road surface by overhead traffic. He looked at his watch. It was almost six. They had 35 minutes at most before first light. Slowly he pushed the cover upwards and looked out until he saw the lighter night sky. He could almost feel the breeze and smell the fresh air inside his helmet and wetsuit but he knew it was only wishful thinking. He ro-tated the cover gently through 360 degrees until he had sur-veyed the whole street and checked it was still empty. He readied himself then slowly slid the cover away from the man-hole and pulled himself out. He plodded stolidly over to the shadow of a near by building and waited. A moment later Roper sprang out like a cat, as though his backpack weighed nothing. He quickly replaced the cover and crossed to the opposite side of the street. They could see the green gates of Gaddafi's safe house only 40 metres away and they hurried towards it, leaving wet, stinking footprints in the dusty street.

Roper had to pass an open hallway and as he did so a black mongrel dog scuttled out in front of him, bared its fangs and began barking loudly. Lynch was glad it wasn't him. He couldn't move like the other man. With a swift, fluid movement Roper's left hand grabbed the dog by the muzzle, clamping its jaws shut while the right, holding the knife, swung up and sliced it neatly across the throat. The dog squirmed for a second then went limp. Roper quickly carried the dead creature over to the manhole, lifted the cover and threw the body inside. It wasn't the prettiest welcome gift to the others but it was better than the dog be found dead to arouse the concern of its owner.

They reached the gates to the house at the same time and Roper pulled the bell. The caretaker and his wife were used to Gaddafi's men arriving at odd hours. They would have to answer the door. They stepped away from the grimy glass peephole in the wooden gate and waited. Nothing happened. Roper counted a minute then gave the bell a long, impatient ring the way he imagined Gaddafi's thugs would. There was another pause, then Lynch heard the sound of a bolt being pulled. A smaller door opened in the frame of the gate and Lynch saw the suspicious face of an old man appear in the crack. Roper didn't give the caretaker time to react. He kicked the trapdoor with vicious force and it flew back, hitting the old man in the face and knocking him sprawling to the ground. Then he leaped through the narrow portal, followed by Lynch. The caretaker's wife stood a few paces away, transfixed, mouth slack and eyes wide with horror. Lynch heard no scream. The woman was utterly petrified and it wasn't hard to imagine why. With their grotesque, metallic bodies, great misshapen heads, the ungodly rattling sound of their breathing, and both of them covered in slime and reeking of excrement, they must have looked like creatures from hell. Roper squelched forward and seized her around the throat with one dripping hand and she folded like a rag doll.

She could have been dead—her heart stopped through terror. Or she could have lapsed into grateful unconsciousness when Roper squeezed her neck and shut off the oxygen to her brain. He laid her beside her husband who lay groaning on the ground, his nose smashed and bleeding. They ripped strips of material from the old couple's nightclothes, gagged them, then carried them into the house and tied them to the bed in their own quarters. Then Lynch and Roper dumped their backpacks, and leaving Lynch to guard the gate, Roper hurried back toward the manhole and signalled to the others. A few minutes later the rest of them shuffled through the gate, lugging the heavy equipment bags. Once inside the small courtyard Lynch bolted the door and they carried everything onto a covered, terracotta walkway down one wall of the house. Then they could begin to take off their gear. Outside, the sky was growing lighter.

The first sensation to impress Lynch as he removed his helmet and took a deep, hungry breath was the bitter-sweet taste of the air. Then he realised the atmosphere around him was competing with the stench that rose from his own rancid clothing.

'Jesus Christ,' Finn gasped near by, letting his helmet fall to the ground with a heavy thud. 'There were a couple of times there, I thought . . .' His words trailed away.

Tuckey, Reece and Bono were slumped against the wall of the house, staring numbly in front of them. Lynch had noticed Tuckey was limping badly again.

'I can't believe I did what I just did,' Reece said. Lynch smiled. Then Reece looked at Bono.

'What happened to you guys?' he asked. 'We thought we'd lost ya.'

Bono didn't even look up. 'We went fishing,' was all he said.

When they had rested they conducted a detailed search and examination of the house. The green double gates were solidly built and reinforced on the inside with steel bars. There was a peephole in the trapdoor set into the gate but its glass was distorted, and it was virtually useless. The courtyard was big for a townhouse. Lynch counted 28 steps across its width and it was 35 steps long. The courtyard walls were thick, and constructed of brick and clay. There was an empty garage to the right of the gates, its cement-slab floor black with oil and dirt. There was a filthy wooden workbench down the back wall of the garage but, more interestingly, the sloping tile roof was supported by a latticework of thick wooden beams where a man could easily perch and hide. A covered walkway ran down the opposite wall of the house, with doors leading to a couple of bedrooms, each furnished with two or three single beds and cheap furniture. The courtyard was empty except for a couple of narrow, cement-walled flower beds containing a few parched shrubs. One of the beds ran the length of the courtyard, parallel to the walkway, and its walls were just high enough to give protection to someone crouched on the walkway's tiled floor. The other flower bed squatted in front of the house with a wide gap in the middle allowing access to the front door.

Once inside the front door there was a wide hallway, paved with more terracotta. To the right a door led to the kitchen and the caretaker's quarters. To the left was a sitting room, sparsely furnished with three single beds, for more of Gaddafi's bodyguards. A curved staircase with peeling varnish led upstairs to five more rooms—three bedrooms, a bathroom and toilet and a study with a tiny balcony facing the courtyard and the green gates opposite. Two of the bedrooms contained more single beds but the third had only one double bed with a thin mattress on a hard wooden frame. It was slightly better furnished than the other rooms in the house, and cleaner. That it was adjacent to the study confirmed it was Gaddafi's bedroom. In the study was a metal-framed, military-style desk, half a dozen folding metal chairs and a small table with a few pieces of crockery.

On the wall behind the desk was a large blown-up photograph of Colonel Gaddafi wearing a white burnous, leaning down from the back of an army jeep to clasp the outstretched hands of a mob of adoring supporters. It was a flattering picture and showed Gaddafi with his face creased by a broad, handsome smile. The top of the desk was clear and in the drawers they found only a few sheets of notepaper printed with indecipherable Arabic script, pens, pencils and a few copies of Gaddafi's *Green Book*.

The bathroom contained an ancient white tub with a bottom stained with rust and a film of dirt. There was a toilet and washbasin in an adjacent cubicle. The towel rails were bare and heavily corroded. The pattern on the mosaic floor was badly faded and many of its small tiles were coming loose, leaving gaps like bad teeth.

Lynch turned one of the taps in the bath. There was a loud, hollow knocking from the pipes then a torrent of brownish water gushed out. After a minute the water cleared. He tried the other tap and it behaved the same way. Either the boiler hadn't been lit for a while or the heating system was unreliable, but even cold water would do. They took turns standing guard on the gate and the old couple until everybody had washed the grime and filth off themselves and their wetsuits. Their Gortex jumpsuits still stank but they would have to live with it for the rest of the day. They still had a lot of work to do in case Gaddafi took it into his head to arrive that afternoon or evening.

For a while it was Finn's turn to take orders as Lynch and Roper supervised the construction of hiding places. They already knew the outside walls of the house were supposed to be a metre or so thick and they confirmed it with some careful probing. When they were satisfied they went through every room moving furniture, peering into every closet and then carefully began to take out the wooden back panelling. They spent the rest of the morning gouging and scraping man-sized hollows into the walls behind each closet and wherever a wardrobe had stood.

Lynch had taken a walk-in closet on the upstairs landing which had been used for storing towels and bed linen. When he was satisfied with the hollow he had carved into the wall he stepped in, pulled the wood panel back over him and made sure it fitted snugly against the sides of the wall. It was almost big enough. He needed a little more room for his rifle and it would be ready. When he was finished he carried the rubble and brick downstairs and, like the others, dug it into the flower beds until it was all gone. The next step was to punch a tiny slit into the wood panelling at eye level so he would be able to see out but no-one would be able to see in. By noon, they were all ready. Lynch had his hiding place on the upstairs landing. Tuckey had a hole behind a wardrobe in one of the bedrooms and Finn had a position behind the closet in Gaddafi's bedroom.

At ground level Roper had dug a temporary grave for himself at the end of the flower bed closest to the main gates. Reece had a hole in one of the downstairs bedrooms. Because of his size, they put Bono in the roof of the garage. He was too big to secrete into the woodwork but he could easily climb onto the bench in the garage and swing up into the roof where the big beams could take his weight. When they were all in position and ready to spring their ambush, Gaddafi and his guards wouldn't know what hit them. Men would literally be coming out of the walls and woodwork at them.

By noon there was still no sign of Mouad Bouraq, the man who was supposed to contact them once they had penetrated the safe house. Roper watched the gate while Finn, Reece and Bono began laying explosive charges around the house. One charge was set into the brickwork above the gates. Another was buried in the ground below them. The gear they wouldn't need again, they buried with another explosive charge in a corner of the courtyard. While the three of them were methodically mining the house and its grounds Lynch went into the caretaker's quarters to spell Tuckey who had been standing guard, resting his injured leg.

Both the old people had revived and their eyes watched Lynch carefully as he walked over to the bed. He looked into their faces, then slowly and melodramatically drew a finger across his throat to make sure they understood. Then he reached down and removed their gags. The old woman was still terrified, though she knew their house had no longer been invaded by demons. Her husband was different. He was afraid but there was hate in his eyes too and when Lynch took the gag away the old man swore at him and began raising his voice. Lynch jammed the gag back into the caretaker's mouth and tied it again. The old woman whimpered and cringed away from him but said nothing.

Lynch turned to look at Tuckey.

'How's the leg?'

'Aching.'

'Need anything?'

They had brought morphine but they all knew its unfortunate side effects, and Tuckey shook his head. They looked around as Finn appeared in the door, sweating, face and hands grimy from helping Reece and Bono with the explosives. He dusted his hands and looked at Lynch.

'We've got a problem,' he said.

Lynch followed him out into the hallway.

'We can't go back through the sewer,' he said. 'We'd never make it through that narrow part in 40 minutes. Not all of us anyway.'

'I know,' Lynch said.

'So we better figure out an alternative escape route.'

'Good idea,' said Lynch. 'When you figure one out, let me know.'

Finn smiled but said nothing. Their thoughts were interrupted by the sudden, loud jangling of the bell in the caretaker's quarters. They both reached for their G11s lying in a pile of open gear bags in a corner of the hall and looked outside. Reece and Bono had disappeared from view. Roper was squinting through the peephole. It was still impossible for him to see anything and he turned and shrugged at them. The bell rang again and they hurried over to join Roper. When they were in position on both sides of the trapdoor he quietly put his rifle down then soundlessly slid back the bolt on the door. He looked up at Lynch and Lynch nodded. In a blur of movement he flung the trapdoor open, Lynch caught it and held it so that it made no noise, Roper reached out, grabbed a startled Mouad Bouraq and yanked him off his feet and into the courtyard. Lynch let the trapdoor quietly fall shut and bolted it. The whole manœuvre had taken perhaps a second. One moment Bouraq had been waiting in front of the gate, the next he had seemingly melted through it and out of sight of anyone in the street.

Bouraq caught his breath and looked at the three of them.

'Nobody saw me,' he said in slightly-accented English. He looked younger than his photograph and they realised he was no more than a kid. If he lived in America he would still be in college instead of helping run Gaddafi's oilfields. He wore cheap sneakers, jeans and a drab black suit jacket over a white shirt. It was almost a uniform among less affluent Arab males and enabled him to blend into the crowd.

'I got the message last night you'd left,' he said. 'But I couldn't get away from work. I have to work at the refinery every day.'

Lynch nodded and they took Bouraq into the house, leaving

Roper at the gate. Bono and Reece reappeared in the courtyard and went back about their dangerous business. They led him into the caretaker's bedroom and Lynch pointed to the elderly couple on the bed.

'The old lady is terrified but the old man isn't too impressed,' Lynch said. 'I'm going to try taking his gag off again. Tell them we won't hurt them if they do what they're told. If they refuse tell them we'll kill them now.'

Lynch removed the old man's gag while Bouraq translated. When he had finished the woman said nothing but the old man spat out a stream of words.

Bouraq looked back at Lynch. 'He says I'm a traitor to the revolution and you're all American dog shit.'

'I thought it was something like that,' Lynch smiled. He replaced the gag then roughly pulled the old man off the bed, dragged him into the kitchen next door and shoved him down into a corner. 'Keep an eye on him,' he ordered Tuckey then returned to the couple's bedroom and living quarters when Finn and Bouraq waited with the woman.

'Tell her if she doesn't do what she's told we'll kill him now,' Lynch said.

Bouraq translated and the woman answered in a trembling, terrified voice.

'She says she'll do what we want,' Bouraq said.

'Good,' said Lynch. He stepped back into the kitchen where Tuckey stood over the old man. 'Put him back on the bed and give him a shot of morphine,' he ordered Tuckey. The old woman watched Tuckey with revulsion as he filled the needle and injected her husband. Gradually the hate seeped out of the caretaker's eyes and he drifted into a drugged sleep. 'Don't worry,' Tuckey grinned at the old woman. 'He'll get to like it.'

'We'll keep him sedated in here,' Lynch told the others. 'When Gaddafi's guards turn up she can tell them he's sick.'

Then he turned to Bouraq. 'It's up to you to explain the rest to her. Tell her all she has to do is go with you when you let the guards in, and bow and scrape to them or do whatever it is she does. Everything you say, she's to nod and agree. That's all. Tell her if she does that we'll let her and her old man live. Tell her if she fucks it up he gets his throat cut.' He looked down at the old woman to make sure she understood his tone. Lynch didn't enjoy frightening old people but unless he secured their cooperation by whatever means the mission would fail. Gaddafi would go on to kill many more innocent people.

'When you've finished, give her some food,' he added. 'Spend some time with her. Get her to trust you, and stay scared of the rest of us.'

Lynch checked his watch and looked at Finn. It was almost three in the afternoon. They hadn't slept or eaten since leaving the *Endeavor*, a lifetime ago.

'Let's see what they've got to eat here,' he said. 'Then we'd better take turns getting some sleep. Gaddafi could get here tonight.'

But Gaddafi didn't arrive that night. So they used the cover of dark to allow Reece and Bono to lay more explosives where it would do the enemy the most harm and themselves the most good when it came to getting out. The two ex-marines crept through the gate after midnight, hurried over to the manhole and disappeared back into the sewer. They spent the next few hours methodically laying the rest of their charges in the tunnel which ran the length of the street. When they had done what they came to do, and if they could get clear of the street somehow, they could make sure nobody would be able to follow them. Their only problem then would be getting the one and a half kilometres through the streets of Tripoli and its hostile crowds to the end of that jetty, and the rendezvous with their rescue chopper.

'We'll just have to take a taxi,' Lynch had decided with Finn as they sprawled on the stairs, working through their options. He picked up his G11 and gave it an affectionate pat. 'I can't see anyone refusing to give us a ride, can you?'

Every 24 hours saw the same routine. Four men would keep watch while two slept in six-hour shifts. Those who kept watch waited with bulletproof wetsuits on and the zippers open to keep them from overheating.

Their helmets had been stripped of the cumbersome aquanites, the faceplates were removed and kept near by, with their rifles and ammunition belts, to double as combat helmets. The backpacks, re-breathers, gear bags and everything else they no longer needed had been buried too and would be destroyed by explosives. Finn never moved without the transmitter for the rescue signal tucked in his belt and Bono kept his own transmitters handy. While the transmitters were tuned to radically different frequencies Bono had warned that if Finn sent his signal first there was a chance it might trigger all the explosives. Under the changed circumstances governing their escape, they all realized, it was a chance they had to take.

The days passed and they supplemented their protein rations with meals prepared by Bouraq from the flour, oil and few other provisions they found in the kitchen. The caretaker was aroused from his morphine-induced coma once each afternoon to take a bowl of homous with some bread and tea. The woman grew more and more wretched with the passing of the days and began to look gravely ill though she dared not complain. The strain began to tell on them too and they wondered whether Gaddafi would indeed come, or instead confound them all by staying away till they were discovered, saving his life through his own erratic behaviour. There was a radio in the house and they listened to it for reports of Gaddafi's movements. The special people's congress he was due to address in Tripoli had been running for 10 days and still Gaddafi hadn't put in an appearance. He had been in Tripoli, they knew, but the announcers only reported his latest statement or address without giving details of his movements. Bouraq threw up his hands after each broadcast he translated for them. It was typical Gaddafi, he said. The colonel came and went, issued a statement, gave a press conference and disappeared. One day he was travelling outside the capital, somewhere in the desert, the next he was at Benghazi and the next he was back in Tripoli. No-one ever knew where he was going, only where he had been. The days stretched into weeks. Bouraq grew increasingly nervous—he had only asked his supervisor at the refinery for two weeks leave to visit his family. Lynch wondered how Halloran was taking the strain of uncertainty. They could be dead for all he knew—though he could have expected to have heard something through Libya's propaganda broadcasts if they had been discovered.

Every day that passed increased the danger of discovery. Still, no-one seemed to notice or care that the caretaker and his wife hadn't been seen for a couple of weeks. No-one called, no tradesmen or random visitors. They listened to the sounds of Tripoli passing them by in the street outside, and four times a day they heard the raucous cries of the mullahs calling the faithful to prayer. They began to run out of food and a couple of the men got stomach cramps. Reece complained bitterly when he lost one of his fake Russian fillings. Much longer and they would have to risk sending Bouraq out to find some food.

As they should have known, Gaddafi came when they least expected it.

The bell rang soon after dawn on the 17th day. Previously, they knew, Gaddafi had always arrived either late in the day or after dark. This time he had elected to drive into Tripoli in the early hours, in convoy, and make the house his base for the day. A car with three of his highly-trained East German bodyguards arrived first to check the safe house while Gaddafi's convoy followed half an hour behind. The ringing of the bell was accompanied by a heavy knocking on the gate and the sound of a voice shouting harshly in Arabic. Finn and Tuckey were on the gate, Lynch and Roper were inside with Bouraq, and Reece and Bono were sleeping in one of the rooms downstairs. Finn woke the two sleeping men and they all hurried to their hiding places. Lynch and Roper woke Bouraq and half-pulled, half-carried the old woman out into the courtyard. The voice outside was growing impatient. Lynch pushed Bouraq and the woman towards the gate, then followed Roper back into the house. He looked into the caretaker's quarters and saw the old man hadn't moved, then he padded upstairs on his rubber-soled dive boots and waited just inside the door to the balcony where he could watch the action at the gate. He looked at his watch. The date said 24 December—Christmas Eve.

Sensibly, Bouraq opened the gate as quickly as he could while the old woman hung back behind him. The moment he slid back the bolt, the trapdoor was pushed roughly open and three men stepped inside, all with weapons drawn, one of them with a walkie-talkie raised in his left hand. They were all dressed similarly in leather-collared jackets with casual pants and sweaters. The man with the walkie-talkie rapped out a few words in Arabic to Bouraq and Bouraq did his best to answer while the other two men strode onto the walkway and began checking the rooms. Lynch saw the woman had still not said anything but stood a few steps behind Barouq and shivered. The man in charge said something to her and she nodded in the direction of the house and said something. He seemed satisfied and lowered the walkie-talkie. He did not seem surprised by the woman's fright. Apparently Gaddafi's guards had that effect on ordinary Libyans.

The two other men continued their noisy search, working their way into the main house and through the ground floor. Lynch listened to them as their voices and clatter echoed up the stairs, then slipped silently into the closet on the landing, leaving the door ajar. He turned and flattened himself into the hollow, his rifle held flat against him in one hand, the other pulling the wooden panelling back flush against the wall. The tiniest sliver of daylight fell across his eye and he squinted through the split he had made in the wood, held his breath and waited.

The two gunmen stamped up the stairs. One of them threw the door to the closet wide open and looked directly at Lynch. He was so close Lynch could smell his sweat. The guard saw only an empty closet and hurried away, pushing more doors open, looking inside cupboards and wardrobes, under beds. To Lynch's relief it was clear they weren't suspicious and were conducting the most basic search. A moment later he heard them tramp downstairs again and then he heard their voices in the courtyard. They spoke German to each other. Lynch carefully pushed the panel aside, stepped out and hurried across the study back to the balcony doorway.

The three guards were standing at the gates. Bouraq was watching near by with the old woman. The guard put the walkie-talkie to his mouth, rattled off a few quick commands in German again then turned to Bouraq, yelled at him and gestured towards the gate. It seemed they had bought the lie but didn't want him hanging around when Gaddafi arrived. Bouraq said something back and the man nodded, then turned away and stepped through the gate back into the street. He was followed by the other two and they left the trapdoor open so Lynch could just see their backs. Bouraq hurried back into the house, bringing the old woman with him, and Lynch padded quietly back downstairs.

'They believed it,' the young Libyan said excitedly. 'Gaddafi's coming.'

Lynch nodded and looked past him through the opening in the gate. Convinced the house was safe, they had taken up guard positions outside.

'They told me to get out,' Bouraq added. 'They don't want me here when Gaddafi arrives. I told them I had to collect my things.'

Lynch pushed the two of them through the kitchen and into the caretaker's quarters.

'Go to the jetty now,' Lynch ordered Bouraq. 'You'll know soon whether we made it or not.'

Bouraq grabbed his jacket, looked at the old woman, patted her on the shoulder and said something reassuring. She looked back at him miserably. Bouraq scurried out of the room and across the courtyard. The old woman climbed back onto the bed and lay down beside her unconscious husband, holding him as close as she could. Lynch looked down at the pathetic old couple, then dragged them both off the bed. The woman screamed faintly but Lynch clamped a hand over her mouth and shoved her under the bed. Next he rolled the heavy body of her husband and then jammed them both in with the blankets and pillows off the bed.

Lynch didn't know if she appreciated it but he was probably saving their lives. He turned and hurried back upstairs.

Outside, Bouraq walked past the three guards, gave them his most obsequious smile and hurried off down the street past the crowds who had already gathered to watch the three men with the Jeep outside the house Gaddafi sometimes visited. He had just reached the corner of the street and turned into one of the wide avenues leading to the sea when he heard the rumble of many powerful car engines. A second later an armoured car came into view, followed by Jeeps with mounted M60s, laden with men, then Gaddafi's armour-plated Mercedes-Benz followed by a truck filled with guards, then more Jeeps and at the end of the convoy, a second armoured car.

Bouraq watched it all roar past, overwhelmed by the number of men and the amount of firepower necessary to protect Gaddafi. Then he thought of the six men waiting in the house and set off in the direction of the sea front again, praying.

As soon as the convoy rumbled into the view of the three men guarding Gaddafi's safe house, one of them climbed into the leading Jeep and pulled away, leaving the door clear. The other two stepped back, flanking both sides of the door, and held their submachine-guns with the barrels pointed up. The first armoured car passed them with a roar and a swirl of dust, then three Jeeps and finally Gaddafi's car. The Mercedes jolted to a halt right in front of the gates and waited while men poured out of the accompanying Jeeps to provide an armed screen around the car. Along the length of the street Gaddafi's Revolutionary Guards pushed people away as they struggled for a glimpse of the colonel.

Upstairs in the safe house, Lynch waited, peering around the doorway looking out over the small balcony.

He heard the choir of car engines and the raucous clamour of Gaddafi's East German bodyguards and the Revolutionary Guards as they cleared the street of protesting people. The man with the walkie-talkie and his friend stepped back through the gate followed by half a dozen similarly dressed men, all wielding SIG submachine-guns. They formed a ragged double line and a moment later the nearest door of the Mercedes swung open and the familiar, arrogant figure of Gaddafi strode into view. He was wearing a grey burnous over his uniform with its cowl pulled up around his face so only his eyes and thick black hair were visible as he passed between the rows of armed guards. As soon as he was inside more guards poured in after him and formed a protective phalanx around him while he marched into the house. Lynch crossed the landing, slipped on his helmet and was back in his hiding place in an instant.

Gaddafi turned neither to the right nor left when he entered the house but stamped straight upstairs. Lynch listened to the babble of the guards as they poured up the stairs with their leader and wondered why they had to make so much noise. The door to the closet was open and through his prism of light Lynch saw a brief flash of grey then a rush of jostling, shoving bodies as Gaddafi walked into the study. Lynch waited. He wanted things to settle down before he made his move but that decision was taken out of his hands when he heard a burst of agitated yelling from downstairs. They must have found the caretaker and his wife. There was a stampede of footsteps outside the closet and Lynch saw another rush of bodies heading back towards the stairs.

He took a deep breath and moved. The men running across the landing towards the stairs had no warning. One moment the closet at the top of the stairs was bare and empty, the next it had erupted in a cascade of splinters and something from the world of science fiction materialised, covered from head to toe in blue-black skin, wearing a black space helmet and holding a space gun. Then the gun blazed and every man on the landing was cut to pieces.

The house exploded into uproar. In the study, Gaddafi and a handful of guards rushed to barricade the door. Two men preparing their leader's bedroom scrambled for their guns but before they could reach the landing the closet wall beside them erupted with a volley of automatic fire. Finn stepped out and saw both men had died with expressions of utter amazement frozen on their faces. In the next bedroom, Tuckey shoved the concealing wardrobe to the floor with an almighty crash and joined Lynch and Finn on the landing.

Lynch nodded towards the study. 'He's in there,' he said. Then he looked at Tuckey: 'Cover the stairs.' When they were in place he looked into Finn's eyes. 'Ready?' he asked.

'Ready.'

The two of them raised their automatic rifles, hosed the study door with bullets and blew it away in a shower of wooden shrapnel. The man standing on the other side screamed and went down, his body pitted with splinters and metal. Inside, Gaddafi had rushed to the balcony and was screaming at his men below but the courtyard was filled with gunfire and panicking, dying men and no-one heard. The two guards still alive threw themselves to the floor and poured everything they had through the open door. Lynch and Finn waited at one side as the bullets smacked harmlessly into the walls and ceiling beyond. When the guards' magazines ran out Lynch swung his G11 around and hosed the room. He stopped to allow Finn past and then followed him in.

One of the guards had been hit across the head and shoulders, the other was squirming back across the floor, legs bleeding, sobbing and struggling to get another clip into his gun. Gaddafi stood in the doorway to the balcony, watching in impotent horror. Finn fired a burst into the wriggling, weeping man on the floor then raised his gun to Gaddafi. Lynch came around from behind him and they both levelled their guns and fired at the same time. The twin fusilade scissored across Gaddafi's body at waist height, lifted him off his feet and dumped him in a bloody heap in a corner of the balcony. And still Lynch and Finn kept firing. They fired until both rifles clicked empty and Gaddafi's corpse looked like a pile of bloody rags. Then Finn looked at Lynch and pulled the rescue transmitter from his belt.

Lynch crossed the room and pulled at the lifeless corpse. 'Don't send that signal,' he yelled over his shoulder to Finn.

'Too late,' Finn said and threw the transmitter to the floor with a heavy thud. 'I've sent it. Now let's get out of here.'

Lynch whirled round and looked at him in disbelief.

'This isn't Gaddafi,' he said and lifted the man's bloodied head up so Finn could see it. 'This is a look-alike . . . a decoy.'

Finn groaned and sank to his knees, oblivious to the battle still going on downstairs and all around, letting his rifle fall. Beside him on the floor, the transmitter pulsed out its unstoppable signal and Finn looked wretchedly across at Lynch.

The realisation of what was happening hit Lynch like a hammer blow. He stood up and looked into the courtyard. The trapdoor in the gate was still open but the woodwork all around it was splintered with bullets. Bodies lay in a heap inside the gate and he could hear heavy firing from the men below. Roper and Reece were behind the cement wall of the flower beds along the walkway. Bono was in the doorway of the garage. They had the courtyard controlled by crossfire. Those of Gaddafi's guards still in the house were trapped downstairs. Nobody could get out. But by the bodies and volume of fire pouring through the trapdoor in the gate, the guards outside still wanted desperately to get in.

Lynch put his head over the rim of the balcony, cupped his hands to his mouth and yelled with all the power he could muster.

'Bono,' he roared. 'Blow the gate.' A volley of shots smacked into the balcony, spraying him with chips and dust. He ducked then tried again. 'Blow the . . .' His words were only half out when the gate vanished in a fountain of flame and smoke and the blast almost burst his ear drums. He looked out and pieces of bodies were still tumbling through the air. The dust and smoke swirled away, leaving a huge crater, half-filled with debris, and where the Merc and some of Gaddafi's jeeps had been there was only burning, blackened metal and more bodies.

Tuckey burst into the room behind them and looked around, taking in the bodies, Finn still on his knees and the winking red light of the transmitter on the floor.

'Did we get him?' he yelled at Lynch.

Lynch shook his head. 'This is a decoy,' he said, nodding at the bloodied corpse in the corner of the balcony. 'Gaddafi's still somewhere downstairs. Probably dressed as one of his own guards.'

Finn's head snapped up.

'You and Tuckey get down those stairs,' Lynch yelled at him. 'Flush the bastards out into the courtyard. I'll get him from up here.'

Finn grabbed his rifle, jumped up and followed Tuckey back out onto the landing. Tuckey leaned over the stair rail and fired a steady spray into the hallway below while Finn crept down the stairs and began aiming concentrated bursts into the rooms on the ground floor. There was a flurry of panicked shouts as the men downstairs realised what was happening. Upstairs on the balcony, Lynch picked his moment then looked over the rim again. The courtyard was still empty except for bodies but the guards outside were re-forming and the fire on Reece, Bono and Roper was heavy again. Then Lynch heard a sound he recognised. He looked out at the street. One of the armoured cars was grinding its way past the wreckage, over the jumbled piles of rubble and fragmented bodies and towards the hole in the wall where the gates had been.

Lynch ran across to the landing. 'Hurry up,' he yelled at Tuckey and Finn. 'We're running out of time.'

Standing near the corner of the stairs Finn looked up at him and nodded. 'See ya,' he said. Then he walked deliberately down the rest of the stairs, away from Tuckey's cover, firing as he went. Tuckey watched only for a second then followed. Finn made it into the middle of the hallway downstairs and fired a steady stream of bullets into the gang of

265

men barricaded into the sitting room. Tuckey was half way down the stairs when he saw Finn hit from behind.

Some of Gaddafi's bodyguards had taken cover in the caretaker's quarters and a hail of bullets poured through the door, striking Finn in the back and throwing him into the wall. Tuckey picked up where Finn had left off, standing at the foot of the stairs, swinging from side to side, firing first into one room and then the other. It worked. Tuckey heard the sound of breaking glass as the guards heaved furniture through the downstairs windows and tried to make a break across the open courtyard. Tuckey chanced a quick look at Finn and saw there was no hope for him. There were no wounds, no blood. As Finn had promised, the suits wouldn't let bullets through. But their impact had pulped his body underneath. Finn's helmet slid slowly off his head and rolled onto the floor and Tuckey saw the thick, dark stream of blood on his chin.

Upstairs, Lynch risked another look over the balcony. He saw the first desperate men try to cross the courtyard for the street but they were all cut down by the crossfire from Roper, Reece and Bono. The armoured car had climbed the pile of rubble in the street and Lynch watched as it bounced heavily forward into the courtyard. There was something familiar about it. Then he remembered their briefing sessions. It was British. An old Ferret scout car. Probably one of a consignment shipped to Libya when the British government had still patronised Gaddafi as a potential ally, 20 years earlier. The armoured car swung around so that its machine-gun was brought to bear on Reece and Roper and began firing. A blizzard of shattered masonry, shrapnel and bullets swept the cement walls of the garden barricade sheltering Reece and Roper. At that range there was nothing they could do except lie flat. At the same time the turret on the scout car began to rotate so that it could bring its light cannon to bear on the garage where Bono hid, less than a dozen steps away. Lynch stood up, ignoring the bullets spattering around him from the guns of the men in the street, and fired a string of bursts at the armoured car, trying to get a shot into one of its eye slits.

The cannon fired and a corner of the garage disappeared, throwing Bono to the floor in a shower of rubble and abruptly silencing him. The car's turret began to rotate again, bringing the cannon around to the man on the balcony. Lynch tore his eyes away as another group of men burst from the ground floor and made a dash for the street. There were six and Lynch stared hard at them but held his fire. With Bono silenced, Reece and Roper pinned down under the barrage of machine-gun fire from the scout car, the men had a clear run and made it safely into the street and the protection of their comrades.

There was a sudden loud crack as the scout car fired again and Lynch threw himself to the floor of the balcony as a torrent of clay and shattered brick cascaded down on him from the hole gouged in the wall of the house over his head. There was a sudden crescendo of firing and yelling from below and Lynch pulled himself back up and looked over the balcony. A large group of a dozen men or more had burst from the house and were running for the street. They stuck together in a clumsy, shambling mob, yelling and firing wildly as they went. In the middle of them, Lynch saw the man he wanted. Wearing a brown leather jacket, his head bare, was the unmistakeable profile of Colonel Muammar Gaddafi.

Gaddafi was stumbling blindly in the midst of his bodyguards as they struggled to rush him from the scene of the ambush under the protective fire of the scout car.

Lynch ignored the bullets spattering around him and the muzzle of the scout car's cannon still pointed his way, climbed onto the stone parapet of the balcony and jumped. As he jumped he fired and his bullets scythed through the men on Gaddafi's left flank. Several fell and the others staggered, stalling the momentum of the rush. Lynch hit the ground and rolled. The scout car revved its engine and tried to turn to bring its machine-gun to bear on Lynch. It was just the break Roper needed. He sprinted out from behind the fragmented cement walls of the flower beds, leaped up onto the scout car, wrenched open its turret lid and fired two rapid bursts at the men inside.

A storm of bullets lashed the gun turret but it was too late. Roper had leaped down and, huddled behind the immobilised scout car, began picking off the men around Gaddafi. Lynch lay on the ground, using the corpse of one of Gaddafi's men for cover, and fired at Gaddafi's stricken phalanx. Tuckey emerged from the house behind him, firing, and Reece poured in his own fire from the covered walkway.

The human shield around Gaddafi melted like snow under the withering hot rain of gunfire. Even the men on the street outside realised there was no longer anything they could do. Slowly the firing faded away as the last man standing next to Gaddafi crumpled. Gaddafi stood, bent and trembling, surrounded by a mound of bodies. It was an apocalyptic image. Everything seemed to come to a halt and an eerie silence settled in the courtyard. After the roar of battle even the din of the city outside seemed no more than distant murmur.

Everyone there knew.

Gaddafi was alone in a sea of blood facing his executioners.

Roper was the first to move. He walked slowly and deliberately up to the colonel, his gun held in one hand, the barrel pointed at Gaddafi's face. Gaddafi straightened and watched him come. His clothes were streaked with blood and there was the blood of other men streaked with dirt on the side of his face, and in his hair.

Roper stepped over the piled bodies until he was only a couple of feet away from Gaddafi. Then he slowly lowered his rifle and poked the barrel into Gaddafi's chest. He pushed, gently almost, and Gaddafi cringed. It was as if Roper had to

268

make sure Gaddafi was real, that they finally had him. Roper looked into Gaddafi's eyes and was enthralled by the fear and dread he saw there. It was as though he couldn't let the moment end. Then Gaddafi swung up his right hand and emptied the magazine of an automatic pistol into his tormentor at point-blank range.

Roper reeled back and sat down in the dust, an expression of mild disbelief on his face. Then he toppled sideways and died.

Lynch hardly heard the scream that came out of his own mouth as he squeezed the trigger and held it. His first bullets sliced across Gaddafi's right arm, almost severing it at the shoulder and spinning him around. Gaddafi tried to raise his good arm as though to deflect the bullets. Lynch kept firing. Behind him Tuckey emptied his rifle at the jerking, twitching figure still upright amongst the bodies. Reece fired and they saw a fine cloud of red spray erupt from Gaddafi's head. Then he sank into the corpses heaped around him and even though the bullets continued to rip through his body he didn't move again.

When Gaddafi died Lynch seemed to come out of a trance. He looked at his watch. Almost 15 minutes had passed since Finn had transmitted the rescue signal. They had less than half an hour to get to the jetty if they were going to make the chopper. Tuckey hit the ground beside him as the enraged Revolutionary Guards in the street poured a furious fire into the courtyard.

'We've got to get Bono's transmitter and blow the street,' Lynch said. Tuckey nodded, pulled a fresh clip from his belt and jammed it into the G11. Lynch yelled to Reece for covering fire and began worming his way around the bodies piled on the ground.

269

A whole corner of the garage had collapsed, burying the hiding place where Bono had been. Lynch scrambled the last few metres on his hands and knees and threw himself over the pile of rubble and into the empty garage. When he looked around he saw one of Bono's legs jutting from the mound of shattered masonry. He began pulling away the lumps of stone and shards of broken timber, then grabbed both Bono's ankles and pulled.

He didn't budge. Lynch pulled again, harder, and Bono groaned. Lynch scrabbled at the debris until he had cleared Bono's head and shoulders. A jagged piece of timber had broken away from one of the collapsed roof beams and was jammed against Bono's helmet. The helmet was badly dented but it hadn't split so miraculously Bono was still alive. Lynch pulled him up and propped him against the wall. He pulled the helmet off and rubbed away the caked dust which had clogged his eyes, nose and mouth. The big man was breathing wheezily and Lynch slapped him roughly, trying to revive him, but he didn't respond. Lynch left him and began raking through the rubble with his fingers for Bono's transmitters. The minutes ticked by but he couldn't find them.

Bono coughed behind him. 'They're in here,' the American said, choking on the dust coating his throat, and he pulled down the zipper on his wetsuit to reveal two transmitters taped to the fleshy folds of his belly.

'Which one for the street?' Lynch asked.

Bono was still groggy but he reached down and ripped one of the transmitters from his gut.

'Do it,' Lynch said.

'Did we get Gaddafi?'

'Yes.'

'We still got time to make the chopper?'

'We're not going anywhere if we don't clear that street,' Lynch snapped.

Bono twisted a small knob on the transmitter then thumbed the button and held it down. An instant later there was a huge, shuddering explosion from the street followed by a chorus of agonised screams and shouts. The floor of the garage shivered and they looked up at the roof as the remaining beams creaked and squealed and a shower of dust drifted down. There followed a series of powerful explosions rippling the length of the street and both men threw themselves to the floor, covering their heads.

The walls of the garage groaned and they felt the tremors from the explosions vibrate up through the floor and through their bodies like pins and needles. Then a sudden lull fell over the street. There was no more shooting, no more yelling. Not even any more screams from the wounded. Lynch stood up and looked at Bono as he pulled himself back against the wall.

'Can you walk?'

Bono looked up and read Lynch's eyes.

'What ... you think I'm gonna be noble and stay here to cover your getaway?' he growled. 'Get fucked.' And he stumbled shakily to his feet.

Reece and Tuckey appeared suddenly outside. Tuckey looked grey. 'We're not going to make it,' he said. Lynch stepped over the debris, pushed him aside and walked across to the gaping hole where the gates had been. When he looked outside it was as if a giant plough had gutted the entire street. An elongated plume of smoke and dust hung in the air, a signature for the long ragged trench that reached from one end of the street to the other. The explosions had collapsed the street in on the sewer tunnel, dragging in men, guns, Jeeps and trucks as devastatingly as any earthquake. There were bodies everywhere ... and pieces of bodies ... but no people. This part of Tripoli had been turned into a war zone and its population had fled.

Right at the northern end of the street Lynch saw one vehicle still standing—the other scout car. The last armoured car in Gaddafi's convoy had been used to form a road-block at the corner and hadn't been caught by any of the explosions. Its hatch was open and there was no sign of its crew. Either they had joined the fight and been killed by Reece and Bono's demolition work or they had fled with the rest in its immediate aftermath.

Lynch looked back at the three dazed and bloodied men. He glanced at his watch. They had 12 minutes. 'Let's go,' he yelled and began a fast, steady lope down the side of the street, close to the buildings where the ground was still level.

Tuckey limped after him, followed by Reece and Bono. The latter was still shaky. He'd lost his helmet and his rifle and his wetsuit flapped open but he kept one hand clasped over the remaining transmitter still taped to his flabby white gut. Reece trotted protectively behind him, rifle held ready, eyes wary.

Lynch reached the scout car, vaulted up and dropped through the hatch. He had never seen the inside of a Ferret before but he suspected the controls were similar to many of the earlier and very basic British armoured cars. He found the ignition, gave it a turn and it coughed, hesitated then roared into life. Lynch fumbled with the controls, aware the seconds were ticking by. When he was satisfied he climbed back up to help the others. The inside of the scout car was cramped. There was barely enough room for three men, one of whom would have been standing in the hatch. With one of those men of Bono's size and build it was hopeless to try to squeeze in four. Lynch pulled Tuckey roughly into the car and pushed him into the gunner's seat. Tuckey winced but said nothing.

'Bono, you'll have to crouch down in the hatchway as best you can,' Lynch yelled. 'Reece, you're going to have to ride on the outside.' Reece clambered up, shouldered the G11 and took a firm hold on two sweat-polished hand grips. When he hunkered down he found himself almost eye-level with Bono.

'Jesus Christ,' Bono muttered.

Lynch gunned the Ferret's engine, pulled hard on the stick and aimed for the nearest main street. Because the Ferret is one of the lightest and simplest armoured vehicles ever made for the British army, it has conventional four-wheel drive on a reinforced chassis and steers like a small truck. But this car was old and Lynch found there was a lot of play in the controls. As he turned the corner into the first main street he clipped the corner of a house and sent stonework flying like shrapnel. Reece swore and hung on outside.

They found themselves in a broad, tree-lined street, deserted except for a scattering of abandoned cars, trucks and buses. Lynch squinted through the driver's window slit and noticed the street was spattered with dirt and lumps of shattered brickwork from Bono's handiwork.

He leaned on the accelerator and sped down the centre of the avenue, trying to thread a course between the abandoned vehicles. As the hijacked scout car thundered down the broad avenue, with its lone rider clinging to the gun turret, they could see crowds of people huddled in the alleyways and the doors and windows of the few shops and small cafés, hiding and watching with disbelieving eyes. Lynch found himself committed to the dead-end of a rapidly approaching T-junction. Two narrower streets led off at right angles but he didn't know where. He made his choice and held his foot firm on the pedal. Tuckey stared through his window slit, eyed Lynch suspiciously and thanked God he wasn't Reece. Lynch had his eyes set on the building dead ahead. It looked like some kind of restaurant and through the tall, flimsily-curtained windows Lynch thought he could

273

make out the glimmer of blue sea on the far side. He yelled at everybody to hang on.

The armoured car was doing more than 50 kph when it bounced up onto the footpath and smashed through the plate-glass walls of the restaurant. They ploughed through the tables and chairs inside, sending shards of broken glass and jagged wooden splinters hissing through the air like javelins. The car erupted through the windows of the opposite wall in a cascade of broken glass, metal and crockery, and hurtled back onto the road on the other side with a roar from its engine like some kind of armoured beast. The Ferret fishtailed wildly, and Lynch almost lost control. Outside on the turret Reece could feel blood streaming from his clenched fists and his back felt as though it had been beaten in half a dozen places with a baseball bat, but he was alive and still hanging on. For the thousandth time that morning he thanked NASA and space technology for coming up with a suit that was meteorite-proof, glassproof and bulletproof. Reece forced himself to open his eyes and despite the tears from the rushing wind he found himself squinting into the sunlit waters of the Mediterranean less than a hundred metres away. He saw something else too—crowds of people with police and soldiers frantically pushing them back, while other troops hurried into firing positions. But Lynch had seen them. He squeezed the trigger on the heavy-calibre machine-gun and watched a long, wicked burst skim down the road in a shower of sparks and flying metal.

The crowd scattered with a roar. The soldiers and police dived for cover and poured a ragged, undisciplined fire on the charging car.

Inside the Ferret, Lynch heard the sudden shower of loud clangs as some of the bullets found their target but caromed harmlessly off the armour plate. Reece lowered his head again and tried to meld into the superstructure of the car. They

274

raced towards the sea-front road and Lynch pulled hard on the stick to cut the corner. The car wobbled sickeningly on two wheels, and outside a shower of sparks streamed from the wheel-housing as the suspension bottomed out. Lynch ground his teeth and held the stick tight. As they rounded the corner Lynch suddenly saw they were confronted by the motionless hulk of an abandoned and empty bus. He wrenched the stick back but not enough, and the right side of the Ferret smashed through the back of the vehicle, ripping it like a bayonet, filling the air with gleaming shrapnel and spilling seats and disembowelled cushions across the road. Lynch heard another intense tattoo of bullets down the right side of the car as the bus slowed them down. He gunned the engine and the Ferret dragged the bus around behind them like a maddening giant anchor trying to hold them back. There was the nerve-shredding scream of tearing metal and then suddenly they were free.

There was a sudden bellow of pain from Reece and he let go with one hand. Bono reached out and grabbed him by the wrist.

'Gettin' a little hairy up here, boss,' the big man called down to Lynch.

Lynch seemed not to hear. He steered the Ferret towards the middle of the sea-front road and they sped along beside the sea. On their right buildings and palm trees flitted past in a blur as he threw all his weight back onto the accelerator. Through his eye slit Tuckey watched in silence as cars and taxis swerved frantically out of their path and the drivers leaped out, panic etched on their faces, and ran for cover. Lynch had his eyes fixed on one precious landmark now racing towards them. The jetty where they were to be picked up by the rescue chopper was in plain sight.

He glanced at his watch. Barely three minutes left. Neither he nor Tuckey could see any sign, any flash of sun on rotor blades to tell them their chopper was out there. Tuckey was the first to see something else on the farthest point of road curving like a scimitar around the great sweep of the sea—the glimmer of sun on hostile metal. Dozens of trucks and troop carriers were speeding towards them.

They came up on the jetty in a rush. Lynch stamped on the brakes, mashed the gears and slewed the Ferret across the road, up over the footpath and down onto the long, wooden jetty with a heavy crash. The thick wooden beams and concrete pilings looked sturdy enough but Lynch didn't have time to gauge the sudden stress of an armoured car. He raced along the wooden jetty and hoped. Dozens of fishing boats were moored inside the quay and their crews looked up in amazement as the car rumbled past. Then they too clambered up onto the jetty and scuttled for the safety of the quayside. At the far end of the jetty, Lynch could see the anxious figure of Bouraq—but still no sign of the rescue chopper. Lynch took his foot off the accelerator for the last time and let the momentum of the heavy car carry them forward, then he jerked the stick viciously back and forth and stood on the brakes. The car seemed to roar in protest but slewed sharply sideways and skidded to a full halt, blue smoke pouring from its engine and rocking crazily on its tortured suspension. Lynch had angled the car to be a natural barricade only a metre or so from the end of the jetty and the now terrified Bouraq. The Ferret was between them and the approaching Libyan soldiers, but they were left with their backs, literally, to the sea. And without the arrival of the rescue helicopter, there was no way of escape.

Bono climbed awkwardly out of the hatch, his fist still wrapped around his buddy's wrist, and let Reece slide gently to the heavy wooden beams of the jetty. Then he knelt down

276

and looked into his face. Reece was ashen. His right arm hung uselessly by his side, shattered by a soldier's bullet and held together only by the indestructible wetsuit. The only sign of the bullet was a dull groove burnt across the upper sleeve. Again, no penetration, as Finn had promised. But by the look on Reece's face, he was suffering massive bone and muscle damage ... and a lot of pain.

It took some effort but Reece opened his eyes, looked up and saw Bono.

'Jesus Christ,' he said and looked away. Bono grinned and stood up, satisfied. Tuckey dropped down beside him a moment later, followed by Lynch.

'Nothin' like a brisk drive to clear the head, huh?' Bono said.

Lynch looked at his watch again. The helicopter was overdue by seconds but they could see nothing. Only the great, blue swathe of the very scenic and very empty Mediterranean. Lynch looked around. Reece had lost his gun. Only he and Tuckey still had their weapons. For a moment the thought crossed Lynch's mind that it would suit Halloran very nicely if Gaddafi had been killed and none of them survived to talk about it.

Bono spat a fat globule of dust and phlegm into the scummy harbour water and wiped some of the grime from his face.

'Cuttin' it a bit fine, ain't they?' he said, echoing the fears of the others. A sharp volley of bullets smacked into the other side of the armoured car and they all instinctively ducked. Bono propped Reece up against one wheel and Bouraq hunkered down in the cover provided by the other. He trembled and even though he said nothing his face was miserable. Lynch could tell the Libyan was wondering whether he'd made the right decision to attempt to leave with them. Lynch picked up his rifle and chanced a quick glance down the jetty. He saw a ragged skirmish-line of soldiers moving warily down the jetty towards them, firing in a disordered but determined manner. Almost nonchalantly now, Lynch fired a long burst into the middle of their line and they fell back, leaving two bodies. The gunfire slackened noticeably, but a few minutes later it picked up again.

Bono stared out to sea but there was still nothing to be seen of the chopper. It was more than two minutes past their pick-up deadline.

'This is bullshit,' Bono muttered. 'They can send a patrol boat and pick us off when they want. We're goin' to have to give 'em somethin' to think about.' He pulled open the flap of his wetsuit, revealing the last transmitter.

'Let's see if this works,' he said and pushed the button. He silently mouthed a count to three then stole a glance around the armoured car at the waterfront. A massive fountain of earth and water was already on its way skywards from the three explosive-packed scooters in the sewer. A moment later the concussion and the thunderclap of the soundwave reached them and Lynch felt a fierce stab of pain in his ears as both ear-drums almost caved in under the impact. The Ferret rocked and the jetty shuddered and groaned beneath their feet. They all stared at each other in appalled silence and waited, but the jetty held. A fine rain of dirt, water and shattered masonry pattered all around them, pockmarking the sea with little splashes. Lynch looked landward and saw a gigantic plume of smoke rising over the waterfront. Directly behind the tunnel the buildings looked as though they had been cleaved by an axe. The whole area looked as though it had been seared by a nuclear blast. Palm trees were burning and he could see a great jumble of smashed cars and trucks along the sea-front road but no-one moving. Then the spray and dust began to settle and as the mist of destruction drifted away, there was a crater at least

278

20 metres wide left on the sea front where the sewer had been.

Then he saw the first signs of movement—uniforms, khaki uniforms, more soldiers flooding in from the alleyways and side streets.

'I can see it,' yelled Bouraq.

The words took Lynch by surprise. He tore his eyes away from the waterfront and looked out to sea. A second later he made out the profile of a green wasp whining towards them at wave height and getting bigger by the second. Lynch forced himself to look back down the jetty towards the renewed activity on the waterfront.

He knew that if the Libyan troops could re-group and launch a fresh assault, this time it would be with everything they had.

'Bono,' he ordered. 'You get the others on the chopper. I'll come last.'

'Fine by me,' said Bono.

Lynch squinted back down the jetty. He could hear the escalating roar of the chopper's rotors as it swooped in towards them. Then he picked out a group of soldiers readying some equipment at the bottom end of the jetty. He struggled to focus but couldn't quite make it out. Then one of the soldiers stood up.

'Shit,' Lynch swore. It looked like they were trying to ready a Blowpipe or an American-made Stinger, a lethal missile launcher which could be fired by one man from the shoulder. He fired a series of short, choppy bursts at the soldiers and they fell back but Lynch could still see the man with the missile launcher.

The chopper arrived with a deafening swoosh of noise and wind. Lynch looked over his shouders and saw one skid resting on the lip of the jetty. He could see the pilot inside waving frantically at them. The helicopter was painted Libyan-green, Lynch saw, but had no other identifying insignia at all. Bouraq

279

was first in followed by Tuckey. Bono picked his buddy Reece up and threw him in like a sack of potatoes. Even above the roar of the chopper Lynch heard Reece's scream. Bono turned back and yelled to Lynch but his words were whipped away. The pilot was waving furiously at him. Lynch took one last look down the jetty and fired off a concentrated burst at the man with the missile launcher, then turned and strode towards the edge of the jetty and the hovering chopper. Almost the moment he got there, the pilot heaved back on the joy stick and the chopper reared wildly up and away from him, leaving him standing alone at the end of the jetty, the purest shock written across his exhausted face. The next moment there was a deafening crack only a few metres behind him as the shoulder-launched missile smacked into the armoured car and blew it apart.

The shock wave blew Lynch off the jetty and into the sea in a long, tumbling arc. He fought the burning pain and unconsciousness that threatened to swamp him but blacked out the moment he hit the water. It only lasted a second or two and when he struggled back to agonising awareness he found himself held afloat on the surface by his wetsuit, floating on his back, body suffused with pain and unable to move. Half a dozen ribs must have gone, he knew, and God alone knew what damage he had sustained to his back. His whole world was filled with noise and the sky wheeled sickeningly above him. His ear-drums too must have gone. A wave splashed over him and he choked and gagged on the salt water. He was dimly aware of the chopper receding somewhere in the distance. The pilot had seen the missile coming and decided to get out, he realised. It was the right decision under the circumstances. He was expendable and now it was his turn. He surrendered himself to the relief that washed over his body replacing the high tension of the past hours, the past days. He began to slip away again.

His mind was wandering, he realised. He was probably becoming delirious from his injuries. Any minute a Libyan patrol boat would arrive to drag him on board. He fumbled painfully for the capsule inside the collar of his undersuit but his fingers wouldn't seem to co-ordinate. He tried again.

A blast of sound crashed over him and he could feel spray stinging his face. He blinked, but still saw only the reeling blue sky. Then a skid of the chopper hove into sight and he felt a powerful hand grab him by the collar and heave him roughly into the chopper.

The last thing he saw before blacking out was Bono's face and the big, wet mouth leering down at him.

'Aren't you glad I came along?' it said.

He was awakened by voices on the radio. The noise flooded back. He could see glimpses of sky spinning over his head between snatches of cabin ceiling and he realised he was still lying on the floor of the rescue chopper.

'Roger, I'll repeat that message,' the voice was saying. 'Two missing, confirmed dead. Two wounded, one serious. One slightly injured, one unhurt. One Libyan national, also unhurt.'

It was the chopper pilot reporting their status over the radio, Lynch realised. He further realised he must be the one described as seriously wounded. He tried flexing his fingers and toes but the effort to draw breath was so painful he decided to wait. He closed his eyes again. The spinning images caused by the loss of balance from his ruptured eardrums was making him nauseous. He lay in agonised silence for what seemed like a long time, then he heard Bono's deep voice.

'Jesus H. Christ,' it was saying. 'Will you take a look at that.'

Lynch struggled to open his eyes again. It hurt to move but he realised there was a blanket acting as a pillow under his head. Tuckey noticed and leaned down to help Lynch turn his head to look out of the open door of the chopper. Lynch fought to focus and the first thing he could make out was Tuckey's great hayseed grin. Then he ignored the wash of the rotor blades and looked down through the chopper door. There, beneath them, was the awesome bulk of the aircraft carrier, USS *John F. Kennedy*, the second most powerful warship, after the *Nimitz*, in the US Fifth Fleet.

It didn't make sense. Where was the *Endeavor*? He wondered what had happened to Halloran's plan. Had they all been sprung somehow and intercepted by the US Navy? Nausea overtook him again and he sank back onto the floor of the chopper, trying to ignore the hostile thoughts that tried to crowd into his tired mind. A moment later the chopper bounced gently onto the flight deck of the *Kennedy* and they were down. Lynch waited. He could hear the grunts of the others as they climbed out and Reece swearing at Bono for his rough handling. Then he felt a flurry of hands reaching in, expertly easing him onto a stretcher and sliding him out of the chopper. They laid him gently on the deck for a moment and Lynch forced himself to open his eyes. The first recognisable face to swim into view belonged to Halloran. He squeezed his eyes shut, then opened them again but Halloran was still there.

'What went wrong?' Lynch wheezed.

Halloran shock his head. 'Nothing went wrong, Lynch.' The voice was still tough and brisk but there was a note of compassion there, too, that Lynch hadn't heard before. 'The State Department was alerted some days ago to the possibility of a

282

coup in Libya. Reports today say that Gaddafi has been assassinated by his own bodyguard. The navy has been ordered to stand by and evacuate all civilians from friendly nations. You are a civilian, aren't you?'

Lynch smiled but the effort made him wince.

'Something else too,' Halloran said. 'Might help take some of the pain away. Less than an hour ago I was talking to another civilian by radio relay back to my office in New York. Don't ask how she got patched-through here but she's a very determined lady and she'll be much relieved to know you got back in one piece.'

'Janice?' Lynch croaked.

A knowing grin crossed Halloran's weather-beaten face. 'When you're up to it, I think she'd like to hear from you personally,' he said.

Lynch managed a faint smile. 'Tell her I'm desperately in need of a skilled nurse. The pay's lousy but the hours are good.'

Halloran nodded and stood up. Then another face materialised beside him. It was the last face Lynch would have expected aboard the US warship in such circumstances. The pink, beaming face of Sir Malcolm Porter, thin white hair whipping in the wind. Lynch sighed. A wave of fatigue swept the pain from his body. He took a deep breath and looked back up at his former boss.

'You managed all of this, didn't you?' he said.

Porter shrugged. 'Not exactly, old boy. But someone had to keep an eye on you from our end. Make sure you didn't get yourself into too much trouble, eh?'

Lynch groaned and looked away again.

'You'll hear all about it soon enough,' Halloran interrupted. 'Right now let's get you down to sick bay and the best medical attention the US Navy can offer.'

The navy medics swept his stretcher off the deck and Lynch

felt himself being carried towards one of the lifts which would take him down to the great warship's surgery. Before they slipped out of earshot, Lynch could still hear Halloran and Porter talking to each other as comfortably as two men discussing the weather.

'Tell me, Porter,' he heard Halloran say in that warm whiskey voice. 'How well do your guys know Beirut?'

Then Lynch slipped gratefully back into unconsciousness.

THE FINEST IN SUSPENSE!

THE URSA ULTIMATUM   (2130, $3.95)
by Terry Baxter

In the dead of night, twelve nuclear warheads are smuggled north across the Mexican border to be detonated simultaneously in major cities throughout the U.S. And only a small-town desert lawman stands between a face-less Russian superspy and World War Three!

THE LAST ASSASSIN   (1989, $3.95)
by Daniel Easterman

From New York City to the Middle East, the devastating flames of revolution and terrorism sweep across a world gone mad . . . as the most terrifying conspiracy in the history of mankind is born!

FLOWERS FROM BERLIN   (2060, $4.50)
by Noel Hynd

With the Earth on the brink of World War Two, the Third Reich's deadliest professional killer is dispatched on the most heinous assignment of his murderous career: the assassination of Franklin Delano Roosevelt!

THE BIG NEEDLE   (1921, $2.95)
by Ken Follett

All across Europe, innocent people are being terrorized, homes are destroyed, and dead bodies have become an unnervingly common sight. And the horrors will continue until the most powerful organization on Earth finds Chadwell Carstairs—and kills him!

DOMINATOR   (2118, $3.95)
by James Follett

Two extraordinary men, each driven by dangerously ambiguous loyalties, play out the ultimate nuclear endgame miles above the helpless planet—aboard a hijacked space shuttle called DOMINATOR!

Available wherever paperbacks are sold, or order direct from the Publisher. Send cover price plus 50¢ per copy for mailing and handling to Zebra Books, Dept. 160, 475 Park Avenue South, New York, N.Y. 10016. Residents of New York, New Jersey and Pennsylvania must include sales tax. DO NOT SEND CASH.